CW01495034

First Edition 2025

Independently published via Amazon KDP

I

Because Of You.

"You taught me love, you taught me pain,
The sweetest poison in my veins.
Because of you, I found my fate—"

—

Alex

I've spent the last five years in a monotonous loop, each day bleeding into the next with a dull, suffocating sameness. Mornings start with the shrill blare of my alarm, a sound I've grown to resent, though I never bother changing it. I shower, dress, force down a coffee that never tastes as rich as the ones I used to make for her, and leave for work with a silence that fills the spaces she left behind. Even the air feels different —heavier, stagnant. Once, life held an edge of excitement, a feeling of possibility. Now, it's a cycle, a routine I walk through without really seeing the world around me.

My circle of friends has dwindled, not through dramatic fallouts or conscious decisions, but simply because they weren't really mine to begin with. They were hers. And when she left, they did too, peeling away like dead leaves in winter. The few that remained became mere acquaintances, people who sent the occasional "How you been, mate?" out of obligation, not genuine care. I don't hold it against them. People pick sides, and I was never the one throwing dinner parties or making grand plans. I was just there. Steady, predictable, forgettable.

At work, I keep to myself. The office is a hive of people who talk just to hear their own voices, conversations laced with artificial enthusiasm and polite laughter. I hear their perfumes before I see them, the sharp notes of citrus and vanilla mixing with the overpowering musk of expensive colognes. It turns my stomach. A nauseating blend of corporate competition and artificiality, much like the interactions themselves. I nod when required, offer half-smiles that never reach my eyes, and bury myself in tasks that mean nothing to me.

The only thing that makes the hours bearable is music. It's been my refuge since childhood, a space where emotions make sense, where every note and lyric forms a kind of language that speaks directly to something inside me. I listen to everything—the poetic melancholy of Sting, the gritty realism of Stormzy, the raw emotion behind Amy Winehouse. Artists who create something powerful from nothing. People who make their pain into something beautiful.

Since she left, I've barely talked to women. Not really talked. Something inside me broke that day, a crack that still hasn't sealed.

It wasn't just the betrayal—wasn't just the fact that she cheated on me with our friend, a guy I had let into my home, my life. It was the slow, deliberate way she had been siphoning away our savings, bit by bit, while still curling into my side at night, whispering how much she loved me. Setting up her new life with him while pretending we still had one together. Looking back, I see it so clearly now—the distance in her eyes, the way she flinched when I reached for her, the way she stopped making plans for our future. I was blind, too caught up in loving her to see the truth staring me in the face.

I don't hate women. I never could. If anything, I still hold onto the idea of love, of something real. I picture a wife, kids, a home filled with warmth. But I'm wary. The idea of trusting again feels like walking barefoot over shattered glass. I still notice women, of course. When a pretty girl catches my eye, the thoughts come—the same thoughts any bloke would have. But then the memories hit, and my mind tightens the leash, pulling me back into the past, reminding me of the pain she caused.

For a while, I tried distracting myself with mindless conversations, diving into the anonymity of sites like Omegle. Late at night, I'd sit in the dim glow of my laptop, talking to strangers from across the world, letting the words flow without consequence. I kept it text-based, preferred it that way.

No awkward video calls, no pressure to show my face. I've always been average-looking at best, and the idea of being judged by a flickering webcam never sat right with me.

Most of the conversations were forgettable —small talk, quick exchanges about music, movies, the mundane details of people's lives. A few girls tried steering the chats in a different direction, sending messages laced with suggestive undertones. I ignored them. I wasn't looking for that and always expected a scam, I was too average to be that appealing. But, even after everything, I still held onto some outdated idea of traditional romance and hoped that someone out there felt the same.

Eventually, I found something better than the anonymous fake connections offered on chat sites—a place where I could talk about the one thing that never let me down. A music platform called 'Noted.' It was like a social media site, but specifically for music lovers. You could create a profile based on your tastes, share tracks, and connect with others who felt music the way you did. I wasn't there for the social side of it. I liked watching my followers grow, seeing the little notifications pop up when people liked my song recommendations. A quiet corner of the internet where my opinion mattered, even if only in a small way.

And that's where I met her. Or rather, where she found me.

It was a normal night. I'd just added a new Imagine Dragons track to my playlist, my headphones snug over my ears, the bass thrumming through my skull as I scrolled mindlessly through the site. A notification popped up.

"Omg, I literally just heard this, it's so good!"

Her profile picture was small, just a blurred glimpse of a girl. Chestnut hair, a hint of a smile. It wasn't unusual for people—women included—to comment on my posts. I hovered over the notification for a second, debating whether to reply.

I typed out a quick "I know, right!" before closing my laptop, ready to lose myself in another round of Call of Duty. Something else that offers me a small solace.

At the time, I had no idea that a simple comment on a song would change everything.

Emma

I love my job—truly, I do. But it's not what I uprooted my life for. Two years ago, I arrived in London with ambition burning in my chest, fresh from music management studies, eager to carve a name for myself in the industry. I imagined myself scouting talent, discovering the next big artist, bringing raw, unfiltered voices into the spotlight. The reality was far less glamorous. The industry was cutthroat, and the doors I knocked on remained firmly shut. So, I ended up here—making cappuccinos and wiping down counters in a coffee shop.

Sure, we hosted open mic nights, and sometimes live music would drift through the air, filling the space with something close to what I wanted. But it wasn't enough. I didn't want to just witness talent—I wanted to shape it.

I knew the power of social media, so I played the game. I used what I had—long brown hair, a slim frame, a knack for makeup that enhanced without overdoing it. I wouldn't sell my soul for likes, but I wasn't above leveraging a little feminine charm. My social media following was decent, but the real gem was my 'Noted' account. That was my passion—an online space where

I could talk about music, review fresh releases, and maybe, just maybe, make a name for myself in the industry. I spent hours scouring for new tracks, reposting hidden gems, trying to stay ahead of trends and be the first to highlight the next viral song.

After a long, uninspiring shift devoid of music, I got home and kicked off my shoes, eager to immerse myself in something more meaningful. I logged into Noted, ready to lose myself in the latest releases. The moment I saw Imagine Dragons had dropped a new song; I pressed play. The beat pulsed through my headphones, wrapping around me, igniting that familiar rush of excitement. Loved it.

Then, I noticed someone had already beaten me to it—posted about it on Noted before I had the chance. I frowned, more intrigued than annoyed, and left a comment.

Curiosity got the better of me, so I clicked on his profile. Alex, from London. His display picture showed a shy-looking guy with a sharp face and glasses, but his music taste? Impeccable. Classic rock, hip-hop, some old-school Sting that made me smile. My dad used to play Sting on road trips, his fingers tapping the steering wheel to the beat.

Engagement was everything when it came to building a profile, so I left a few more comments, casually liking some of his posts. A few minutes later, a notification popped up.

"I know, right!"

Just a simple reply, but there was something about it. No forced enthusiasm, no flexing—just genuine appreciation for the music. That was rare. I logged off for the night, uploading a couple of pictures to Instagram and Snapchat before bed. Nothing too revealing—I had a hopeful brand to maintain—but just enough to keep my followers engaged.

Alex

My morning routine was as predictable as ever. The alarm dragged me from sleep, I fumbled through my usual motions—shower, coffee, scrolling through social media with bleary eyes. But today, something different. More notifications than usual.

Emma.

She'd commented on my Imagine Dragons post last night, but now, she'd liked a bunch of my songs and left a few more comments. "Love this song too!" and "You've got the best taste!!"

I clicked on her profile, curiosity winning out. Her tiny profile picture hadn't done her justice. She was beautiful—not in an unattainable, airbrushed kind of way, but effortlessly. Her chestnut brown hair cascaded over her shoulders in waves, her eyes, like liquid silver caught in the light. A faint line of freckles dusted her nose, and her lips were slightly parted, frozen mid-laugh. Something about the photo felt real, like she wasn't posing but just existing in the moment. I caught myself staring and quickly backed out before I felt like too much of a creep.

Instead, probably like a creep, I scrolled through her posts. She had playlists for every mood, every occasion, each one crafted with care. Her reviews weren't surface level; they had depth. She wasn't just someone who listened to music—she *felt* it, the way I did.

I should have been getting ready for work, but instead, I sat there, caught in a moment, lingering just a little longer.

I got to work late, blaming traffic, but the truth was, I got lost in her. Not just for a few minutes —no, I had fallen headfirst down the rabbit hole, three years deep into her post history, scrolling through every snapshot, every caption, every thought she had ever decided to share with the world. I barely heard my boss when he called my name, snapping me out of the trance.

"Alex, that report—tell me it's done."

Shit. I hadn't even started.

I cleared my throat, forcing out a lie that felt smooth from years of practice. "Just putting the final touches on it now."

He nodded, accepting my excuse without a second thought. I was good at my job, which meant I could get away with this kind of thing. Still, I shoved my phone into my drawer, willing myself to focus. But it was no use. The damage had already been done. Emma had taken up residence in my mind, and she wasn't leaving anytime soon.

All day, she lingered in my thoughts like a song stuck on repeat. A particular image of her, one from a year ago, stood out the most. It was taken in a small music studio, bathed in a deep red glow that painted the walls in temptation. She stood in the doorway, a silhouette against the rich crimson light spilling in from behind her. The contrast sharpened every curve, every delicate angle of her frame. Her long thick hair cascaded over one shoulder, catching just enough of the glow to shimmer. Shadows kissed the arch of her exposed neck, the slope of her shoulders, making the image almost intimate in its intensity. She wasn't posing in the way other girls did—no forced pout, no rehearsed expression. She simply stood there, effortless, magnetic.

Emma wasn't like the others. Her pictures weren't thirst traps, and her words weren't empty. She didn't seek attention with skimpy outfits or meaningless captions. She was thoughtful, sharp, and her love for music ran deeper than just curated playlists. It was stitched into everything she shared, every post, every comment. She wasn't just another pretty face— she had substance. And for the first time in a long time, I felt something real stir inside me.

I had to message her today.

Emma

There was a guy at the coffee shop today, perched on a stool with a sticker covered acoustic guitar, pouring his soul into a string of Ed Sheeran covers. He wasn't half bad

—confident, easy-going, the kind of guy who looked like he belonged under a spotlight. I admired that about him, that self-assurance. We talked briefly, and I learned he was playing for free, just to build experience. I respected the hustle. Confidence is key, even if you have to fake it until you make it.

We exchanged Instagram handles before he packed up, but he was a little too forward for my taste—too quick with the winks, the playful smirks that felt just a little too rehearsed. I preferred men who were quieter, more introspective. The ones who didn't need to put on a show.

After my shift, I headed home, eager to sink into the digital world where I felt most at ease. I made a quick pasta dinner, nothing fancy, just something to keep me going. Then, with my laptop open and a fresh cup of tea in hand, I settled in for my usual nighttime routine— checking notifications, responding to messages, curating content. Building.

I had a few pictures ready to post, ones I'd taken on a day when everything felt right—hair, makeup, lighting. That's the trick, really. You rarely post in real time. You stockpile the good days and use them to cover the bad ones. A little social media sleight of hand.

Then I saw it—a new message on Noted.

From Alex. The Imagine Dragons guy.

"So, I just wanted to say you've got the best music taste! I've spent ages listening to your suggestions and reading your reviews, and honestly, I agree with you on everything!"

It was simple, sincere. Not the usual nonsense I got—no over-the-top compliments, no cringey attempts at flirting. Just genuine appreciation. *That* was a rare thing.

Alex

I wish I could say I played it cool, but I didn't. I sat there, agonising over every word, rewriting the message at least a dozen times before finally forcing myself to hit send. I wanted to make an impression but not come on too strong. To show interest, but not desperation.

I went with something safe, complimenting her taste in music, mentioning how I'd spent hours listening to her recommendations. As soon as I sent it, regret hit me like a truck. It sounded forced. Too eager. I should've kept it shorter, wittier—should've said something that stood out.

Before I could spiral any further, a notification popped up.

"Thank you, Alex! That means a lot coming from someone with such a diverse taste. I saw you're into everything—quite the range! What's your all-time favourite song? xx"

Immediate response. A double 'xx.' Interest, or just politeness?

I stared at my screen, pulse quickening, knowing one thing for certain.

This was the start of something.

I stared at the message, my fingers hovering over the keyboard. How do I even begin to answer that? There were too many songs I loved for too many different reasons. Some reminded me of childhood road trips, my dad's off-key singing filling the car. Others took me back to late-night drives, the windows down, the city lights streaking past. And then there were the songs that held something deeper—songs I couldn't explain why I loved, only that they made me feel something real.

This felt like some sort of test, like my response would set the tone for whatever this conversation could become. I couldn't help but stare at the 'xx' at the end of her message. Was that just her usual way of signing off? Or was she trying to tell me something? My mind worked overtime, overanalysing every little detail, but I forced myself to focus on the question at hand.

After a moment's hesitation, I started typing.

"That's a tough question! But if I had to choose, I'd probably go with 'Every Breath You Take' by The Police. It's a classic, and there's something about the melody that just gets me every time. What about you?"

The second I hit send, regret crept in. Had I really just picked *that* song? The one universally recognised as an anthem of obsession and borderline stalker behaviour? Brilliant. Real smooth, Alex. I braced myself for a sarcastic reply, maybe even a full ghosting.

But before I could dwell on it too much, her response came almost instantly.

"Oh, great choice! Sting's voice is so iconic. For me, it changes all the time, but right now, it's 'Clair de Lune' by Debussy. It's so calming and beautiful. Perfect for winding down after a long day xx"

I exhaled, tension leaving my shoulders. She didn't think I was a psycho—at least not yet. Instead, she'd hit me with a choice so effortlessly elegant, so unexpected, that it made me smile.

Classical music, huh? There was definitely more to Emma than I'd initially thought.

"Debussy, wow. I didn't expect that! I guess you really do have a wide taste in music. Do you play any instruments, or?"

This time, there was a slight pause before her reply, as if she was thinking carefully about what to say next. I sat watching the screen, impatiently waiting for the typing bubble to reappear, hoping I hadn't already bored her to death.

"I used to play the piano when I was younger. I'm not very good, though. But yeah, my dream is to manage and discover new artists. I studied it at Uni, but I'm working at a coffee shop right now. Hoping to get into artist management someday. What about you? Do you play any instruments or sing? xx"

I chuckled to myself. She was ambitious. There was something about the way she phrased things—like her dreams weren't just dreams, but inevitabilities. She didn't say *I hope*, she said *I'm hoping*—like she was already halfway there. That kind of quiet confidence was rare, and it made me like her even more.

I quickly typed back.

"I tried learning the guitar in college, but it didn't stick. I'm more of a listener. I work in a dull office

16

job, so music is my escape. Speaking of, any new artists you're excited about?"

As I waited for her response, I realised how easy this conversation felt. Normally, I'd be overthinking every reply, worried about coming across as boring, but with Emma, there was none of that. I could talk to her. And I *wanted* to talk to her. I'd almost forgotten how absolutely stunning she was, but the small profile picture beside her name was a constant, subtle reminder.

Her next message pinged onto my screen.

"Absolutely! There's this indie band called 'The Violets'. They have a unique sound—kind of a mix between folk and alternative rock. I think you'd really like them. I'll send you a link to one of their tracks. xx"

Those kisses. I clicked the link she sent, and as the music filled my room, I found myself nodding along. They were good, really good. Their sound was raw, unpolished, but packed with emotion. I could see why she liked them.

"These guys are awesome! How did you find them?" I typed back, genuinely curious.

"I saw them at a small gig in a pub. They were amazing live! I guess I've got an ear for these things xx" she replied.

Our conversation continued late into the night, exchanging songs and video suggestions. She told me about gigs she'd been to and made a playful comment about taking me to one because I said I'd never been. I learned that Emma wasn't just a casual music lover; she had an encyclopaedic knowledge of artists and genres. She was witty, effortlessly funny, and a little sarcastic—a combination I found dangerously irresistible. Her passion bled through every word, and I found myself inspired by her in a way I hadn't felt in a long time.

By the time she finally said she had to go to sleep, it was well past midnight, and I was exhausted, but I knew I could've stayed up all night talking to her. As I lay in bed, phone resting on my chest, I felt something I hadn't in years—a spark. Emma had reignited something in me. Something I hadn't even realised had gone out.

I didn't know where this would lead, but for the first time in a long time, I felt hopeful. Maybe it was the music, or maybe it was Emma, but something inside me felt lighter, more alive. The dull routine of my life—wake up, work, go home, repeat—suddenly didn't seem so monotonous. It was as if someone had turned up the volume on everything, making colours brighter, sounds richer, and the future a little less predictable.

As I closed my eyes, my thoughts were filled with her silhouette standing in that red-lit doorway, the image already cemented in my mind. The way the glow outlined her figure, the way her hair cascaded over her shoulders—it was hypnotic. I knew I'd be thinking about her long after sleep claimed me.

Emma

Chatting with Alex was a breath of fresh air. Most guys I spoke to online had an agenda—some were blatant about it, others tried to dress it up with compliments and charm—but Alex? He seemed different. Sincere, almost shy. He didn't bombard me with personal questions or try to steer the conversation towards anything sordid. Instead, he spoke about music with such unfiltered enthusiasm, and I liked that. It made me curious about him, about who he really was beyond the messages, the profile picture, the carefully chosen words.

When I logged off, I lay in bed replaying our conversation, letting the details settle. His taste in music was broad, which I respected. His choice of The Police's 'Every Breath You Take' had made me smile. Most people see it as obsessive, but I understood why he picked it. He wasn't thinking about the lyrics necessarily, although that may be something he relates to—he was drawn to the melody, the nostalgia, the feeling it evoked. That kind of innocence, that unguarded way of expressing himself, was rare. And, if I was being honest, kind of sweet.

I found myself smiling as I thought about how his messages had shifted, his words becoming more confident the longer we talked. He'd started off hesitant, overly careful, but by the end, there was ease between us. I liked that. And I made sure to add two kisses to each message, a subtle reassurance that I was enjoying the conversation just as much as he was.

The next morning, I woke up to the soft vibration of my phone. My hand instinctively reached for it, my heart skipping just a little when I saw his name on the screen. I tapped the notification, anticipation humming through me.

"Good morning! Hope you had a great sleep! I'm

still thinking about our chat. So much music to listen to now, thanks to you! Any plans for the day?"

I hesitated for a moment, my fingers hovering over the keyboard. I didn't want to seem too eager. There's a fine balance in these things— keep him interested, but don't lay all your cards on the table. It was a rule I'd learnt the hard way.

Instead of replying straight away, I set my phone down, focusing on my morning routine. I applied my makeup with slow precision, ran a brush through my hair, and picked out an outfit for my shift at the coffee shop. Only then did I allow myself to type out a response.

"Morning! Just the usual—work at the coffee shop. But I'm looking forward to listening to some new music later. I'll let you know if I find anything good! xx"

I hit send, and within seconds, the screen lit up again.

"Have you heard of The Kinks? I checked them out recently, and they're amazing! Thanks for the recommendations, by the way—it was fun chatting to someone so in the know!"

I bit my lip, amused at how quick he was to respond. He was reading my messages the second I sent them, waiting for my replies. That kind of eagerness was sweet. Endearing, even.

But I knew better than to reply instantly every time. I'd made the mistake of being too keen before, and history had taught me that guys lost interest when they felt like the chase was over too soon.

So, I left it for a little while, sipped my coffee, double-checked my outfit in the mirror.

"I'll check them out! I'm glad you liked my suggestions. Send me anything you think is good —I'm always up for discovering new music xx"

I hit send, knowing he'd be waiting for it. It's been a while since I've felt that hint of excitement just from talking to someone.

-

I spent the morning busy at the coffee shop, moving through the usual rhythm of serving customers, wiping down tables, and refilling coffee cups, but my mind was only half on the tasks at hand. My thoughts kept drifting back to Alex, to the way he had responded to my messages with such enthusiasm. There was something refreshing about his innocence, a stark contrast to the brash confidence of the musicians and wannabe managers I usually dealt with. He wasn't trying to impress me with empty bravado or reel me in with overused lines—he was just... himself. And I liked that.

During my break, I scrolled through his profile again, letting my curiosity take over. His posts, his playlists—they all painted a picture of someone who genuinely loved music, not just for the status or the scene, but because it meant something to him. It mirrored my own passion, and that realisation tugged at something inside me. I wondered what he would be like in person, whether his voice would have the same quiet intensity as his words, whether his eyes would light up when he talked about his favourite bands. I pictured us in a quiet pub, sharing a drink, conversation flowing effortlessly between us. The thought made me smile.

On impulse, I took a sip of my coffee and snapped a selfie with the window behind me, soft light catching in my hair. I sent it to him with a simple message: "Really like The Kinks!" I hadn't actually listened to them yet, but I would on the way home so I could back up the white lie. The truth was, I just wanted to make sure he was thinking about me.

Alex was interesting, but there was something else, too—something vulnerable. And the more I thought about it, the more intriguing he became.

Alex

As soon as I woke up, I messaged Emma. I didn't even go through my usual routine of scrolling through social media or checking emails. She was the first thing on my mind, and I was eager to talk to her again. I told myself to play it cool, to not seem too desperate, but the truth was, she was the most exciting thing in my life right now. I wanted to keep the conversation going, to see where it might lead.

At work, the monotony set in within minutes of sitting at my desk. The dull hum of computers, the clatter of keyboards, the low murmur of colleagues discussing deadlines—it was all just background noise. My thoughts kept drifting to her, but I was so caught up in work that I didn't get a chance to check my phone until my afternoon break.

Then I saw it.

She was sitting at a table in the coffee shop, cupping a large white coffee cup that made her hand look delicate, almost fragile. Her eyes met the camera—met mine—with an effortless kind of intimacy, and the soft glow from the window behind her framed her in light, creating an almost angelic aura. She was breathtaking. And for a brief moment, I forgot to breathe.

My mind raced. The photo was innocent, but was it for me? Had she taken it just to send to me? Or was I one of many who had received it?

I had no idea how to reply. I was glad she liked The Kinks, but ignoring the picture felt impossible. At the same time, I didn't want to sound creepy. I typed out a message, deleted it. Typed another, deleted that one too. Everything either felt too much or not enough.

Eventually, I settled on: "You have really nice eyes! And that coffee looks hugeee."

I hit send before I could overthink it and immediately put my phone on silent, face down on my desk. A ridiculous smile tugged at my lips, one I had to suppress around my coworkers. This was ridiculous. I shouldn't be this giddy over a girl I hadn't even met yet. And yet, I couldn't help myself.

That evening, once work was over, we fell into conversation again—longer, deeper this time. The casual small talk melted away, replaced with something more personal. We talked about everything—music, life, our hopes and dreams. She told me about her plans to break into the music industry, her desire to find and manage new talent, her belief that there were voices out there waiting to be heard. I told her about my dull office job, my love of gaming, my quiet hope that one day I'd do something more meaningful with my life.

She listened. Really listened. She asked questions, gave thoughtful responses, encouraged me in a way that felt genuine. I found myself opening up to her in ways I hadn't with anyone in a long time. And for the first time in what felt like forever, I felt understood. Like I mattered.

Emma

The more I talked to Alex, the more I found myself enjoying his company. He was sweet, thoughtful, and genuinely interested in what I had to say. It was refreshing, really, to have someone eager to listen for a change, rather than just waiting for their turn to speak. Most people wanted to talk about themselves, but Alex was different. He asked about my day, my interests, my dreams, and he actually cared about the answers. It was nice to feel heard.

When I saw his reply to my photo—"You have really nice eyes! And that coffee looks hugeee"— I couldn't help but smile. There was something so endearing about his awkwardness, the way he tried to compliment me without coming on too strong. He was careful, deliberate, trying to strike the right balance, and I appreciated that.

I typed back quickly, keeping the tone light. "Thanks, Alex! And yeah, our coffee cups are massive—perks of the job, I guess! I'm glad you liked the pic! xx" Then I set my phone down and forced myself to focus on my work.

That evening, our conversation took on a more personal tone. We talked about music, our favourite bands, and the things we'd do if we could do anything in the world. Alex confessed he'd always wanted to travel, to see the world beyond the confines of his office cubicle. He spoke about faraway places—sun-drenched beaches, misty mountain trails, cities alive with neon and noise. His words painted vivid pictures, and I could hear the longing in his messages. It was clear he craved something more, something beyond the monotony of his daily life.

"You should go for it," I told him. "Life's too short to stay stuck in a job you don't love. You deserve to be happy, to do what you want. xx"

And I meant it. There was something about him, something restless and uncertain, like he was just waiting for someone to push him in the right direction. I could be that person. I could give him that push.

His response came quickly, filled with hesitant hope. "Maybe one day. It's just hard, you know? Responsibilities and all that. But talking to you makes me feel like anything is possible."

I smiled to myself, a warmth spreading through me. I liked knowing I had that effect on him, that I could make him feel more confident, more alive. There was a quiet power in that, in being a person who makes others see the world differently.

"Anything is possible, Alex. You've just got to take the leap! xx" I added the kisses deliberately, knowing he'd notice. I liked the way he responded to me, the way he became more open, more willing to share. And the more he shared, the closer we became.

Over the next few days, our conversations became a constant in my life. I found myself reaching for my phone first thing in the morning, waiting for his messages, eager to keep talking. It felt natural, effortless. Like having a friend who genuinely cared about my day, my thoughts, my dreams. And in return, I found myself caring about his.

We exchanged songs, sending each other music we thought the other would like. It became our thing. He sent me tracks from obscure indie bands, heartfelt acoustic ballads, classic rock anthems. I sent him my favourites in return, the ones that spoke to me the most. It felt like we were building something, weaving an invisible thread between us, one song at a time.

I started noticing a pattern in his choices. His favourite lyrics always carried a darker undertone, an underlying sadness I hadn't expected. He once quoted a John Lennon song —*"You may say I'm a dreamer, but I'm not the only one. I hope someday you'll join us, and the world will be as one."* Another time, he sent me a line from Billie Eilish— *"Can't shake the feeling that I'm just bad at healing."*

I found it interesting, this glimpse into another side of him. It made me wonder what lay beneath his easy-going messages, what thoughts lurked behind his carefully chosen words. There was more to Alex than he let on, and I wanted to understand him better.

Sometimes, I'd catch myself imagining what it would be like to meet him, to see him in person, to hear his voice not just through text but in real life. I pictured us at a concert, lost in the music, or sitting by the river, talking about everything and nothing. It was a nice thought, a comforting one. I didn't know where this was going, but I liked the direction it was heading.

Emma

I was careful, too. I made sure to keep things balanced, never too eager, never too distant. It was a delicate game; one I had learned to play well. Keep just enough mystery, just enough intrigue, and they'll always come back for more. It wasn't about manipulation—it was about allure. About keeping the spark burning, about making sure I stayed in his thoughts even when I wasn't there.

One evening, as we drifted from films into the comfort of late-night conversations, Alex's message popped up, tentative but unmistakable.

"I've been thinking about you a lot lately."

I paused, my fingers hovering over the screen,

rereading his words.

There was something vulnerable in them, something raw. Like he had hesitated before hitting send, unsure if it was too much, too soon. It was a bold move for someone like him—a quiet risk, a step closer. And for the first time in a long time, I felt something stir, a pang of something I couldn't quite place.

I let a slow smile curl at my lips before I typed my reply.

"That's sweet, Alex. I've been thinking about you too! It's nice to have someone to talk to, you know? Someone who gets it. xx"

I watched the message deliver, then leaned back against my pillows, my heart beating a little quicker than I cared to admit. Would he overthink it? Read too much into it? His reply came almost instantly.

"Yeah, it's really nice. I feel like I can be myself with you, Emma. Like you really see me, you know?"

I bit my lip, staring at the words, feeling their weight. He was pulling back the curtain now, showing me more of who he was, how he felt. A little intense, maybe. A little too eager. But there was something kind of beautiful about it, something real.

I typed, then deleted, then typed again.

"I do see you, Alex. And I like what I see xx"

As soon as I hit send, I exhaled, feeling warmth spread through me. This was going well—better than I had expected. And I wasn't sure what that meant yet.

Later that night, as I lay in bed, my phone resting beside me on the pillow, I let my thoughts drift to him. Alex was… different. He had a quiet intensity about him, a need to be understood, to be seen. And I liked the way he made me feel —like I was something rare, something worth holding onto.

For now, I was happy to let things unfold. No rush, no pressure. Just the slow burn of something that felt like it could be real.

Alex

I couldn't stop thinking about her.

It was ridiculous, really. I barely knew her, not in the way that truly mattered. But still, she was there, lingering in my mind like the chorus of a song I couldn't shake.

Every morning, my first thought was her. My first instinct—reaching for my phone, hoping for her name on the screen. And when it was there, when I saw that notification light up, it was like the world had cracked open just enough to let a little bit of light in.

Her words stuck with me, playing on repeat in my head.

"I do see you, Alex. And I like what I see xx."

She liked me, for me.

The words felt like a lifeline, a thread pulling me closer, making me want more.

I tried to play it cool. I told myself I wouldn't check my phone too much, wouldn't obsess over every message, wouldn't read into every emoji, every kiss at the end of her texts. But I was failing miserably.

I barely touched my games anymore. My usual distractions—TV, scrolling endlessly through social media—felt empty now. Nothing held my attention the way she did.

And the worst part? I wanted to know more.

I shouldn't have, but I couldn't help myself. I found myself searching her online, clicking through her social media, piecing together the parts of her life she hadn't yet told me about.

Her Facebook was private.

But her Instagram wasn't.

I scrolled through her posts, my eyes drinking in every detail, every moment frozen in time. There she was at a music festival, arms raised, her face alight with unfiltered joy. There she was at work, laughing over a coffee cup too big for her hands. A candid shot of her staring off into the sunset, looking lost in thought. Her captions were simple, sometimes just a lyric, sometimes nothing at all. But each post felt like a glimpse into who she really was.

I lingered on one picture—her in the crowd at a gig, eyes closed, swaying to the music.

She looked free. Alive. Happy.

I tried to imagine what it would be like to be there with her, standing beside her, feeling the bass vibrate through our bones, her voice in my ear as she sang along.

Would she reach for my hand? Would she smile at me the way she did in those photos?

Would I ever get the chance to find out?

A message notification pulled me from my thoughts.

Emma.

My pulse quickened as I opened it.

"Just heard a song that reminded me of you. Sending it your way xx."

I swallowed hard, staring at the screen.

She thought about me too.

And that thought alone was enough
to make my whole world tilt just a
little bit more in her direction.

I wanted to know her. All of her.

I told myself it was innocent curiosity, just the natural way of things when you liked someone. But the truth ran deeper than that. The more I learned about her, the more I wanted. It wasn't enough to just talk to her, to wait for her messages to appear like small gifts in the palm of my hand. I needed to fill in the gaps, to understand the spaces in between the words she chose to share.

I scrolled through her followers, my eyes skimming over names, profile pictures, connections. Who were her friends? Who was just a stranger pressing 'follow' on her life? Were there exes lurking there, watching her the same way I was? I looked at the comments beneath her photos, analysing the way people spoke to her, how familiar they seemed. How she responded.

She didn't give much away. A few laughing emojis here, a simple 'miss you xx' there. But that didn't mean anything. It was a puzzle, and every piece slotted together gave me more of the picture.

One evening, as we drifted into another easy conversation about our favourite films, she mentioned a small gig she was thinking of going to in a few months. It was casual, offhand, the kind of thing you could miss if you weren't paying attention. But I was paying attention.

My heart kicked up, my fingers tightening around my phone. Was this a hint? Was she testing the waters, waiting to see if I'd pick up on it?

I had to be careful.

"That sounds amazing!" I typed, keeping my tone light, like it was just an idea I was open to, nothing serious. "I've been wanting to go to a gig for ages. It would be great to experience it with someone who knows their music."

Seconds passed. The typing bubble appeared.

"We should go together! It would be so much fun. I'd love to meet you too! xx"

My breath caught.

I reread the message three times before responding, my pulse thudding in my ears.

This was it. This was what I'd been waiting for.

I clenched my jaw, steadying myself. Play it cool Alex. Don't let her see how much this means to you.

"I'd like that," I replied, my fingers trembling slightly as I typed. "It would be great to hang out in real life, see if we vibe as well in person as we do online."

A few seconds later:

"Definitely. I have a feeling we'd get on just fine xxx"

I noticed the extra kiss.

I wasn't imagining this.

I closed my eyes, drifting away and picturing it —us in the crowd, standing side by side, the bass vibrating through our bones. Her face turned up to the lights, her body moving with the music, lost in the moment. And me, right there beside her. Close enough to reach for her hand. Close enough to really see her, to know her in a way no one else did.

The idea of it settled deep in my chest, something warm and bright blooming inside me.

But I had to be patient.

She liked me. That much was clear. But I couldn't push too hard, couldn't make the wrong move. I needed to let things happen naturally, even if every part of me was screaming.

Still, I tried to put my phone down, but I couldn't help myself.

I opened her profile again, scrolling through her photos, each one a window into her world. I zoomed in on the small details—her jewellery, the books in the background of her selfies, the posters on her bedroom wall. I wanted to absorb every little thing, to know her better than she knew herself.

Then, I saw it.

A picture from a gig last summer. Her hair was messier than usual, strands sticking to her sweat shined face as she smiled, her arm slung around some guy's waist. He was smug-looking, his hand resting comfortably against her hip, *too* comfortable.

A sharp pang shot through me, something bitter and unwanted curling in my stomach.

I stared at the photo longer than I should have, my mind running in circles. Who was he? A friend? An ex? Was he still in her life? Had she loved him? Why was he touching her like that? Why did he look so smug?

I tried to shake it off, telling myself it was an old photo. It didn't mean anything. But the feeling lingered, gnawing at the edges of my thoughts. I scrolled down, looking for something to distract myself, and that's when I noticed something I hadn't before.

A tattoo on her wrist.

Small, barely visible in most pictures—a tiny star, inked just above the curve of her palm.

I zoomed in, tracing the outline with my eyes. I wondered what it meant. If it had a story. If she'd tell me, when I asked. And if she didn't—would I be able to find out anyway?

I started to make a list in my head; a growing catalogue of things I wanted to know about her. Her favourite food, her favourite book, the little things that made her laugh. The way she took her coffee. Whether she preferred the sunrise or the sunset. I wanted to know it all, to fill in every blank space until I had a complete picture of who she was. A full, unfiltered image of Emma.

I knew I should just let things unfold naturally, that over time these details would come to light. But patience was never my strong suit. She was like a puzzle, and I was desperate to solve her, to piece together every fragmented part and hold the whole thing in my hands.

The more I learned, the more she consumed me. She was kind but sharp, with a dry wit that sometimes caught me off guard. She had a dreamer's heart, always talking about places she wanted to visit, the experiences she longed for. I imagined us travelling together—walking foreign streets at night, her hand slipping into mine, the glow of unfamiliar cities reflected in her eyes. The thought settled in my chest like a permanent fixture, warm and inviting. And then there was that photo of her in Greece, stretched out on golden sand, sun-kissed and utterly at peace. The image burned itself into my mind, a quiet promise of something that could be.

Every night, as I lay in bed, I replayed our conversations, dissecting every word, every moment.

She was the first thing I thought about when I woke up, the last thing before I drifted off. My world, once predictable, had tilted on its axis, shifting its focus entirely to her. I knew it was quick, reckless, irrational even, to let someone occupy this much space in my mind. But I didn't want to stop.

Emma was different. She made everything brighter, more vivid. I know I probably shouldn't, but all I could see was potential and possibilities. Life has been hard, and I sometimes wondered if

I wasn't meant to find love, at least not the kind I dreamed of.

Emma

I couldn't get him out of my head. His messages, the way he spoke to me—it was addictive. He had a way of making me feel seen, like I was the only person in the world who mattered when he talked to me. And I liked that feeling. I liked that he made me feel important.

Every time my phone buzzed; my stomach flipped. When it wasn't him, I felt the smallest pang of disappointment, something I'd never admit aloud. When it was, a quiet thrill shot through me. Our conversations flowed effortlessly, as if we had always known each other. He was careful, not too eager, but I could see through it. He was holding back, pretending not to be as invested as he really was. Trying to play it cool.

The idea of meeting him in person had started to linger in my mind. I wondered if he would be the same—if he would still have that softness, that subtle intensity, when we were face-to-face. I wanted to see how he looked at me in real time, to hear his voice, to feel the weight of his attention on me without the barrier of a screen.

That morning, as I got ready for work, I decided to push things forward. Just a little. A gentle nudge. I picked up my phone, turned to the mirror, and snapped a quick selfie—nothing too staged, just a glimpse of me before heading out.

"Hey, just heading to work. If you're ever in the area, you should drop by! I make a mean latte! xxx"

I hit send and smiled to myself, already anticipating his reaction.

It was a test, really. A way to gauge just how eager he was. Would he pick up on the invitation beneath the words? Would he jump at the chance? The idea of him coming to the coffee shop, watching me from across the counter, made my heart beat a little faster. It felt like control.

His response was instant. "I'd love that! Maybe one day soon. Would be great to see you in person!"

I could almost hear the edge of excitement in his words. He was careful, keeping it light, but I knew. I could feel it.

And just like that, I had him exactly where I wanted him.

I spent the rest of the day thinking about him, wondering what he was doing, what he was thinking. I pictured him sitting at his desk, his eyes lighting up every time he saw a message from me. It was a nice thought, knowing that I had that effect on someone. It made me feel special, important even.

By the time I got home, I was already planning our next conversation. I wanted to keep things light and fun, but I also wanted to hint at something more.

Alex

Emma's message had me fidgeting with excitement. The thought of seeing her in person, of actually being near her, was intoxicating. I could picture it so clearly: walking into the coffee shop, the scent of fresh coffee in the air, seeing her behind the counter in that apron I knew she wore, her smile lighting up when she saw me. It felt like something out of a movie—a meet-cute, a Hallmark moment. The kind of moment you remember forever. The kind of moment you tell your children and grandchildren about.

I couldn't help myself. I found myself thinking about her all the time, wondering what she was doing, who she was with. It wasn't enough just to talk to her; I needed to know more. I started checking her social media more often, looking for any new posts, any updates. I wanted to understand her in a way no one else did. I convinced myself that was what she needed. That was what she wanted.

One evening, as I was scrolling through her Instagram, I noticed something I hadn't seen before. A comment on one of her older photos, from a guy I didn't recognise. It was a simple comment about how she looked, nothing too obvious, but the phrase 'my girl' caught my attention. My stomach twisted. I clicked on his profile, my curiosity getting the better of me. Again.

His account was public, and as I scrolled through his posts, a picture started to form. There were photos of him and Emma together, smiling, looking happy. But there were also posts that hinted at something darker. Comments that suggested things hadn't ended well between them. My heart pounded as I pieced it together. This was her ex. The guy she'd been with before. Before me.

A tight, unfamiliar sensation coiled in my chest. I didn't know much about him, but I didn't like him. The way he looked at her in the photos, the way he talked about her in his posts—it was possessive, smug. He had her once. He didn't deserve her. The thought of anyone else knowing her the way I wanted to made my skin crawl.

I spent the next few days digging deeper, finding out more about their relationship. From what I could gather, it hadn't ended well. There were rumours, comments from mutual friends that hinted at problems, at things not being as perfect as they appeared on social media. I read between the lines, piecing together the story. He hadn't been good to her. That much was clear. There were whispers of infidelity, of him taking her for granted. Like she was someone you could take for granted. Like she wasn't the most important thing in the world.

Then I found something that made my blood turn cold. A comment, buried in a conversation on her Facebook page, vague but unmistakable: 'He was rough with his ex too. She just doesn't talk about it.'

A hot wave of anger surged through me. He was violent to Emma like his ex? The thought of anyone hurting Emma, of making her feel small, made my hands shake. What kind of man thought it was okay to put his hands on her? To make her feel anything less than adored? I stared at his profile picture, feeling something dark and unfamiliar bloom in my chest.

The more I found out, the more determined I became. Emma deserved better. She deserved someone who would treat her right, who would cherish her for who she was. Someone who could love her the way she needed to be loved. Someone like me.

Maybe she already knew that. Maybe that's why she wanted me to come see her so soon. Maybe she was waiting for me to show her what real devotion looked like.

Our conversations continued, and I made sure to I dropped hints about wanting to see her, about being there if she ever needed someone to talk to. I wanted her to know that I was different, that I cared. That I could be the man her ex wasn't.

One evening, we were chatting when she brought up the idea of meeting again. This time, it wasn't just a casual suggestion—it was real.

"I've been thinking" she said. "We should meet up soon. It feels like we've been talking for ages, and it would be nice to actually hang out in person. What do you think? xxx"

My heart leapt from my chest. This was it. The moment I'd been waiting for. I forced myself to stay cool, not to let my excitement come off as too eager but also let her know I wanted to. I instantly noticed the extra kiss on the message too.

"I'd like that" I replied, keeping it short, controlled. "Name the time and place, and I'll be there."

"How about next weekend? We could grab a coffee after my shift, maybe go for a walk. Nothing too fancy, just a chance to hang out xx."

I agreed instantly, but inside, my mind was racing. This was happening. We were going to meet, and I had to be ready. This wasn't just any coffee date—this was the beginning of something bigger. And I couldn't afford to get it wrong.

~

The lead up to our meeting felt like an eternity. I tried to focus on work, to lose myself in routine, but Emma was always there, lingering in the back of my mind. Her smile, her laugh, the way she spoke. I imagined how she would look when she saw me, how her eyes might widen with excitement or how her lips might part slightly in surprise. I craved that moment. I also worried that I wouldn't be interesting enough, or she'd be turned off at the sight of me, but I just knew I needed to meet her.

I spent hours poring over her social media, memorising every post, every caption, every tagged location. I traced the names of her friends, noted where she liked to go on weekends. I knew her favourite bands, the way she liked her coffee, the books she'd been reading. But it wasn't enough. I needed more. I needed to know her beyond the surface, beyond what she chose to share with the world. I needed to understand her better than anyone else ever had.

And yet, despite all that knowledge, there was one thing I couldn't predict—how I would actually feel when I saw her in person. What if I messed up? What if I said something wrong, or worse, what if I froze completely? The idea of disappointing her, of her realising I wasn't what she wanted, gnawed at me.

I needed reassurance. I needed to see her, just for a moment, before the big day. Just to be sure. Just to prepare myself.

That's how I found myself standing outside the coffee shop where she worked, my heart pounding against my ribs. I'd taken the afternoon off, spinning some lie about a dentist appointment. The deception barely registered, seeing her was far more important.

I had been here for almost an hour, pacing up and down the street, stealing glances through the large glass windows. I walked past, slowed near the entrance, then looped back around. My palms were damp, my nerves electric. I felt ridiculous, but I couldn't leave. Not until I saw her. Not until I had something real to hold onto before our meeting.

Finally, on my fifth pass, I spotted her, and it was like time stood still. She was behind the counter, her hair swept up in a messy bun, strands curling loose around her face. She laughed at something a coworker said, her entire presence glowing with warmth.

My breath caught in my throat. She was even more beautiful in person. The screen didn't do her justice. The way she moved, the way she smiled—it was effortless, hypnotic. I stood frozen, watching her hand a coffee to a customer, her fingers brushing the cup with delicate precision. She was right there, so close, yet so far and completely unaware of my presence.

I felt a surge of emotion, a mix of longing and something heavier that settled in my chest, pressing against my ribs. It took me a moment to place it. Fear. A cold, creeping fear that whispered doubts in my ear. She looked so happy. So effortlessly light and at ease. What if I couldn't make her feel that way? What if I wasn't enough? The thought twisted inside me like a knife, burrowing deep and making my stomach flipped. My breath came shallow, my pulse a frantic drumbeat beneath my skin.

Then, as if the universe was truly testing me, a man approached the counter. He was smiling, easy, familiar. Emma greeted him warmly, her eyes lighting up as they spoke. Something in me snapped tight, my jaw clenching as my hands curled into fists, nails biting into my palms. Who was he? A regular? A friend? Something more? The idea of her laughing with someone else, of her giving her attention so freely, made my vision blur. My chest rose and fell, too fast, too sharp. I had to remind myself to breathe. To stay calm. I couldn't let jealousy get the better of me. Not now. She was too perfect to ruin it before I'd even met her.

The man eventually left with a takeaway coffee in hand, strolling out the door without a second thought. Emma turned back to work, her smile lingering, unshaken. The relief was instant, the tension in my muscles easing ever so slightly. I exhaled slowly. It had been nothing. Just her being friendly like I expected her to be. That's all.

I watched her for a few more minutes, memorising every detail. The way she tucked a stray strand of hair behind her ear. The way she tilted her head when she listened. The tiny movements, the unconscious gestures, all of it captivating. Then she disappeared into the back room, and I knew she'd be finishing soon. That was my cue.

Slipping away, I moved across the high street to a bus stop that gave me the perfect vantage point. Partially hidden, I had a clear view of the coffee shop's entrance. I settled in, the anticipation curling tight in my stomach.

Eventually, she stepped outside, bag slung over her shoulder, her eyes flicking up as if scanning the street for something—or someone.

My breath caught. But then, she glanced down, attention shifting to her phone as she typed. My fingers twitched at my sides. Was she messaging me? Was she thinking about me right now? I hoped so. I needed her to be, but my phone soon told me she wasn't. Who was she talking to?

She started walking, her steps light and my feet moved before I could stop them, falling into pace at a distance. Not too close. Just enough.

I wasn't following her. Not really. I just… needed to know where she went. Her routine. Her habits. It wasn't about control; it was about understanding. Preparation. That was all. Soon I'd be a part of those routines.

As I moved, shadowing her path, a strange calm settled over me. Seeing her in person, knowing she was real and not just pixels on a screen, made everything clearer. It was grounding. This was meant to be. Our meeting, our connection— it was all leading to something bigger. I just had to show her. Had to make her see.

She turned into a small park, settling onto a bench. She pulled out a worn-out book, that looked like she'd read it a hundred times. She crossed her legs beneath her as she lost herself in the pages.

My heart was bursting, watching her like this, so peaceful, so perfect. She had no idea how much she meant to me, how deeply I understood her. Despite this being so fast, I knew she was the one. She was the total opposite of my ex, and I knew Emma would be good for me, good to me. And after everything I've learnt so far, she needed me just as much. I would treat her the way she deserved, always.

A slow exhale left my lips. Our meeting was only the beginning, the first step in something far greater. I was ready now. I think.

She hadn't seen me. I knew that much for sure. The park was quiet, the late afternoon sun casting long shadows across the grass. I stayed back, out of sight, watching as her face softened with focus while she opened her book. Her fingers brushed over the pages, her eyes flickering back and forth as she read. She looked so peaceful, so content. I could have watched her like that for hours. My imagination conjuring up thoughts of our lives together. Creating memories on holidays, watching sunrises and sunsets and experiencing life's journey together.

But then my phone buzzed in my pocket, making my heart pound for a minute, snapping me out of my trance. I pulled it out, my breath hitching as I saw her name on the screen.

"Can't believe we're meeting soon! I'm actually

really excited, hope you are too! xx"

A rush of adrenaline surged through me. She was thinking about me. Sitting there, lost in her book, she was still thinking about me. Just as I was thinking about her. I forced myself to keep my reply casual.

"I can't wait! Counting down the days to be honest! What are you up to?"

I hit send and watched, barely breathing, as she pulled out her phone, her lips curving into a small smile. Then she lifted it slightly, tilting her head just so, and snapped a selfie. My phone vibrated again. Her picture filled the screen, the golden light of the setting sun catching in her hair, her eyes alight with something playful, something real. She was so breathtaking.

"Just enjoying a bit of peace and quiet reading my book at the park after work. What about you? xx"

My fingers hesitated over the screen. I didn't want to lie to her, but I couldn't exactly tell her the truth either.

I wanted to see her face when she read my reply.

"Just finished work, heading home now. Wow you look beautiful Emma. Wish I could join you! Looks so relaxing there!"

I watched as she read my message, her smile

widening to show her perfect white teeth. Another reply came almost instantly.

"Aww thanks! Only a few days! We can hang out in this park or go for a drink, whatever you like! xx"

She wanted to spend time with me. She wanted to be with me. That was all that mattered. I had to do this right. I had to make sure everything was perfect when we finally met. I clenched my phone in my hand, resisting the urge to run to her, to sit beside her, to breathe the same air.

She stayed on the bench a little longer, her attention shifting back to her book. I let myself watch her, drinking in every detail, every tiny movement. Eventually, she slipped her book into her bag and stood, stretching slightly before heading towards the park exit. I waited, giving her a few seconds of distance, then followed.

She walked with an easy confidence. She didn't know I was there, that my eyes never left her. I wasn't following her. Not really. I just needed to see where she went, to understand her routine, to be prepared for when our worlds finally, properly collided.

She turned a corner, heading down a quieter street lined with terraced houses. My breath caught when she slowed, stopping in front of a small home with a red door. She pulled out a key, unlocking it with effortless familiarity, and stepped inside. Just before she disappeared, she glanced over her shoulder, scanning the street. But she didn't see me.

I stood still, staring at the door long after it closed behind her. That was her home. The place where she lived, where she woke up in the morning, where she lay in bed at night thinking about me. A deep sense of satisfaction settled in my chest. I knew something real about her now, something intimate. This wasn't just an online fantasy. It was real. She was real.

And soon, she would know just how real I was too.

I turned and forced myself to walk away, but in my mind, I could already picture it: us, together, behind that red door. Not hers. Ours.

I should say at this point that I was very aware that what I was doing might have seemed a little strange or overbearing, but I have only had one serious relationship, and we know how that went. I can admit I am a jealous person, but it is never without reason. I want to keep her safe from harm, and sometimes that requires a little bit of a possessive nature. I know once she is mine, and we are together that I won't feel like this. It's just because I wanted to be with her so much that it drove me a little crazy, but it would all be perfect soon.

Emma

Work was busier than usual today, the steady stream of customers leaving me with little time to think. But even as I poured coffee, handed out change, and wiped down tables, my mind kept drifting back to Alex. I enjoyed my job, some of the regulars were always nice and we even got tips and Christmas presents from our favourites.

After my shift, I decided to head to the park. The weather was nice, and I needed some fresh air, a change from the smell of coffee. I found a quiet bench under a tree and pulled out the book I've probably read twenty times but still love. The peace and quiet was a welcome relief after the noise of the coffee shop all day, and I let myself relax, losing myself in the story for a while, but then, inevitably, my thoughts wandered back to Alex.

I pulled out my phone and sent him a quick

message, letting him know I was excited to finally meet him. I couldn't help but grin at his reply, feeling a flutter of anticipation in my stomach. He seemed just as eager as I was, counting down the days.

Looking around the park, I saw the perfect opportunity to send him a little something. I snapped a selfie, making sure the soft evening light highlighted my best features. I looked cute, and I sent it to him with a smile. His response came almost immediately, a mix of compliment and humour that made me full smile. I could imagine him sitting there, his face flushing red when he saw my picture, maybe trying to hide his smiles for those around him to avoid questions. The thought made me feel warm inside.

I could imagine him staring at the photo, lingering on it a little longer than most would. He always responded quickly, but sometimes, I wondered what ran through his mind before he hit send.

"Soon! We can hang out in a park or go for a walk, whatever you like! xx" I messaged, hoping he'd take the hint. I didn't want to sound too forward, but the truth was, I was looking forward to seeing him in person, to feeling the connection we'd built online translate into real life. I knew it would continue, that wasn't a worry for me.

The relax and read for little while then I headed home, my mind still on Alex, on our conversations. I cooked a quick pasta dinner, settled on the sofa, and picked up my phone again. This time, I wanted to know more about him, to peel back the layers and understand the person behind the messages. I wanted to find out more about his past.

"So," I typed, "what's your relationship history like? I feel like I've told you loads about me, but I don't really know much about you in that way! xx"

His reply took a little longer this time, and for a moment, I wondered if I'd hit a nerve. I'd just started to type that he didn't need to tell me, but then my phone buzzed, and his message appeared. I smirked to myself—of course he'd tell me.

"Not much to tell, to be honest. Had a long-term girlfriend and we lived together, but that didn't end well for me, and I've been single since. I guess I've just been waiting for the right person. What about you?"

I smiled, imagining the slight blush I could almost see on his face as he typed. His honesty was refreshing, and it made me want to be honest with him too. My past wasn't as simple, as clean.

"I've had a few relationships," I began, choosing my words carefully. "My last one was… complicated. He wasn't a good guy, you know? Things got really bad towards the end. I was scared for a while, but I got out of it. It's all behind me now, but it made me a bit wary of trusting people. xxx"

I hit send, my thumb hovering over the screen for a second longer than necessary. My stomach twisted slightly. I hadn't meant to get so deep, but it felt right to share this with Alex, to let him see a part of me I didn't show to anyone. I already felt safe enough with him.

His reply came quickly, and the protective edge in his words took me by surprise. I'm not sure if he meant it in a light-hearted jokey way, but I didn't take that from it.

"I'm really sorry to hear that, Emma. You deserve so much better. If anyone ever tries to hurt you again, I'll make sure they regret it!"

I always sensed there was a seriousness in his words, but that felt intense, a promise laced with something darker. Yet, instead of unsettling me, it made me feel safe, like he cared enough to mean it. "Thank you, Alex. That means a lot," I replied. "I feel safe talking to you, like I can trust you. xxx"

"You can," he replied without hesitation. "I'll always be here for you, Emma. No matter what."

I smiled, warmth spreading through me. There was something about Alex, something that made me feel seen, understood. He was different from anyone I'd met before, and I found myself looking forward to our meeting even more. Three days. Three days, and I'd finally see him, be able to look into his eyes and see the person behind the screen. I couldn't wait. When I wake up, it's two days, I told myself as I drifted to sleep.

Alex

Seeing her in the flesh had made her real, more than just a series of messages on a screen. It had grounded me.

But that had faded the second I opened my eyes to the morning sun, replaced by a growing restlessness that was more intense than before. The more I thought about her, the more I needed to see her again. Just once wasn't enough. The coffee date was two days away, but it felt like an eternity. I couldn't wait that long.

So, of course I went back to the coffee shop.

I told myself it was just to get a coffee, but I knew that was a lie. I had absolutely no intention of walking inside, of letting her see me. Not yet. Not like this. Not so desperate.

Standing across the street again, my eyes scanned the shop, searching for her. And there she was. Behind the counter, elegant and perfect as ever, laughing at something her colleague said. My fingers curled around my phone, tightening instinctively. Who was making her laugh? Did she smile at everyone like that?

The sight of her should have eased the tightness in my chest, but instead, it made it worse. This was why I couldn't wait two days. She was out here in the world, interacting, existing, being seen by other people. And they didn't even realise how lucky they were.

I forced myself to stay seated at the bus stop, pretending to scroll through my phone while keeping my eyes fixed on her. Telling myself I was just checking, just watching over her—that was all. And that was okay, wasn't it?

After an hour, and several showers, I was cold and wet, so I was about to leave, thinking I'd seen enough for today, when movement on the other side of the street stopped me cold. A man was walking towards the entrance.

Tall. Dark hair. There was something about him —something that made my skin prickle before I even placed it.

Then, it hit me.

My stomach twisted, ice flooding my veins. It was him. The guy from her online posts. Emma's ex. The one who had hurt her. The one she told me about.

My jaw clenched so hard it ached, and my teeth crunched. My fingers dug into my palms, nails pressing deep. The world around me dulled, fading into irrelevance. He was here. He was walking into her space, into her life, like he still had the right. Did he have the right to? Did Emma tell me everything?

For a brief, burning moment, I imagined what it would feel like to rip that right away from him.

I watched as he approached the counter, his eyes locked onto Emma like a predator closing in on prey. She froze, her smile vanishing in an instant, replaced by something raw—fear. Even from across the street, I could see the stiffness in her posture, the way her fingers tightened around the cloth she'd been using to wipe the counter.

He started talking, his voice low but insistent. I couldn't hear every word, but the tone was unmistakable, laced with frustration. Emma shook her head. Even from this distance, I could see the way her body subtly leaned away from him, recoiling.

He wasn't backing down. Emma's colleague—a blonde girl with a no-nonsense stance—stepped forward, presumably telling him to leave. He ignored her. The tension grew, the air between them practically crackling. And then—a bang. A slammed fist on the counter. The entire shop flinched with it.

I saw Emma take a step back, her face pale, her breathing shallow. The bastard turned on his heel and stormed out, shoving the door open with unnecessary force. Emma crumbled, her colleague wrapping a protective arm around her, guiding her toward the back.

I sat frozen, my hands clenched into fists so tight my knuckles ached. Half of my instinct telling me screamed to go to her, to pull her into my arms and promise her she'd never have to deal with him again. The other half telling me to tackle him and beat him to a bloody pulp in her honour. But I couldn't. Not yet. She'd know I was here.

The sight of her crying, so vulnerable and small,

made my blood burn. He had no right to make her feel like that. He had no right to even breathe the same air as her.

There was only one thing I could do. I had to stop him.

I saw him turn left down the street, walking away with that same arrogant hunch of his shoulders, as if he was the one who'd been wronged. My jaw tightened as I moved, my pace mirroring his.

He didn't notice me. He had no idea who I was, but I was tracking his every step, memorising the way he walked, the way his fingers twitched at his sides. I followed him through the city, past crowded streets and alleyway shortcuts, until he finally stopped outside a converted house. His grubby little flat.

I stood across the street, staring at the place he called his home.

Now I knew where to find him.

A part of me wanted to move now, to walk up behind him and show him what it felt like to be powerless. But I needed to be smart. Careful. He wasn't going to just get a warning—he was going to learn.

I wouldn't let him hurt her again.

Emma

The moment Bradley walked through the door; my body reacted before my mind did. My breath caught in my throat, my fingers clenched tighter around the cloth I'd been holding. A month. It had been a whole month since I'd seen him, since I'd finally gathered the courage to leave.

I thought I was free.

I thought he was gone.

But he stood there, leaning against the counter like he had every right to be in my world again.

"Emma," he said, voice smooth, easy. As if he hadn't ripped my life apart. "We need to talk."

I forced my shoulders back, tried to keep my voice steady. "There's nothing to talk about, Bradley. It's over."

He smirked, tilting his head like he found me amusing. "Come on, babe. Just give me five minutes. We can't end things like this."

I knew that tone too well. It was the same one he'd used every time he'd convinced me to stay, every time he'd made me doubt myself. For years, I had been trapped in the cycle—his apologies, his promises, the nights spent crying, the bruises hidden under sleeves.

Not this time.

I swallowed hard, gripping the edge of the counter for stability. "Bradley, you need to leave. You're not supposed to be here. The court said—"

His expression darkened in an instant, the charm slipping away like a mask discarded. He leaned closer, and my stomach lurched. "You don't get to just walk away after what you did," he hissed. "You owe me a conversation. You owe me that much."

Lucy, my colleague, stepped forward. Brave, despite the slight tremor in her voice. "Hey! She asked you to leave!"

Bradley's glare flicked to her, but only for a second. His focus was on me, always on me. "This isn't over, Emma," he murmured.

Then—bang! His fist slammed onto the counter, rattling the cups and spilling fresh drinks. I jumped, my breath hitching, my pulse roaring in my ears.

And then he was gone, storming out the door like a thunderstorm.

As soon as he left, I deflated, the adrenaline draining from my limbs. My body shook. Lucy wrapped an arm around me, guiding me to the back as other coworkers rushed to clean up the mess.

Tears I had fought so hard to hold in spilled over.

"Do you want to call the police?" Lucy asked gently, pressing a tissue into my hand.

I shook my head. "No. He'll leave me alone. He always does... eventually."

But even as I said the words, I knew they weren't true.

Bradley never let go that easily.

And for the first time, I wished Alex was here. I hadn't met him in person yet, but something about him—his words, his energy—felt like safety. And right now, that was all my mind could think about. The last time we spoke.

"If anyone ever tries to hurt you again, I'll make sure they regret it!"

I left work early; well, my boss sent me home. My nerves still on edge when I got there but, I was grateful for the silence. I didn't tell anyone what had happened—not my friends, not my family. I didn't want them to worry, to tell me what I already knew—that I should have done more to get away from Bradley or got away earlier. I just wanted to forget, to pretend the day had been normal.

I curled up on the sofa, my phone in my hand, and texted Alex. We just needed to get Friday out of the way, and we'd be together on Saturday. The thought of seeing him in person, of talking to him face-to-face, was the only thing keeping me sane at this point. I was almost glad I'd be working all day so it would go quicker. Almost.

"Hey, just one more day! I can't wait to see you! How's your day been? xx" I typed, trying to keep my tone light, hiding the turmoil inside me.

He replied almost immediately, as always. "Can't wait to see you too! My day's been good, just thinking about our coffee date. How about you?"

I hesitated for a moment before replying. "Same here. It's been a long day at work, but only one more day to do before the weekend! It feels like it's been forever since I've been able to relax and just enjoy someone's company xx"

I left out everything about Bradley—the fear, the way my hands were still shaking. Instead, I asked Alex about his day, about his plans for the evening, anything to keep the conversation going, to distract myself from the dark thoughts creeping in. As we talked, the tightness in my chest eased, replaced by a warm, comforting feeling. Alex was sweet, kind, everything Bradley wasn't, and I found myself wanting to open up to him, to tell him everything.

Alex wasn't like Bradley. He wouldn't hurt me. If anything, he'd protect me, keep me safe. And maybe, just maybe, that was exactly what I needed.

Alex

From the moment Emma started messaging me after work, I knew she was lying. Her words had that forced fake cheerfulness to them, like she was trying to convince both of us that everything was perfectly fine. But I knew better. I had seen her in the café, the way her face went pale when Bradley walked in. The tension in her shoulders, the way she looked around as if searching for an escape.

She didn't mention Bradley at all when we talked. Not a single word about him showing up, the argument they'd had, the way he'd cornered her behind the counter. I'd seen the fear in her eyes. It took everything in me to stay hidden, to not rush in and punch him for making her look so terrified.

She didn't tell me any of that. Instead, she talked about how tired she was, how she couldn't wait for our coffee date the day after tomorrow. I listened, quietly angry at the secrets. I knew she was trying to protect me from the truth—or maybe just trying to protect herself. I wanted to ask her about Bradley, to demand why she hadn't told me what had happened, but I couldn't. What if she thought I was being too intense? Too controlling? Too... Bradley?

Maybe I was overreacting. Maybe I was the problem. I was the one following her, watching her every move. Was I any better than Bradley, showing up uninvited, lurking around? I didn't want to be that kind of guy. I didn't want her to see me as someone to be afraid of. But I couldn't help it. The thought of Bradley being anywhere near her made my skin crawl. I wanted to protect her, to keep her safe from him.

I could feel myself spiralling and caught myself. I just hated Bradley for what he'd done to her, for the pain he'd caused.

The more I thought about it, the more I wondered if I was any different. She was my everything and she didn't even know it—my perfect girl—and I couldn't lose her. Not to Bradley. Not to anyone. I pushed my doubts to the side, continued the evening texting back and forth until she fell asleep. I'd been so tired trying to match her late nights, so I crashed as soon as I knew she was gone. I kept up my usual positive attitude and decided to allow her the benefit of the doubt. She was just protecting me from her messy past, but she would learn in time that I accepted all of her, and she didn't need to fear anything anymore.

It was the last day before we'd meet in person. I had it marked in my mind, on my phone— hell, I'd probably have carved it into my skin if that wasn't insane. I counted down the hours, the minutes, the seconds. The way Emma had hidden what happened with Bradley gnawed at me like a dull blade against bone.

I needed to check on her. To hear her voice, to see her, to know she was okay. But I knew I had to play it cool. I couldn't afford to scare her off, not now. Not when we were so close.

The day crawled by, every second stretching into

eternity. My boss, in typical fashion, decided to pile on extra tasks, keeping me late. Some new big contract, some deal that was apparently life or death to the company. I couldn't have cared less. My focus was elsewhere.

I tried to stay professional, to act like I gave a damn, but my thoughts drifted. To Emma. To Bradley. To the way she had looked in the café —small, tense, searching for an exit. My jaw clenched at the memory. Had he tried to contact her again? Had he been waiting outside her flat, lingering in the shadows? The thought made my stomach churn.

I wasn't a fighter. I had never really been in a proper fight. The last time I'd thrown a punch was over a decade ago, and it hadn't even been serious. But the way I felt about Emma—the way I *needed* to protect her—made my fingers itch. I wasn't sure what I would do if I saw Bradley again, but I knew I wouldn't just stand there this time.

By the time I finally got home, the city outside had settled into its quiet, late-night hum. I collapsed onto the couch, feeling the weight of the day press down on me. My first instinct was to reach for my phone.

There it was. A notification. A message from Emma.

My pulse jumped as I opened it.

Hey! How was work? I'm just winding down for the night. Can't believe tomorrow's the day! xx

Attached was a photo.

I inhaled sharply as I tapped on it, the image filling my screen.

She was lying on her bed, hair fanned out over the pillow, soft waves framing her face. A simple t-shirt draped over her, and even though it was casual, it still made my breath catch. Her expression was peaceful, content. Her lips curved into a small, sleepy smile; her eyes half-lidded. The warm glow of her bedside lamp bathed her in gold, making her skin look like it was glowing from within.

She looked so soft. So perfect.

For a moment, I just stared.

I imagined being there, lying beside her. Reaching out, spinning a lock of her hair around my finger. Feeling the warmth of her skin under my touch. I could almost smell the faint trace of her perfume, something light and floral, something that would cling to my clothes if I pulled her close.

I swallowed hard, dragging myself back to reality.

I needed to stop doing this—falling into these thoughts, letting my mind drift into places it shouldn't. Tomorrow, I'd see her for real. Not through a screen. I would hear her laugh in person, see her eyes light up when she spoke. I didn't need to *imagine* anything anymore.

But then came the doubt.

What if I wasn't what she expected? What if I messed it all up? What if she took one look at me and realised she'd made a mistake?

No. That wouldn't happen. I wouldn't let it.

I typed out my response carefully, making sure every word was right.

Work was hectic, boss kept me late, but honestly, I can't wait for tomorrow! What time by the way? You look so relaxed! I wish I could be there to unwind with you!

I stared at the message for a second before hitting send.

Her reply came quickly. We talked for a little while longer, mostly about how excited we both were, and with every text, my chest tightened in that familiar way—the kind of ache that only she could cause.

I wasn't imagining this. The connection. The chemistry. She felt it too.

When she finally said she was going to sleep, I lay in bed, my phone resting on my chest, my thoughts running wild. I scrolled through our old messages, reading over them like a student studying for an exam. I memorised the details, the little things she liked, the words she used most often. I wanted her to know I paid attention. That I *knew* her.

I pictured it. The moment she saw me. The way her lips would part in surprise, the way her voice would sound when she finally said, *hey* for the first time. I imagined her smile when I said something to make her laugh, the way her eyes would linger on mine when I talked about music and *us*.

I wanted it to be perfect.

I *needed* it to be perfect.

Because Emma was already everything I had dreamed of.

And I would make sure I was everything she needed, too.

Tomorrow was our day.

No pressure.

Alex

The morning of our date arrived with a jolt of adrenaline. My phone buzzed me awake, the alarm I'd set for the day blaring like a warning siren. I turned it off, staring at the ceiling for a few moments, trying to steady my breathing. Today was the day. The one I'd been waiting for, planning, obsessing over. And now that it was finally here, I felt like I was unravelling. Sleep had been an impossible task the night before—every time I closed my eyes, I saw her. Imagined her walking towards me, imagined her voice, imagined the way her hand might feel in mine. I had built up this moment in my head for so long, and now that it was happening, it was almost too much.

I forced myself to move, dragging my body out of bed, my limbs feeling heavier than usual. I went through the routine automatically—shower, brush teeth, trim the barely-there beard I kept just to look older. As I stood in front of the mirror,

I examined myself with a new intensity, seeing myself through her eyes. Would she like what she saw? Would I measure up to the version of me she'd imagined? I'd chosen my outfit carefully—jeans and a navy button-down shirt, something safe but presentable. I didn't want to overdo it, but I needed her to see I'd made an effort.

After getting dressed, I found myself back at my desk, staring at my open laptop. I needed to feel prepared, to have control over something—anything. I pulled up Emma's profiles, scrolling through her pictures and rereading her posts. I had seen them all before, but today, they felt heavier, more important. Like I was studying, cramming for the biggest test of my life. Her favourite books, the music she loved, the little details she had shared with me late at night. I wanted to have everything fresh in my mind, ready to bring up in conversation so that I could keep her interest, so there wouldn't be awkward silences. So, she'd see how much I cared. And how different I was.

But as I scrolled, an uneasy feeling crept in. A whisper of doubt, nagging at the edges of my excitement. What if she didn't like me? What if, the second she saw me in person, she felt nothing? I had built her up as this perfect, unattainable woman, and now, for the first time, I had to confront the possibility that I might not live up to whatever version of me she had in her head. The thought twisted my stomach.

I slammed the laptop shut, trying to shake the negativity away. She had agreed to meet me. That meant something. That had to mean something.

My phone shook across my desk, snapping me out of my downward spiral. I snatched it up, my pulse kicking into overdrive when I saw her name on the screen.

"Hey! Just wanted to say I can't wait to see you today! I'm so excited!! xxx"

A grin tugged at my lips before I even realised it. Three kisses. That was something, wasn't it? I had started to notice that when she really wanted to emphasise something, she used three. My chest loosened slightly, the tension ebbing away just a little. She was excited. She wanted this too.

I quickly typed out a reply, my fingers trembling slightly as I hit send.

"I can't wait either! Counting down the minutes!"

The nerves weren't gone, but her message helped. If she was this excited, maybe I wasn't crazy. Maybe I wasn't the only one who had been overthinking every little thing.

The next hour dragged. I paced my apartment, checking my phone every few minutes. I rehearsed conversations in my head, picturing how it would all go. I imagined the way she would smile when she saw me, the way she'd tilt her head when she was really listening. But then, intrusive thoughts slithered in. What if she looked at me with indifference? What if she checked her phone every few minutes, already making up an excuse to leave? I shook my head, trying to banish the images. Focus on the good. Focus on her message. Focus on those three little kisses.

Finally, it was time to go. I grabbed my jacket, stealing one last glance in the mirror. My reflection stared back at me—eyes a little too wide, hair slightly messy. I ran a hand through it, trying to smooth it down, then took a deep breath. I could do this. I had to do this.

The coffee shop was only a short walk away, but it felt like the longest journey of my life. My mind raced with last-minute doubts and reassurances, a constant battle between anxiety and hope. I forced myself to breathe, to keep my steps steady. Be cool. Be confident. Girls don't like nervous, awkward guys. I repeated it like a mantra, even though my hands wouldn't stop clenching into fists at my sides and my armpits were already feeling sweaty and sticky.

As I reached the shop, I stopped just outside, taking a moment to gather myself. *Girls don't like nervous, awkward guys.* Through the window, I spotted her instantly. Emma was behind the counter, mid-conversation with a customer, her face lit up in a warm, easy smile. Her hair was pulled back into a messy bun, loose strands framing her face, making her look effortlessly beautiful.

And in that moment, my breath caught. She was real. Right there. Just a few feet away. And she was waiting for me to enter her life.

The weight of the moment settled on my shoulders as I exhaled the long breath I didn't realise I'd been holding, but instead of fear, I felt something steadier. This was it. No turning back now. Girls don't like nervous, awkward guys.

I took the deepest breath of my life and pushed the door open. The bell jingled softly as I stepped inside, the unexpected chime making my entrance feel louder than I wanted. I hadn't accounted for a bell. I wanted to slip in unnoticed, compose myself before she saw me, but before I could even gather my thoughts, Emma looked up. Our eyes met for the first time.

"Alex!" she called, waving me over with a smile that sent a rush of warmth through my chest. "You made it!"

I forced a casual smile; despite the fact my heart was trying to hammer its way out of my ribcage and bounce across the floor in front of her. "Yeah, of course I did," I said, walking over to the counter and taking a seat at the bar. "How's your shift been today?"

She shrugged, her eyes bright and lively as she looked at me. "Not too bad. But I've been looking forward to this all day. I've been checking the clock every five minutes."

God, she was cute—the way she admitted that and looked away sheepishly, her fingers idly fidgeting with a napkin.

"Me too," I admitted, though my voice came out more breathless than I wanted. I cleared my throat, trying to sound more composed. "I barely slept, if I'm honest. I kept checking my phone like a lunatic."

She laughed, a soft, musical sound that made something inside me melt. "Well, you're here now," she said. "Just give me a few minutes to finish up, and then we'll go. There's a place around the corner I think you'll like."

I nodded, watching as she moved behind the counter, tidying up, talking to customers, smiling like she was in her element. This was real. This was happening. After all the messages, all the planning, all the waiting, I was finally here, with her, and I hadn't messed it up. Yet.

When she was done, we stepped out into the evening air, the crisp breeze swirling around us as we walked side by side to the café she'd mentioned. Every step felt loaded with something I couldn't put into words. I stole glances at her, taking in the way her hair caught the light, the way she gestured animatedly as she talked. She told me about the coffee they served, how it was imported from Spain and "somehow just better," and how an elderly woman had tipped her ten pounds earlier for being "lovely." I wasn't surprised. Emma was lovely.

The café she chose for us was small and cosy, with warm lighting and the scent of fresh coffee thick in the air. We found a corner table, tucked away from the bustle, and she ordered us both lattes without hesitation.

"So," she said as we settled into our seats. "This is nice, huh? Us. In person."

Girls don't like nervous, awkward guys still ringing in my ear but the intimacy of the moment got the better of me. "Yeah," I said, stumbling over my words. "It's… it's really great to see you, Emma. You look… amazing."

She blushed slightly, and it was the most beautiful thing I'd ever seen. "Thanks, Alex. You look great too. I like your shirt!"

I glanced down, suddenly self-conscious but desperate to appear calm and cool. "Oh, uh, thanks. Just threw this on."

She laughed again, her eyes crinkling at the corners. "Well, it works. You should throw things on more often."

Our coffee arrived, and the conversation flowed as easily as it always had. We talked about everything and nothing—our days, our favourite films, the weird little things that made us laugh. I hung onto every word, every smile, every glance. I wanted to memorise the way she tilted her head when she was thinking, the way she played with the rim of her cup absentmindedly.

Still, my nerves weren't completely gone. There were moments where I second-guessed myself, worried I was talking too much, or not enough. I wanted to get everything right, but I knew I was overthinking, and my armpits were now swimming which constantly bothered me.

Then, out of nowhere, Emma broke a comfortable silence. "You know," she said, her voice softer now, more thoughtful, "I've really enjoyed talking to you these past few weeks. You're… different. In a good way."

She held my gaze, her expression sincere. "I'm really glad we're doing this, Alex. It's been a long time since I've met someone who just… gets me."

My chest tightened, something overwhelming and electric flooding through me. "To be honest Emma, I get that," I murmured. "I feel the same."

We stayed there for hours, long after the sky outside had faded into deep twilight. The café started emptying out from its dinner service, but neither of us made a move to leave. I could have stayed there forever, caught in this beautiful moment.

Every now and then, I found myself getting lost in her eyes, in the way she spoke, in the way she looked at me. I wanted to reach across the table and take her hand, to show her somehow that I wasn't just infatuated, I was hers. I knew I loved her. Maybe it was too soon to say it, but I knew. And I had known for weeks.

Eventually, the café staff began closing, and we took that as our cue to leave. We walked back to her car in a comfortable silence, the city lights casting a golden glow around us. I kept glancing at her hand beside mine, aching to reach for it, to feel her fingers laced with mine. But I held back.

When we reached her car, she turned to me, that same happy light still dancing in her incredible grey eyes. Sparkling for me in the moonlight. "This was really nice, Alex. I'm so glad we did this."

"Me too," I said, my voice thick with sincerity. "I had a great time. Really."

Then, before I could react, she leaned in and wrapped her arms around me. It was quick, a fleeting moment of warmth and softness, and before I could properly return it, she was already pulling away. No, come back.

"I'll see you soon, yeah?" she asked, her voice light, hopeful.

"Yeah," I nodded, trying to keep my grin in check. "Definitely."

I watched her drive away, my entire body buzzing, my mind spinning with everything that had just happened. I felt high. Weightless. Like I had just lived a moment that would be imprinted on me forever.

She was everything. And I knew, deep in my bones, that she was the one.

Emma

I checked my reflection in the backroom mirror for the hundredth time, trying to steady my nerves. My shift was almost over, and I could feel the anticipation building. I'd sent Alex a text, saying how excited I was for our date. The thought of finally meeting him in person had my stomach in knots, in the best possible way.

I pulled out my phone again, my eyes drifting to his reply.

"I can't wait either! Counting down the minutes!"

Every time I read it; a butterfly took flight in my stomach. It felt good knowing he was just as eager as I was. We'd been talking for weeks, and now that the day was here, I was both thrilled and a little scared. What if he wasn't what I expected? What if I wasn't what he expected? I felt like maybe I'd made myself sound too interesting or intelligent and he'd realise now I was just a girl working in a coffee shop.

I shook my head, pushing the doubts aside. Alex seemed sweet and genuine. His messages were always thoughtful, and he remembered the little things I told him. That was rare—most guys I'd met just talked about themselves, or tried to make it all sexual, but Alex actually listened. He made me feel important, like I mattered.

As the minutes ticked by, I kept glancing at the clock, willing my shift to end. Finally, it was time. I started tidying up the counter, my hands shaking slightly with nerves. The bell over the door chimed, and I looked up just as Alex walked in.

My heart skipped a beat. He was taller than I'd imagined, with messy brown hair and glasses that gave him a cute, nerdy vibe. There was something endearing about the way he looked around, a little unsure of himself, like he was searching for something—or someone—to anchor him. I couldn't help but smile, waving him over.

"Alex!" I called, trying to sound casual. "You made it!"

He smiled back, hesitant but genuine. "Yeah, of course I did," he said, coming over. "How's your shift going today?"

Always thinking about me. "Not too bad," I said with a slight grin, looking him in the eyes. "I've been looking forward to this all day."

"Me too," he replied, his voice a little shaky. "Really, I've been counting down the hours." His gaze flickered away briefly. I think he finds eye contact a little intimidating. I kind of like the nervous, awkward types. It's cute really.

I laughed, feeling a bit more at ease. "Well, you're here now. Just give me a few minutes to finish up, and we can go."

As I wrapped up my tasks, I caught him stealing looks at me, as I stole glances at him. He looked good, in a slightly boyish way. The dark blue button-down shirt he wore made his eyes stand out, and his hair had that just-got-out-of-bed look that was surprisingly attractive. He was definitely nervous, shifting and fidgeting on his stool, but I found it adorable instantly. It was nice to know I had that effect on him.

We left the shop together, heading to the café I'd picked out. It was only a short walk, but it gave me a chance to get a feel for him in person, away from the prying eyes of colleagues.

He moved with a kind of quiet confidence, though I could sense the nervous energy humming beneath the surface. He didn't talk much on the way, and I had to keep the conversation going, but I didn't mind. He seemed sweet, just a little reserved. I'm sure he'd relax once we sat down.

At the café, we found a small table in the corner. It was cosy and felt a little more private, away from the other customers. I ordered us both lattes and we settled into an easy conversation. At least, I tried to make it easy. Alex was still a little tense, his eyes darting around the room like he was trying to take everything in at once. Like he was studying the space. Or looking for an escape. I wanted to make him feel comfortable, so I asked him about his day, his job, his hobbies —anything to get him talking.

I caught him off guard when I said during a slightly awkward silence, "You know, I've really enjoyed talking to you these past few weeks. You're… different. In a good way." I needed to let him know he didn't need to be nervous with me and he could let his guard down, "I'm really glad we're doing this, Alex. It's been a long time since I've met someone who just... gets me."

And it worked, because something about his demeanour changed when hearing those words, like he woke up and remembered this was real. His reply came without hesitation and sounded slightly pained, but deep. "To be honest, I get that," his eyes suddenly boring into mine with an intensity that made me tingle a little. "I feel the same Emma."

Okay, he was good looking when he was being serious, and my name sounded like so nice on his lips!

There was something genuine about him, a sincerity I found refreshing. I'd had my share of dates with guys who only cared about one thing, but Alex seemed different. He actually cared about who I was, not just what I looked like. It was rare, and it made me want to know more about him.

As we talked, I found myself liking him more. He was smart, with a quirky sense of humour that made me laugh. He wasn't as smooth as some of the guys I'd dated, but that was part of his charm. I had to lead the conversation a bit, asking questions, keeping things flowing, but I could tell he was trying. And that was enough for me. He was clearly inexperienced, but I liked that. I could teach him.

The café started to empty out, signalling it was time to go. Alex insisted on walking me to my car, which I thought was very traditional. But I've always liked a protective guy. We walked in comfortable silence, the city lights flickering above us, casting elongated shadows on the pavement. I could feel his tension beside me, the way he kept glancing at me, his hands shoved into his pockets. It was cute, how unsure he seemed. I wondered what he was thinking.

When we reached my car, I turned to him, smiling. "This was really nice, Alex. I'm glad we did this."

"Me too," he said, his voice sincere. "I've had a great time, Emma. Really."

For a moment, I considered kissing him. I knew he wouldn't make the move, and the thought was there, lingering in my mind. But I hesitated. Not yet. I didn't want to move too fast. I didn't want to scare him off or give him the wrong idea, so instead, I stepped forward and gave him a quick, tight hug.

"I'll see you soon, yeah?" I said, stepping back, meeting his eyes.

"Yeah," he nodded, beaming a nerdy smile I don't

think he knew he was wearing. "Definitely."

As I slid into my car, I glanced at him in the rearview mirror. He was still standing there, watching me. A small, satisfied smile tugged at the corner of my lips as I pulled away. The date had gone better than I'd hoped. Alex was sweet, kind, and he made me feel good about myself.

I could see this going somewhere.

When I got home, I couldn't stop smiling. I changed into my pyjamas and curled up in bed with my phone. I typed out a quick message to Alex.

"Had a great time tonight! Maybe next time we can go somewhere a little more… romantic? xxx" I wanted to be clear that I saw him in that way, I think he needed it.

His reply came almost instantly. Of course.

"Sounds perfect. I'm already looking forward to it. I had the best time!"

We spent the next hour texting, talking about where we could go for our next date, sharing little jokes and stories. As we talked, I felt a warmth spreading through me, a happiness I hadn't felt in a long time. Alex was different, special. I could see a future with him, something real. It seemed so easy and simple, the way it was supposed to be.

As I lay in bed, the lights off and my phone resting on my chest, I felt a sense of peace. This was just the beginning, the start of something good. I didn't know where it would lead, but I was excited to find out.

Tomorrow could come with all its uncertainties, but for now, I was happy, and that was more than enough.

I stretched out in bed, savouring the feeling of having the whole day to myself. No work, no obligations—just a Sunday to relax and do whatever I felt like. The date with Alex had gone so well last night. I couldn't stop thinking about it, replaying every moment in my mind. The way he looked at me, nervous but sweet, the warmth of his presence. It felt good, knowing that I had someone like him in my life. Someone kind, someone safe, someone reliable.

I got up and headed to the shower, letting the hot water wash away any lingering sleepiness. My mind drifted to Alex as I enjoyed the steam, wondering what he was doing right now, if he was thinking about me too. I hoped so. I thought about sending him a message, something to let him know I was thinking of him. After last night, I wanted to keep that connection going, to let him know I was interested. So, after my shower, I wrapped myself in a towel, the steam billowing around me. I caught sight of myself in the bathroom mirror, my skin flushed pink from the heat, my hair damp and curling around my face. Feeling a little bold, I grabbed my phone and took a quick selfie, my towel wrapped tightly around me, just hinting at something hotter. Nothing too much—just a tease, something to keep him wanting more.

I typed out a quick message: "Morning! Just got out of the shower and thought of you! What are you up to today? xx"

I hit send and smiled, imagining his reaction. Alex was shy, but I could tell he liked me and found me attractive, even if he was a little uncomfortable or intimidated by me. The way he looked at me last night, his eyes lighting up whenever I spoke—it made me feel good, made me feel seen. I went back to my room and got dressed, feeling a lightness in my step. Today was going to be a good day, I could feel it.

I spent the next hour tidying up the house, humming to myself. It was nice to have a day to myself, to just relax and not have to worry about anything. I was just finishing up the dishes when I heard a knock at the door.

I put down the dish I was holding, walked to the door, and peered through the peephole, my breath catching in my throat.

Bradley.

For a moment, I just stood there, staring. My heart was jumping out of my chest, my mind racing. Why was he here? He wasn't supposed to be here. He wasn't even allowed to be here. I took a deep breath, trying to steady myself. Maybe if I just ignored him, he'd go away.

The knock came again, louder this time. More insistent. I bit my lip, fear clawing at my stomach. I couldn't ignore him, not without him making a scene to the neighbours. I unlocked the door and opened it a crack, my voice shaking.

"What do you want, Bradley?"

He pushed the door open, stepping inside without waiting for an invitation. His eyes were wild, his jaw clenched. I backed away, terror setting in.

"We need to talk, Emma," he said, his voice low, dangerous.

"There's nothing to talk about," I said, trying to keep my voice steady and confident. "You're not supposed to be here. If you don't leave, I'll call the police."

His eyes flashed with anger. "Call the police? You think that scares me? You think I care?" He stepped closer, his presence overwhelming, suffocating. "You've always been a liar, Emma. Always playing the victim. You made me crazy, you know that? This is all because of *you*."

I flinched, his words hitting me like a physical blow. "Bradley, stop, please, just go. I don't want to see you. You can't be here."

He laughed, a harsh, bitter sound. "You think you can just get rid of me? You think you can just move on, pretend like I never existed?"

I felt my phone vibrate in my hand, Alex's name flashing on the screen. I ignored it, too focused on Bradley, on the fear twisting in my gut.

"You need to leave," I said, my voice trembling. "Now."

Bradley's eyes narrowed, his hands clenching into fists. For a moment, I thought he might hit me. Instead, he turned and grabbed the TV remote, throwing it across the room. It hit the TV, the screen shattering with a loud crack. I flinched, my heart pounding in my chest.

"You're nothing, Emma, you're sick." he spat, his voice filled with venom.

He stormed out, slamming the door behind him.

I stood there, shaking, my eyes fixed on the broken TV. My phone vibrated again, a reminder of the text I'd received, so I pulled it out with trembling hands.

"What are you up to right now?" Alex's text read.

I stared at the screen, the words blurring through my tears. My fingers trembled as I clutched the phone tighter, my pulse a frantic drum against my ribs. I couldn't let him know how scared I was. The thought of Alex seeing me like this —broken, vulnerable—twisted something in my stomach. I took a shaky breath, forcing air into my lungs, trying to quiet the panic that threatened to choke me. I needed to keep it together. I needed to stay strong.

I wiped my face with the sleeve of my hoodie, but my hands wouldn't stop shaking. I double locked the front door, like it mattered now. The tightness in my chest didn't ease. I felt like I was shrinking into myself, folding inwards under the weight of it all. The room felt smaller, like the walls were pressing in on me, suffocating me. I needed to move, to get away from the silence, but my body felt heavy—like lead, like I was sinking into the floor.

I stumbled toward my bedroom, every step an effort. The second I reached my bed, I collapsed onto it, pulling the covers over me, as if they could shield me from the world. From him. From myself.

I lay there, curled up, my mind racing in endless circles. The confrontation replayed over and over, each word sharper, cutting deeper. Bradley's face, twisted in anger. His voice, rising, full of entitlement. The way he shoved his way into my home like he still had a right to be there. I clenched my fists, nails digging into my palms. He didn't get to do this to me anymore. He didn't get to walk into my life and shake the ground beneath me like an earthquake I couldn't outrun.

I reached for my phone, my fingers fumbling over the screen as I tried to type. My head felt foggy, my body drained, but I needed to tell Alex. He would worry if I didn't. He always did. I swallowed hard, my throat dry, and forced myself to focus.

"Just had my ex turn up, looking for an argument. I'll talk to you in a little while and tell you more. I want you to know, I just need a little time x"

I hovered over the send button, hesitation twisting in my gut. Alex cared so much—too much, maybe. Would he see this as a test? Would he think I was pulling away? I didn't want to deal with his questions, his insistence that he could fix things. I just needed quiet. A moment to breathe.

I hit send.

Then I curled into myself, my phone clutched tightly in my hands, as if holding onto it would keep me grounded. I squeezed my eyes shut, willing myself to disappear into the darkness. Just for a little while. Just until I could face it all again.

Alex

I was there. I heard him. I saw him, hurting her, again.

I woke up restless, my mind tangled in the echoes of last night. The warmth of Emma's touch, the way she'd smiled over dinner—it played on a loop in my head. She was soft, trusting. Perfect. I needed to see her again.

She'd said she was spending the day at home, unwinding. I pictured it—Emma curled up under a blanket, lost in a book, maybe humming some song I showed her without even realising it. It felt safe. Right. I wanted to be part of that, even if just from a distance. Maybe then, I'd finally be able to relax.

I dressed quickly, barely noticing my own movements, like I was being pulled forward by something beyond me. I told myself I was just going for a walk, just stretching my legs. But I knew exactly where I was going. My feet carried me toward Emma's street, as if drawn by some invisible force.

When I reached her road, I slowed my pace, keeping my head down, my hood up. Her house was still, the curtains drawn. No sign of movement. I walked past, casual, like I wasn't watching. Like I wasn't waiting for a reason to stay.

Then, I saw it.

A car mounted the curb, engine cutting off sharply. My stomach twisted. I turned, about to walk the other way—until I saw him step out.

Bradley.

A hot, sharp pulse of rage shot through me.

I ducked behind a parked car, my breath shallow, eyes locked on him as he marched up to Emma's door. Even from a distance, I could see the way he moved—tense, charged, like a snake coiling before the strike. He knocked, then pounded when she didn't answer fast enough. My fists clenched. He wasn't supposed to be here. He wasn't supposed to be anywhere near her.

The door opened just a crack. Emma's face appeared, pale, her shoulders hunched inward. I could see the way she held herself—rigid, small, like she was trying to disappear.

I inched closer, crouching behind a black car parked next door.

Then I heard them.

Her voice, soft but strained.

His, low and sharp.

A crash. Something breaking inside.

I didn't realise I'd moved until I was gripping my phone so hard my knuckles turned white. My hands were shaking, but not from fear. From fury. My vision blurred at the edges, red-hot anger rising like bile. I forced myself to take a breath, to think.

I typed out a message.

"What are you up to right now?"

Sent.

I waited. Eyes flicking between my screen and the house. She would answer. She had to. She would tell me what was happening. She would let me be the one to save her.

But nothing came.

Silence.

Then the door burst open. Bradley stormed out; his face twisted with anger. He kicked the doorframe on his way out, shaking the frame.

I watched, every muscle in my body tight, my hands curled into fists. He muttered something under his breath as he climbed into his car, slamming the door so hard the windows rattled.

He sped off.

I stood there, my pulse pounding in my ears. My breath came fast, uneven, but I forced myself to steady it. The house was silent again, as if nothing had happened. But I knew better.

I wanted to go to her, to knock on the door, to see if she was okay. But I couldn't. Not yet. Not when she'd chosen to handle this alone. Again.

I pulled out my phone. It vibrated in my palm before I could type.

"Just had my ex turn up, looking for an argument. I'll talk to you in a little while and tell you more, I want you to know. I just need a little time x"

One kiss. No warmth.

It was like a confirmation.

Bradley was a problem.

And I would take care of it. For her. For *us*.

~

I stormed into my apartment, slamming the door so hard the walls shook. My whole body was vibrating with anger, my pulse hammering in my ears, my mind still reeling from what I'd seen. Bradley. That prick. The way he'd barged into Emma's house, invading her space, like he owned her. Like she was his possession. I felt sick, my stomach twisting with the helpless, boiling rage clawing at my insides.

I paced the length of my living room, back and forth, my movements jerky, restless. I couldn't sit down. I couldn't be still. Every time I closed my eyes, I saw his face contorted in fury, his body looming over Emma. And her—so small, so fragile in that moment. I should've done something. I should've ripped the door open and dragged him out of her house. I should've beaten him to a bloody mess and made sure he knew to never come near her again. But I hadn't. I'd crouched there, watching, hiding like a coward.

The shame burned almost as much as the rage.

I collapsed into my desk chair, my fingers digging into my scalp. I wasn't good with this kind of emotion. It buzzed inside me, too much, like a live wire sparking uncontrollably. My thoughts raced in frantic circles, leaping from one desperate idea to the next. How could I protect her? How could I stop him? How?

I glanced at my laptop, the dark screen staring back at me. Emma needed space. I knew that much. I couldn't bombard her with messages, not now. Not when she was already dealing with him. But I couldn't just sit here, doing nothing. I had to act. I had to prepare.

I cracked my knuckles and opened the laptop, my fingers flying over the keyboard. If I couldn't fight him physically, I'd fight him another way. I'd dig up everything there was to know about Bradley—his past, his present, his fucking future if I could. There had to be something. A weakness. A mistake. Something I could use to destroy him.

His Facebook was private, but his Instagram? Wide open. Fool. I scrolled through his feed, scanning picture after picture. Gym selfies, nights out, posing with his mates, flexing, always flexing. A guy desperate to look tough. Desperate to be seen. My lip curled as I kept digging, finding old posts with Emma, back when they were together. They looked happy. Like a perfect couple. And the way he had his arm around her, clinging, claiming, made my stomach churn with disgust. She must have hated it. She must have felt trapped.

I kept scrolling, kept searching. Then I found it—an old news article. A pub fight. Bradley's name listed in passing, no charges pressed. Of course. The kind of guy who got away with things. The kind of guy who thought he was untouchable.

I leaned back, closing my eyes for a second, my mind drifting. I imagined confronting him, standing over him, telling him to stay the hell away from Emma. And when he laughed? When he refused? I'd break him. I'd make him regret every time he laid a hand on her, every time he made her feel small. In my head, I saw it so clearly—him on the ground, bloodied and weak, and me, standing victorious. The hero.

But reality was different. I knew that. Bradley was built like a tank, and he was comfortable in a fight. I wasn't. The only fight I'd ever been in was years ago, and I'd lost. Badly. I needed to be smarter than him. I needed to be calculated.

My phone buzzed.

I jolted, heart lurching as I saw her name. Emma. My hands trembled as I clicked open the message.

"Hey Alex, Sorry about the weirdness. I've been wanting to tell you something... It's about my ex, Bradley. I feel like I need to tell you about it, especially since you care about me, and I really appreciate that. I just need to be honest, even though it's hard to talk about. I don't want you thinking it changes anything about me and you, and I don't want you to worry.

So, Bradley and I were together for a while, but over time, things got bad. He became controlling and jealous, always questioning where I was or who I was with. It was like he didn't trust me, no matter what I did, and it got worse. He'd show up at my work, at my friends' houses, just to check up on me. I felt like I was being suffocated.

He'd get angry over the smallest things, and sometimes, it would turn into a huge argument, and he would be violent. He'd say I was the one making him crazy, that I was the one playing games. He'd twist everything around to make me feel like it was my fault. There were so many times I was honestly scared of him.

When I finally got the courage to leave him, he didn't take it well. He'd call me, show up at my door, begging me to take him back one minute, then threatening me the next. I ended up having to go to court to get a restraining order. He's not supposed to come near me, but that hasn't stopped him from trying. He still turns up sometimes... It's like he doesn't care about the law. He just wants to make sure I can't move on.

I'm sorry for not telling you all this sooner. I guess I didn't want you to see me as a problem. I've been trying so hard to put on a brave face, to act like everything's fine, but the truth is, I'm scared, Alex. Every time I see him, it brings back all those memories, all that fear. I just want to move on, but he keeps pulling me back.

You mean a lot to me, and I don't want you to get dragged into this mess, but I also don't want to keep secrets from you. I hope you understand. I REALLY hope this doesn't change how you feel about me! I really like you. Talk soon, I hope! xxx"

I read the message again. And again. My grip on the phone tightened.

He wasn't supposed to go near her. There was a fucking restraining order. And yet, he was still pushing, still forcing his way back into her life, into her mind. She was scared. She was afraid.

I felt a huge sense of relief at her message—she let me in and opened up, so she trusted me. On the other hand, my rage was more powerful than ever, but now I finally knew. I could help. I could show her how perfect I am for her. I didn't reply to Emma; it was too late, and I was too caught up in my plans.

Bradley had no idea what was coming.

Within a few hours of pacing in my room, the plan was decided. It wasn't pretty, and it certainly wasn't what I had imagined when I first started talking to Emma, but it was necessary.

I had seriously considered more drastic measures. Thoughts of knifing Bradley in the street, catching him off guard one night and ending him where he stood played through my mind. The idea of finally freeing Emma from his grip, of never having to worry about him hurting her again, was intoxicating, but I knew the consequences of that path. I'd end up in prison. I couldn't be with Emma if I was locked away, my life ruined because I let my emotions take control. No, I needed to find another way, a less extreme way to rid her life of him. I needed to be smart.

In the hours I spent online, waiting, sifting through every scrap of information I could find about Bradley, I'd found out where he worked. His Instagram was like a goldmine of bad decisions—pictures of him at construction sites, bragging about the latest project, trying to show off his muscles in a high-vis vest, his location tagged in every post like he was begging to be tracked. One photo showed him in front of a sign for a specific construction company, the name and logo clear as day. Idiot. A few more clicks, and I had the address of the site he worked at, just a few miles from Emma's place.

Next, I needed drugs, preferably cocaine. Something that would land him in serious trouble if he was caught. That's where Sam came in. He wasn't really a friend, more like a guy I knew at work. Sam was the type who lived for the weekends, for the parties and the highs that came with them. He wasn't shy about his usage, and everyone in the office knew he was a regular user. The management didn't care, as long as he showed up to work on time and got his job done. Which, to be fair to him, he always did.

Satisfied with my nights work and it being too late to message Emma now, I closed my laptop and lay back on my bed. But sleep didn't come easy. My mind raced through every detail, every possibility, every risk. I imagined different scenarios, different ways this could play out. Each time, I convinced myself that this was the right thing to do. Emma needed me. I had to protect her. At some point, exhaustion finally won, dragging me into a restless sleep filled with fragmented dreams of Emma, of Bradley, of the moment he'd finally be out of our lives for good.

After a day at work where my thought were consumed by my plan and all the intricacies of it, I caught Sam, just as he was heading out. He looked at me with surprise when I pulled him aside, but he was more than happy to help when I told him what I needed. Sam liked to talk, and he was always looking for an excuse to show off and appear connected. I told him it was for a group of friends at a party, and they knew what they were doing, just their normal dealer wasn't around. We went to his car, and he definitely sold me enough to look bad if I got caught—tiny, tightly packed little bags of white powder, sealed and ready to go. The whole transaction took less than five minutes. I handed him the money, and he handed me the drugs, a quick exchange in the back of the office car park after work. No questions asked.

I'm still waiting for Emma's name to pop up on my phone, and I'm literally dying. Is she waiting for me to message? She did message last, I've just been so distracted with the matter at hand.

Next was a slightly more difficult task. Planting it in Bradley's car. I knew where he parked when he was at work. One Google Maps search, and I could clearly see the staff car park for the site; I had a perfect eagle-eye view on how I'd get in and out. All I needed to do was find his car.

It would be easy enough to slip the drugs into his car when he wasn't around. I'd already made a mental note of the car's make and model, its faded red paint and the dent in the passenger-side door. I'd even memorised the registration when I saw him pull up. Luckily, it was an old model—so old, in fact, that the door locks were quite easily picked, apparently. There was a video to prove it, using a butter knife and a large paperclip. It looked easy enough, but I didn't exactly have time or opportunity to practice. I'd have to take my chance. The ignition was still more advanced, but I just needed to get inside for ten seconds.

Once the drugs were planted, all I had to do was make a call. I'd act like a concerned member of the public, someone who had seen him in the Sainsbury's car park around the corner, wearing a company high vis, sniffing something suspicious. I'd sound worried, earnest, like I was just doing my civic duty. I had a good telephone manner, and I could easily pass for much older than I was. I'd call his company, the police, and let them know what I'd seen. Hopefully, that would be enough to get him fired, at least. Hopefully arrested.

I got home and found myself staring at the bags of cocaine in my hand, feeling the weight of them, the cold reality of what I was about to do. It wasn't a perfect plan, and it wasn't without risks. If it went wrong, I could get caught, and then everything would come crashing down on me, but if it worked…if it worked, Bradley would be out of the picture. It would give Emma the space she needed, the freedom to finally live her life without looking over her shoulder. She could concentrate on me, on us.

It would give us a chance. A real chance to be together.

Tomorrow, I would plant the drugs and make the calls. Hopefully, by the evening, Bradley's world would be far too messy to even consider going near Emma again. I was almost excited to bring him down.

I messaged Emma back before I got into bed, I didn't mean to make her wait for a reply, she must have been worrying that I did feel differently, but I was just so focused on a solution to her problem.

"Hey, I know I should've replied sooner. Just been caught up with a few things, thinking stuff through. Didn't want to half-answer you when you deserved more than that. I read your message a few times. Every word. I get it. I get all of it. And I need you to know—I'd do anything for you. Some things don't need to be said out loud, you just know, right? I don't think any less of you, I promise! You can't control the actions of someone else.

I don't want you worrying if I go quiet again. Not for long anyway. Just trust me on this one. It's all gonna work out the way it should.

I'll see you soon Emma."

That night, I barely slept. I lay awake in bed, staring at the ceiling, my mind running through every possible outcome. I imagined Bradley getting dragged away by the police, Emma finally free, finally safe. But doubt crept in too—what if something went wrong? What if I got caught? I turned over, checking my phone, hoping for a message from Emma, but there was nothing. Eventually, exhaustion won, and I drifted off into restless sleep.

I'd managed to get away from work just after lunch. I'd fabricated some excuse about an appointment I needed to attend—nobody questioned it because I rarely took time off, and my work was always up to date. In the staff room,

I grabbed one of the high-vis vests normally assigned to the fire marshals. I figured it was a reasonable precaution—there likely wouldn't be a fire today, but it could come in handy.

Blending in was key. If I looked like I belonged, no one would ask questions about why I'm in the car park. A high-vis vest was practically an invisibility cloak on a construction site—people would assume I was just another worker.

Back at my flat, I changed into a set of clothes that would blend in on a construction site—worn jeans, a faded t-shirt, and, of course, the high-vis vest. I took a moment to look at myself in the mirror, adjusting the vest and trying to steady my nerves. I looked ridiculous and certainly didn't belong on any building sites. I checked Google one last time to review my entry and exit plan. The site's address was still fresh in my mind. I then took a final glance at Emma's picture, the one of her sitting in the coffee shop. That image was my reason for everything—the motivation behind this desperate act.

I hopped on my bike, the most efficient way to navigate the city and make a quick getaway if necessary. As I pedalled towards the construction site, my mind raced. The thought of silencing Bradley, of planting the drugs in his car, filled me with a mix of dread, resolve, and satisfaction.

Arriving at the site, I noted the coast was clear. There were no security guards or workers milling about, just a few cars parked haphazardly. I spotted Bradley's car right where I expected, the faded red paint standing out even in the dim light of the afternoon. I wanted to slash the tires too, cut the brakes, set it on fire maybe.

I left my bike a little distance away and approached the car, adrenaline coursing through my veins as I crouched down and fumbled with the lock, feeling the cool metal of the paperclip in my hands. The initial few attempts to pick the lock were shaky; I dropped the paperclip twice and nearly panicked when I heard a car, but I took a deep breath, forcing myself to calm down.

Finally, with a quiet click, the lock released as did the breath I was hoping. I slid low into the driver's seat, quickly checking to make sure no one was watching. I pulled the drugs from my pocket and placed them carefully in the glove box, tucking them under some napkins and straws.

With the drugs in place, I took a moment to relish the gravity of what I'd done. It felt surreal, like I was on the edge of something big, something that could change everything. I reminded myself why I was doing this— to protect Emma, to give her the freedom she deserved.

I must admit, it was a thrill I'd never felt.

After a few seconds, I pulled myself together and closed the glove box. I glanced around once more to make sure I wasn't being watched and slipped out of the car. My heart still raced, but I felt a strange sense of relief.

Everything had gone perfectly. And I'd even be home before I'd be finishing work.

I made my way back to my bike, the weight of the high-vis vest suddenly feeling heavier as the adrenaline began to wear off. I pedalled away from the site, heading back towards home. The plan was set in motion, and now all I had to do was make two phone calls and wait.

I imagined Emma's reaction—relieved, grateful, finally free. I was riding back home feeling like I was Superman, and she was my Lois.

Emma

I woke up feeling heavy-headed and immediately remembered recent events. I reached for my phone, looking for Alex, but he hadn't messaged since he sent me a slightly cryptic message telling me everything would be work out and to trust him. Before I got too caught up in my thoughts, I saw a text from my friend Lauren. It was a short text.

"Hey, you'll never guess what happened. Bradley got arrested last night! Possession of something, apparently. Maybe now he'll finally leave you alone."

I stared at the message, reading it over and over. Bradley, arrested. It seemed almost too good to be true. Part of me had expected him to spiral down this path, but hearing it actually happened was something else. Relief washed over me, a wave of lightness I hadn't felt in so long. I closed my eyes and took a deep breath, feeling the tension slowly leave my body.

I should have felt some kind of sympathy, maybe, but all I felt was joy. This was it. Maybe now he'd be out of my life for good. Maybe I could finally stop looking over my shoulder, wondering when he'd show up again. The thought made me smile for the first time in what felt like ages.

My mind immediately went to Alex. With Bradley out of the picture, things would be so much simpler. I wouldn't have to hide anything or worry about explaining the past. I could be with him, really be with him, without all this fear hanging over us. I reached for my phone, my fingers already typing a message.

"Hey you! So, I just heard some good news, for me at least. Bradley got arrested last night. Honestly, I feel like I can finally breathe again. We should celebrate, don't you think? xxx"

I hit send and waited, my heart beating a little faster. I was excited to see how he'd react. A few moments later, my phone buzzed with his reply.

"Hey! Really? That's great news! I'm so happy for you, Emma. You definitely deserve to celebrate. How about dinner tomorrow night after we finish work? My treat."

I grinned at the screen, a flutter of excitement in my chest. Dinner with Alex sounded perfect. I could already picture us, sitting across from each other, laughing, holding hands across a candlelit table, talking about us. For the first time in a long time, I felt like the future was now something I could look forward to.

"Dinner with you sounds perfect, Alex. I can't wait. Have the best day and we'll talk later about where and when! xxx"

I set my phone down and got up, feeling lighter than I had in weeks. I still had a whole day of work ahead of me, but it felt like I was floating. I made myself some coffee, humming softly to the song on the radio as I moved around the kitchen. Everything seemed brighter, the colours more vivid. I couldn't remember the last time I felt this happy.

Bradley was gone, at least for now, and I had Alex. The thought made my heart flutter. He was so sweet, so caring. Sure, he was a little awkward and nervous, but I found it endearing. I loved the way he looked at me, like I was the most important thing in the world, the way his energy was also focused on me. I enjoyed the attention, I admit it. Being with him was easy—he made it easy.

I couldn't wait for tomorrow. To see him again, to celebrate, to start this new chapter. Everything was finally falling into place, and I was ready to grab hold of it with both hands.

Standing in front of the bathroom mirror after a hot shower, I held my phone up, angling it just right to capture my reflection. I tilted my head slightly, letting my hair fall over one shoulder, and gave the camera my best 'come to bed' look. I wanted to look sexy, irresistible. My eyes were half-closed, lips slightly parted, as if I was lost in a delicious daydream.

Click.

I looked at the photo and smiled. Perfect. I quickly sent it to Alex with a little note.

"Thinking about you this morning Alex... xxx"

I hit send, feeling a thrill of excitement rush through me, a sense of power. Alex would love that. I could already imagine his reaction, the way he'd probably blush and stutter over his words. He was so adorably shy, but I loved that. Something about his lack of confidence was attractive in a strange way. Maybe I knew he'd be too nervous to talk to other girls, or maybe it was the way he seemed to always need a subtle hint that he was doing good. It was reassuring to know he needed me that way. It was cute.

I put my phone down and finished getting ready for work, still feeling like I was floating on air. Bradley being arrested had lifted a weight off my shoulders, and with Alex, I felt like things were finally going to go right. After everything that had happened to me, I deserved this. I deserved to be happy.

The walk to work was short, and I hummed happily to myself, enjoying the late morning sunshine. The world was full of possibilities, and I was ready to seize them all.

As soon as I walked into the café, I could sense something was off. My boss, Mr. Harris, was behind the counter, wiping it down with a cloth, a frown creasing his forehead. He looked up as I entered, and for a moment, our eyes met. There was something in his expression that made me realise the day was, once again, about to be spoiled.

"Emma, can I see you in my office for a minute?" he asked, his voice stern.

"Uh, sure," I replied, trying to keep my tone light. I followed him into the back office, my good mood slipping away with each step. The office was small, cluttered with papers and receipts, the faint smell of coffee lingering in the air. Mr. Harris sat down behind his desk and gestured for me to take a seat.

"Look, Emma," he began, rubbing the back of his neck. "I hate to do this, but we've been having some difficulties lately. The cost of running this place is getting too high, and we need to make some cutbacks."

I felt a cold lump of dread settle in my stomach. "Cutbacks?" I repeated, my voice sounding small and insecure.

He nodded, avoiding my gaze. "I'm afraid we're going to have to cut your hours in half. I know this is sudden, and I wish there was another way, but… there isn't."

I barely heard the rest of what he was saying. My mind was reeling. Cut my hours? How was I supposed to manage that? Mortgage, bills, groceries—all of it ran through my head like a rapid-fire slideshow. I needed those hours. I needed the money; I couldn't just ask Dad like I used to. The image of Bradley's smug face flashed in my mind, and I clenched my fists. This was his fault. He'd shown up, caused a scene, and now this.

"Is this because of what happened the other day?" I asked, my voice sharper than I intended.

Mr. Harris shifted uncomfortably in his seat. "That didn't help, I'll admit. But the main issue is financial. I hope you understand."

I nodded. At least he was honest, but I didn't really understand. I just wanted to get out of there, to go somewhere and scream. I finished my now shorter shift in a daze, barely registering the customers or the orders I was taking. I couldn't get out of there fast enough. I practically ran home, my mind buzzing with anger, frustration and hopelessness.

Once I was home, I sank onto my bed, staring at the ceiling. The excitement I'd felt earlier was gone, replaced by a heavy sense of dread.

My mind replayed Mr. Harris's words, the sheer finality of them pressing against my chest. My hours were cut. Bills would pile up. Everything I had just started to piece together felt like it was unravelling again.

I needed to talk to someone, to let it all out. I grabbed my phone and texted Alex.

"Hey, can I call you? There's too much to type. I really need to talk, I've had a day xx"

His reply was almost instant. Obviously.

"Of course you can. Call me anytime."

When he answered, I could hear the nervousness in his voice, the way he hesitated for a split second before speaking.

"Hey, Emma. What's up?"

I could picture him sitting there, probably fidgeting with something, trying to sound casual. The sound of his voice was comforting, and I felt a lump form in my throat.

"Alex... I just... everything's a mess," I began, my voice cracking. I told him about work, about my hours being cut, because Bradley showed up and caused trouble. I told him about my TV and how it happened. My voice trembled as I talked about how stressed I felt, about the bills piling up, about feeling like I was losing control.

Alex listened quietly, his occasional murmurs of sympathy encouraging me to keep going. I felt a tear slide down my cheek, and I wiped it away, feeling foolish for crying. "I just don't know what to do," I finished, my voice barely above a whisper. "Everything's falling apart, and I don't know how to fix it."

There was a pause on the other end of the line, and I could hear Alex taking a deep breath. "Emma, I'm so sorry you're going through all this," he said, his voice soft but strong and full of conviction. "You don't have to face this alone. I'm here for you. Whatever you need, I'll do it. I promise."

His words wrapped around me like a warm blanket, and I felt some of the tension ease from my shoulders. I didn't know what I'd do without him. He was my anchor, my support. Knowing he was there made everything a little more bearable.

"Thank you, Alex," I whispered, my voice thick with emotion. "I don't know what I'd do without you right now."

He hesitated, then said softly, "You'll never have to find out. I'm not going anywhere."

A small smile tugged at my lips, despite the tears. Maybe things were a mess, but those words helped more than he'd ever know. Alex always had a way of seeming capable when I needed him —it was comforting.

I didn't know what I was going to do, but somehow, I had a feeling I'd be okay.

Alex

I stared at the phone screen long after the call had ended, my pulse still uneven, my mind still spinning. Emma's voice lingered in my ears, soft but strained, edged with that raw vulnerability that made me want to wrap her in my arms and never let go.

She was struggling. Hurting. And I couldn't stand it.

I imagined her sitting there in her small house, shoulders curled in, head resting against the wall, her lip caught between her teeth the way it always was when she was thinking too hard. Her hair would be slightly messy, strands falling out of whatever attempt at a bun she'd made. She'd be wearing one of those oversized sweaters that swallowed her up, sleeves tugged over her fingers.

God, I loved her like that. Soft. Real. Mine.

A sudden, electric determination buzzed through me. I had to do something. Fix this. Fix everything. It wasn't just about proving myself anymore—it was about making sure she never had to feel this way again. She deserved better. She deserved security, comfort, and to know, without a doubt, that someone in this world would always be there to catch her when she fell. And that someone was me.

I pushed up from my chair, pacing the room. My mind raced, searching for solutions. Money. She needed money. Not just a little, but enough to make a difference. Enough to stop the constant stress, the weight pressing down on her shoulders. The bills, the broken TV, the hours being cut at work—each one was a problem, and I needed to be the answer.

The old version of me—the one who blended into the background, who let life just happen to him —would have felt helpless. But not anymore. Not after what I'd done, what I'd proven I could do. I wasn't afraid to get my hands dirty. For her.

Setting Bradley had been the first step, but now, I had to think bigger. Smarter.

I woke up to the familiar ding of a text message, the weight of the last few days still clinging to me. Groggy but eager, I reached for my phone, and the second I saw Emma's name, a surge of energy cut through the fog of sleep. I opened the message, and there she was—a vision so effortlessly beautiful, it stole the breath straight from my lungs.

She was leaning against her bathroom counter, a towel wrapped around her body, her hair still damp, cascading over one shoulder in loose, glistening waves. My weakness. The dim bathroom light cast a soft glow over her skin, making her look impossibly fresh, impossibly real. Her eyes, deep and knowing, locked onto mine through the screen, like she could see straight into me. And that smile—just the barest hint of mischief playing at the corner of her lips —like she knew exactly what she was doing to me.

I could almost smell the faint scent of her shampoo, feel the lingering warmth of the shower clinging to her skin. She was everything. Everything I wanted, everything I needed, right there in my hands. I smiled, unable to help myself. She was becoming mine more and more every day.

"Good morning, thinking about you this morning Alex... xxx."

I stared at the message, my fingers hovering over the keyboard as I tried to conjure the perfect response. Something that would match the way she made me feel. But nothing seemed good enough.

"Wow, just wow, Emma."

It was all I could manage. I hit send and put my phone down, my chest still heavy from the seductiveness of her message. Clearly, my plan had worked perfectly, and Emma was already showing signs of feeling better. Bradley was out of the picture—for now. That was all I needed. With him gone, she could focus on us, on me. I could make her really see me now and finally make her mine.

Work was its usual monotonous blur, but I floated through it, untouched by the dull hum of office chatter and the rhythmic clatter of keyboards. Even the hissing of the coffee machine faded into the background. None of it mattered. I was invincible. I had done something real, something powerful. I had protected Emma, ensured she was safe. And the best part? No one knew. No one would ever suspect quiet, unassuming Alex—the one with the glasses and the oversized sweaters. The guy who never raised his voice, never drew attention to himself. They'd never believe what I was capable of. Anything for her.

I struggled to focus on my tasks; my mind pulled back to Emma over and over again. The way she had smiled at me on our date, the way her laughter had lit up the night, the way she looked in that towel—every part of her filled me with purpose. With drive. I deserved her love. More than ever, I knew that now.

I had proven myself. I wasn't just some lovesick fool. I was a protector. A guardian. A real man.

By the time I got home, the rush of it all still lingered, thrumming beneath my skin. The sense of accomplishment, of control. I had been nervous, uncertain even, but I had done it. I had followed through, and it had worked. Perfectly. The adrenaline still pulsed through me as I locked the door behind me and sank onto the couch, a slow, satisfied exhale escaping my lips.

Then I saw her message.

"Hey, can I call you? There's too much to type. I really need to talk. I've had a day xx."

My heart skipped. She needed me. Without hesitation, I replied, agreeing immediately, even as a familiar unease coiled in my stomach. I *hated* phone calls.

When I answered, her voice came through the speaker, soft but strained, edged with exhaustion. "Alex, I just... everything's such a mess."

Her words wavered, unsteady, and I could hear the weight pressing down on her. She spoke about work—her hours being cut because of him. She told me how he turned up to her work and house, how the stress was piling up, her life slipping just out of reach. She just needed to release it all, to let it spill out into the open.

She told me about the bills stacking up, the broken TV, the overwhelming pressure closing in around her. Her voice cracked, and I could hear the tears she was trying to hold back. The sound of it twisted something deep in my chest. I wanted to reach through the phone, to pull her into me, to take it all away. I had already done so much for her, but clearly, it wasn't enough. I needed to do more. Wanted to.

I leaned back in my chair, closing my eyes, letting the sound of her voice echo in my mind. The way it wavered. The way she had thanked me for listening. She was adorable when she was grateful. That feeling it gave me, the way it stirred something warm and powerful inside me —I liked it.

I wouldn't let her down.

After we hung up, I sat in the darkness of my room, the only illumination coming from the pale glow of my phone screen. Emma's voice still echoed in my mind, trembling with exhaustion, raw with fear. It wasn't just the words she had spoken—it was the way they had cracked under the weight of everything she was carrying. It did something to me, fractured something inside. I hated that she was struggling, that she felt so alone. I wanted—no, needed—to be the one who made it better.

I thought about the broken TV, about the way Bradley had left her, crying and afraid in her own home. It wasn't just about shielding her from him anymore. It was about ensuring she never felt that kind of helplessness again. Emma deserved someone who put her first, who went out of their way to make her happy, who made her feel safe. I wanted to be that person. I had to be.

I opened my laptop, my fingers moving instinctively across the keys, pulling up online stores. TVs flickered across the screen—brands, sizes, prices—none of it really mattered, only that she had one by tomorrow. It was a small thing, but it was something tangible, something she would see and know someone was looking out for her. I found one—decent enough, nothing extravagant, but a perfect replacement. My hands were unsteady as I typed in her address, a nervous energy buzzing through me as I clicked 'Order Now.' By tomorrow afternoon, she would have a new TV. She would know someone cared.

A familiar thrill rushed through me; the same

one I'd felt after setting Bradley up. It wasn't just about being kind. I knew it was about control, about fixing things, about knowing that because of me, her life was going to be just a little bit better. But that mattered. She mattered.

Yet it wasn't enough. A TV wouldn't make her problems disappear. I thought about the money sitting in my savings account, gathering dust, waiting for a purpose. What better purpose than this? She was drowning in stress—bills, rent, uncertainty—I could take that weight off her shoulders for a while. And I would.

Tomorrow morning, I'd offer her five thousand pounds. No strings attached. Just to help her through, to give her some breathing room until she was back on her feet. She'd refuse, of course —prideful, stubborn, independent. But I'd find a way to make her see reason. I'd joke about it, make it light, make it impossible for her to say no. I'd playfully threaten to cancel our next date if she didn't accept. She'd roll her eyes, laugh maybe, but in the end, she'd agree. She'd understand that I wasn't just helping her—I was proving something. To her. To myself.

It was insane, really, how deeply I felt for her already. We barely knew each other. And yet, when I thought about her—about the way her smile tilted slightly before she laughed, the way her eyes darkened when she was deep in thought

—I knew. I was already falling. Hard.

That night, I lay awake, staring at the ceiling, picturing her reaction. The way her face would light up when she saw the TV. The way she'd argue about the money, then ultimately relent, thanking me in that soft, breathless way that made my chest tighten. I imagined the way she'd look at me—not with obligation, but with gratitude, with something deeper. With something real.

When morning came, my confidence was high. Today, I'd show Emma how much she meant to me, how far I was willing to go to make her happy. As I got ready for work, my mind was already rehearsing the conversation. I'd be smooth, confident. I'd make her see that she wasn't alone anymore.

Before I left, I grabbed my phone and typed out a message.

"Hey, I've got something I want to talk to you about later. Nothing bad, promise. Just something important. Let's chat at lunch?"

I hesitated, then added:

"PS: Hope you're having a good morning. Can't wait to see you tonight!"

I hit send, my pulse quickening. I wanted her to know I was thinking about her. That I was always thinking about her.

Work was the usual tedious corporate bore. My body went through the motions, but my mind was like always recently elsewhere, locked on Emma. Every passing hour brought me closer to lunch. Closer to her. Closer to proving that I was the person she could rely on.

When lunchtime finally arrived, I stepped outside, finding a quiet corner of the car park. My fingers gripped my phone a little too tightly as I called her number. She answered on the second ring, her voice lighter than last night, carrying a hint of warmth that sent a ripple of satisfaction through me.

"Hey, Alex," she said, and I could hear her smile. God, I loved when she sounded like that.

"Hey, Emma. How's your day going?" I kept my voice casual, easy.

"Not bad," she said. "Just finished work, actually. I only had to do a few today. You know, the budget and everything"

"That's good," I said, then winced. "I mean, not the cut hours part—just that you're free now. We can talk?"

"Yeah, sure. What's up?" Curiosity edged her voice.

I exhaled slowly. "I've been thinking... I know things have been tough for you, and I want to help. There'll be a little something arriving this afternoon, and also... I have some savings I don't really need right now. About five thousand. I want you to have it. No pressure. No repayment. Just... let me do this for you."

Silence. Just the faint sound of her breathing. My heartbeat thundered in my ears.

"Alex..." Her voice was barely above a whisper. "That's... that's so generous, but I can't—"

"Please," I interrupted gently. "I *want* to do this. For you. You don't have to do this alone. Just think of it as a loan if that makes it easier. I'll cancel our next date if you say no." I forced a teasing edge into my voice, but my throat was tight. I *needed* her to accept.

A long pause. Then, finally, she sighed. "Okay, Alex... Thank you. I don't know what I'd do without you. I mean that."

Relief crashed through me, warm and overwhelming. I smiled. "Good thing you'll never have to find out," I said with a self-assured tone.

We talked for a little while longer, setting plans to message after I finished work, dinner booked for eight o'clock. I let her go reluctantly, my fingers lingering over the screen after we hung up.

Satisfaction pulsed through me. I was doing the right thing. Helping her, fixing things, proving myself. And yet, even as I basked in the glow of it, a thought crept in, quiet and insistent.

I'd given her money. A new TV. My support. But was it *enough*? Could I do more?

Emma

I woke up feeling lighter than I had expected. Last night's phone call with Alex had been... nice. Comforting, even. How I was able to tell him everything that had happened, His voice had wrapped around me like a cocoon, steady and warm. He was so caring, so eager to support me. It felt good to know someone had my back for a change. Someone who wasn't Bradley. A soft smile crept onto my lips as I stretched, remembering we had a date tonight.

Rolling out of bed, I let the sheets fall away, the chill of the morning air nipping at my bare skin. I shivered but didn't mind. Today felt different. My shift was only a half-day—thanks to my hours being cut—but maybe that was a good thing. More time to think, to figure out what I really wanted. Maybe a new job, something in music, something that made me feel alive again. My Noted profile had gathered dust since meeting Alex, but I didn't mind. Not anymore. It seemed insignificant right now.

His name popped up on my phone as I slowly got ready,

"Hey, I've got something I want to talk to you about later. Nothing bad, promise. Just something important. Let's chat at lunch?"

"PS: Hope you're having a good morning. Can't wait to see you tonight!"

The tone of the message got me excited, and I was curious what he was thinking, but I'd have to wait until lunchtime.

Work was uneventful. The café was quiet which gave credence to the budget excuse. The early rush fading into a slow hum of background noise. I went through the motions—pour, stir, smile, repeat—but my thoughts were elsewhere. Every glance at the clock was a silent plea for time to move faster. The anticipation was getting unbearable.

When my shift finally ended, I peeled off my apron, grabbed my bag, and stepped outside. The cold air hit my face, crisp and refreshing, grounding me in the moment. I pulled out my phone, about to text Alex, when it shook in my hand.

Alex.

My lips curled into a small smile before I even realised it.

I answered, unable to keep the warmth from my voice. "Hey, Alex."

"Hey, Emma. How's your day going?" His tone was casual, easy, but there was something underneath it—something that made me feel like this wasn't just a check-in.

"Not bad," I said. "Just finished work, actually. I only had to do a few today. You know, the budget and everything."

"That's good," he said, then hesitated. "I mean, not the cut hours part—just that you're free now. We can talk?"

A small frown tugged at my lips. "Yeah, sure.

What's up?" There was curiosity in my voice now. Whatever this was, it was important to him.

I heard his slow exhale before he spoke again. "I've been thinking... I know things have been tough for you, and I want to help. There'll be a little something arriving this afternoon, and also... I have some savings I don't really need right now. About five thousand. I want you to have it. No pressure. No repayment. Just... let me do this for you."

Silence stretched between us. My own breath felt louder than usual.

Five thousand pounds. Just like that.

"Alex..." My voice barely carried over the phone. "That's... that's so generous, but I can't—"

"Please," he cut in, gentle but insistent. "I want to do this. For you. You don't have to do this alone. Just think of it as a loan if that makes it easier. I'll cancel our next date if you say no." His tone turned light, teasing, but there was something in it—something tight. He needed me to say yes.

I hesitated, letting the moment breathe. Then, finally, I sighed. "Okay, Alex... Thank you. I don't know what I'd do without you. I mean that."

A beat of silence. Then, his response, smooth and certain. "Good thing you'll never have to find out."

Warmth settled in my chest. We talked a little longer, setting plans to message later, dinner booked for eight. And when we finally hung up, I stayed there for a moment, staring down at my phone. My fingers hovered over the screen as if I could still feel the conversation lingering in the air.

He made me feel light again, just like that.

Sliding my phone into my pocket, I headed home, my steps quicker, more buoyant. My mind rushed with possibilities. The money, the gift— whatever it was—tonight's dinner.

Everything was falling into place.

As I reached my front door, I fished for my keys, already imagining what the surprise would be. A present maybe flowers, something thoughtful. Something only Alex would think to send.

But then—

I hesitated.

My fingers tightened around the key, my breath stalling.

When did I give him my address?

A chill ran down my spine, cutting through the warmth like a blade.

I stood there, staring at the lock, my pulse a quiet, steady drum in my ears.

Did I give him my address?

I let the door swing shut behind me, the familiar silence settling over me like a well-worn coat. The stillness wasn't loneliness—it was comfort. A rare, welcome kind of peace. I dropped my bag by the door, kicking off my shoes, savouring the weight of the afternoon stretching before me. And tonight, I'd be with Alex. That thought alone sent a ripple of anticipation through me. It was just a simple dinner, nothing extraordinary, but with him, everything felt new. Different. Like stepping into sunlight after too long in the shade.

I moved through the living room, straightening things up—tossing stray clothes into the laundry basket, stacking magazines and letters into a neat pile, brushing away the remnants of last night's snacks.

A small smile curled at my lips. A present, he'd said. What could it be? He was thoughtful in a way that felt almost unreal, like something out of a dream I wasn't ready to wake up from.

A knock at the door jolted me from my thoughts, my pulse stuttering. For a fleeting second, cold panic gripped me. Was it Bradley? Had he found out about Alex? Was he back to cause more trouble? My mind jumped ahead, conjuring a dozen worst-case scenarios, but then I remembered—Alex had mentioned a surprise. A delivery. I exhaled slowly, pressing a hand to my chest as I peered through the peephole. A uniformed delivery man stood outside, a large box resting at his feet.

I pulled the door open, composing myself. "Hi," I said, forcing casualness into my voice.

"Delivery for Emma?" he asked, checking his clipboard.

"That's me."

He set the hefty package down in the middle of my living room as I signed for it. "Have a good one," he said with a nod before heading off.

I shut the door and turned to the box, my curiosity spiking. The label read an electronics store. My breath caught as I peeled back the flaps, revealing a sleek, brand-new TV.

"Alex," I whispered, shaking my head, a stunned laugh escaping. Of course, he had. My hero.

Warmth flooded my chest. No one had ever done things like this for me before, not without expecting something in return. But Alex... he just did.

I reached for my phone, my fingers hovering over the screen. How do you even begin to thank someone for something like this? Then, a thought struck me. A way to show him, not just tell him, how much I appreciated him.

I slipped off my top and tossed it aside, standing in front of the mirror. The deep red lace of my bra hugged my curves, a perfect blend of softness and seduction. I ran a hand through my hair, tousling it just enough, then lifted my phone and snapped a picture—my best 'come to bed' eyes locked on the camera.

"Thank you so much Alex!! You're amazing! Can't wait to see you tonight and say thank you in person.. xxx"

I hit send, a thrill tightening in my stomach as I imagined his reaction. I could practically see the way his jaw would clench, the way his eyes would darken with hunger. The thought sent a shiver through me.

I spent the rest of the afternoon trying to keep busy, but my mind kept drifting back to him. To tonight. To us. I pictured laughter over candlelight, the warmth of his hand on mine. What would life with Alex be like? Music playing softly in the background, lazy Sunday mornings wrapped in sheets, the feeling of belonging to someone who actually wanted to be there. Maybe

—just maybe—he was what I'd been searching for all along, without even realising it.

Hours passed in a haze of anticipation, and then my phone shook across the coffee table. Alex.

"Hey, can't wait for tonight! I've got us a table at that Italian place in town, eight o'clock. Want me to pick you up, or should we meet there? Wow Emma, you look incredible!"

I paused, frowning slightly. Had I given him my address? I couldn't remember doing it, yet the TV was here. How else could he have sent it? It didn't matter, not really. I'd ask casually tonight, just to see what he said.

"Let's meet there. I can't wait! See you soon xxx."

Setting my phone down, I felt excitement bubble up inside me. Tonight was going to be perfect. Alex was perfect.

I turned to my wardrobe, fingers trailing over the hangers. Tonight felt important—more than just another date. This was about showing Alex what he meant to me, showing him that I saw everything he was doing, and that I wanted this. Wanted him.

My eyes landed on a dress I hadn't worn in ages. Midnight blue, shimmering in the light. Elegant yet sexy, just like I wanted to feel tonight. I pulled it out and held it against my body, turning to the mirror. I hadn't changed size since I was sixteen —I knew it would still fit. And it did, hugging my curves in all the right places, flowing just enough at the hem to brush teasingly above my knees. The neckline dipped, hinting at just enough to keep him wanting more, while the open back revealed the soft curve of my spine, delicate straps crisscrossing like whispers of silk against my skin.

I smiled at my reflection, my confidence surging. This dress was more than just an outfit—it was a statement. A silent message to Alex that I saw him. That I wanted to be everything he needed, just like he was becoming everything I needed.

I slipped on a pair of strappy heels that made my legs look impossibly long, added a silver necklace to highlight the neckline, and kept my earrings small—just enough sparkle without distraction. My makeup was subtle, except for the deep red on my lips. A bold, teasing colour. A promise.

Tonight, I wanted him to kiss me.

I took a final look in the mirror, smoothing my hands over the fabric. My heart pounded with anticipation. Tonight was about us. About letting Alex in. About showing him that I wasn't just grateful—I was his.

I grabbed my clutch, a sleek blue piece with a silver buckle, and headed for the door.

Tonight, I was going to be unforgettable. For him.

Alex

The afternoon was a grind. Reports, emails, meetings—none of it held my attention. My thoughts kept drifting to Emma, replaying our conversation from earlier. Every word, looped in my mind like a song I couldn't shake. I couldn't wait for tonight. It felt inevitable, like everything before now had been leading to this. I wanted to tell her things, to see if she felt the same way I did, to finally understand where we stood.

My phone buzzed across my desk, snapping me out of my trance. I glanced around the office to make sure no one was watching before picking it up. Emma's name lit up my screen, sending a quick rush of adrenaline through me. My pulse kicked up a notch as I unlocked my phone.

There she was, staring back at me. My breath

caught in my throat.

Emma had sent me a selfie, and she was wearing nothing but a red lace bra. My God. My mouth went dry. Her hair was slightly tousled, as if she had just run her fingers through it, and her eyes shimmered with a teasing, almost wicked glint. The bra clung to her perfectly, the delicate red lace framing her in a way that made my chest tighten. Her lips were curved in a playful smile— the kind that said she knew exactly what she was doing to me.

"Thank you for the TV! You're amazing! Can't wait to see you tonight and say thank you in person... xxx," the message read.

I stared at the picture, as if trying to burn it into my memory. Emma wanted me. *Me.* The thought made my head spin.

The rest of the afternoon was a blur. I worked on autopilot, my mind stuck on Emma, on that picture, on the way she made me feel. I caught myself grinning at random moments, lost in the high of knowing that she was thinking about me too. My colleagues probably thought I was losing it, but I didn't care. I had something real to look forward to—something that mattered.

When work finally ended, I practically bolted out of the office, the excitement in my veins making it impossible to move at a normal pace. This wasn't just another date. This was my chance to show Emma how serious I was about her; how much I wanted to be the man she could rely on.

At home, I showered quickly, the scalding water doing little to calm the restless energy pumping through my body. I stood in front of the mirror, assessing myself. I needed to look good for her, to show her that I was worth this.

I picked out a crisp white shirt—casual, but with just enough effort—and paired it with dark jeans. A suit blazer added a polished touch. A man should always have something in case his lady gets cold, right?

Running a hand through my perpetually unruly hair, I took a steadying breath. This was it. Tonight, could change everything.

One last glance around my apartment, one last deep breath. Then I grabbed my keys and stepped out the door.

Tonight was going to be perfect.

The restaurant was quieter than I expected, which suited me just fine. I was already nervous, and a packed place full of noise would have made it worse.

Emma's last text told me she was already here.

As I stepped inside, the warm, intimate atmosphere settled over me. Candles flickered on each table, their soft glow casting a golden hue over the room. The scent of garlic, tomatoes, and freshly baked bread drifted through the air, mingling with the faint sound of soft Italian music playing in the background. This was a real date.

I scanned the room, searching for her, my stomach twisting with nerves… and maybe a little with hunger. But the second I saw her, everything else disappeared.

She was sitting at a small candlelit table near the window, waiting for me.

My breath stalled in my throat.

She stood as I approached, and for a moment, I lost my ability to think.

She was wearing a midnight-blue dress that shimmered under the candlelight, hugging her body in all the right places. The plunging neckline showed just enough to set my pulse racing, the delicate straps crisscrossing over her shoulders in a way that made it impossible to look anywhere else. Her hair was down, soft waves cascading over one shoulder, catching the light in a way that made her look almost ethereal. She was stunning—so stunning that it physically hurt to look at her.

I forced myself to breathe, to focus, to act like a normal, composed human being and not a man who was rapidly losing his grip.

"Hey, Emma," I said, my voice lower than I intended.

She smiled, and for a moment, my entire world tilted.

God help me.

"Alex! You made it." Leaning in, Emma kissed my cheek, the warmth of her skin sending a shiver down my spine. The scent of her perfume—something floral with a hint of spice—wrapped around me, intoxicating. For a second, I forgot how to exist.

"Of course. You look… amazing," I said, my voice feeling like it wobbled with nerves. She always had this effect on me.

Her lips curved into a knowing smile as she gave me a once-over. "You don't look so bad yourself."

We sat, and for a moment, there was a brief, almost fragile silence between us. I was never great at first dates, never quite knew how to navigate them without fumbling through the awkwardness. But Emma? She was effortless, confident.

"So, how was the rest of your day? Boring, I hope," she teased, her eyes glinting as she smirked at me from across the table.

I chuckled, grateful for the opening. "Boring as hell. Couldn't focus on anything. Kept thinking about tonight. So, technically, that's your fault."

She laughed, the sound like music to my ears. "I'll take the blame for that."

The conversation flowed after that, easy and natural. We talked about everything—music, travel, childhood stories, even our strangest dreams. I told her about a ridiculous dream where I was chasing a flying pizza, expecting her to roll her eyes, but instead, she burst into laughter, resting a hand lightly on mine as she shook her head.

"A flying pizza? Really, Alex? That might be the weirdest one I've heard," she said between giggles.

"Hey, I don't control my thoughts," I grinned, enjoying the way her fingers lingered against my skin before she pulled back.

As the night unfolded, I felt myself relax. Emma was easy to be around, the kind of person who made the world feel lighter, who made you want to open up. She ordered bruschetta to start, followed by tagliatelle with truffle oil and mushrooms—elegant, rich, exactly like her. I went for something heartier, rosemary focaccia and lasagna, The soft clink of silverware, the quiet hum of conversation around us, the flickering candle between us—it all felt perfect.

But then, just as I was beginning to believe nothing could go wrong, she set down her fork and tilted her head slightly, studying me.

"Hey, Alex," she started, her tone light, but her eyes sharp. "How did you know my address for the TV?"

My stomach turned to ice. The fork in my hand suddenly felt too heavy. I hadn't expected her to ask that.

Stay calm. Don't overthink it.

I forced a casual smile, shrugging as if it was nothing. "You told me, obviously. How else would I have known?"

Emma's brows knit together for a split second, like she was trying to remember. My pulse pounded in my ears. I could see the thought forming in her mind, the question hovering on the edge of her tongue.

But then she let it go. Laughed lightly, shaking her head.

"Yeah, I guess so. I must be losing it," she murmured, sipping her wine. "Been so all over the place lately."

I let out a slow breath, steadying myself. That was close. Too close.

Luckily, we moved on, the conversation shifting into something safer, easier. She told me about her dreams of breaking into the music industry, how much it meant to her. I listened intently, nodding at all the right moments, absorbing every word. She was magnetic when she talked about her passions, and I wanted to be the person who helped her reach them.

As the night went on, we shared a tiramisu for dessert, both of us scooping from the same plate, laughing as we argued over who got the last bite. She ended up winning that little battle, but I didn't mind. Watching her smile as she enjoyed it was better than any dessert.

When the bill came, she reached for it before I could. "No way, Alex. You've done enough already," she said, shaking her head.

"Emma, come on. I asked you out. It's my treat," I insisted, holding firm.

"But—"

"No buts. I'm paying," I said, smiling as I handed

my card to the waiter without even glancing at the amount. I knew I could cover it, I did my research on the menu beforehand and transferred more than enough to cover the most expensive options. She rolled her eyes but gave in with a smile, clearly not used to someone insisting on taking care of things.

As we got up to leave together, I couldn't help but feel like the night had been perfect. Emma was everything I'd hoped she'd be and more. Funny, smart, beautiful, and easy to talk to. I felt lucky to be the one standing beside her as we walked out of the restaurant, into the cool evening air.

I didn't wait for her to hint that she was cold. I simply placed my jacket over her shoulders as we started walking to her car around the corner. She looked up at me as if I was Prince Charming, and I loved the way it made me feel—to protect and provide for her.

She took my hand as we walked, her fingers lacing perfectly with mine. It felt natural. Right. We talked about the meal, how much we both enjoyed it, and casually agreed to meet up again next weekend—she'd have to check her shifts first, but the intention was there.

We reached her car, and I could almost feel my heart in my mouth. This was the part where I was supposed to confidently pull her close and kiss her. The meal, the conversation—none of it mattered as much as this moment. This kiss. This is what she will judge me on for the rest of her life. This is a moment she'd tell our children about.

I was in the middle of thanking her for a wonderful night, trying to subtly work up the courage, when she grabbed my face with both hands and kissed me hard. I was stunned, caught completely off guard, and for a split second, I think I forgot to kiss her back. By the time I caught up, she was pulling away, smiling at me in a way that made my head spin.

"Thank you," she murmured, her voice soft. "For everything."

I wanted to do that again. A million times. But before I could, she got into her car, gave me one last smile and a cute little wave, and drove off into the night.

The journey home was a blur, my mind playing that kiss over and over. The best kiss of my life, and I didn't even see it coming.

Emma

I arrived a little early, which is typical for me. Being closer to the restaurant definitely helped, but if I'm honest, I wanted a few minutes to myself before Alex got here. I chose a table near the window, where the soft candlelight flickered in the centre, casting a romantic glow. Perfect for a first date.

I checked my reflection in the window, smoothing down the midnight-blue dress I'd chosen, hoping it was enough to make an impression. The plunging neckline was daring for me, but I wanted to feel confident tonight. I wasn't going to let my nerves ruin this. My hair was behaving for once, the waves falling over my shoulders perfectly. I looked good, at least. That was one less thing to worry about.

I kept my eyes on the door, waiting for him to walk in. I didn't know why I was so nervous. Alex seemed great and, honestly, like the least threatening guy ever. We'd been chatting for a while now, and he was always funny, sweet, and attentive. I liked that. But first dates are weird, aren't they? No matter how comfortable you feel with someone online or over the phone, in person is just different. It's more real. And even though we'd met before, this felt much more formal.

Then, I saw him. My stomach did a little flip as he walked in, scanning the room before his eyes found mine. I watched him for a second before he spotted me, and when he did, his expression softened into a smile that made me feel like I'd made the right choice being here. He looked good, too—better than I remembered. Crisp white shirt, jacket, that effortless kind of put-together. I liked it.

I stood up to greet him, hoping he liked my dress. "Alex! You made it," I said, leaning in to kiss his cheek. I could tell he was nervous too, which for some reason made me relax a little. We were both feeling it, not just me.

As we sat down, there was a brief moment of awkwardness, but I expected that. First dates always have that strange "What do we talk about now?" phase, even when you've been chatting for weeks. But once we got into the swing of things, it was easy. He made me laugh, really laugh, the kind where you don't care how you look. When he told me about his dream of chasing a flying pizza, I nearly spat my drink at him. It was so ridiculous, but so funny.

It felt natural, the way we just slipped into conversation about everything and nothing—music, travel, even dreams for the future. He was genuine, trying not to try too hard, and I liked that. I could tell he was still a little nervous, but it was cute. He wasn't one of those guys who pretended to be super confident or cool. He was real.

The food arrived, and we started eating, still chatting between bites. I went for the bruschetta and the tagliatelle, something that felt indulgent but not too heavy. He ordered lasagna, which made me smile. Classic guy. I liked that he didn't try to be fancy just for the sake of it.

As the meal went on, I found myself feeling more at ease. The restaurant had this beautiful, cosy atmosphere, the kind that makes you feel like you're in your own little world. For a while, it felt like it was just the two of us. I kept catching myself thinking, *I could get used to this.*

Then, halfway through the meal, a thought popped into my head—how did he know my address to send the TV? I hadn't given it much thought since that initial moment, but suddenly

I was curious. I didn't remember telling him, but it must've happened during one of our conversations, right? Still, I had to ask.

"Hey, Alex, I've been meaning to ask... how did you know my address for the TV?" I asked, trying to sound casual and light.

For a split second, I saw something in his face —panic? But it disappeared so quickly, I thought maybe I imagined it.

"You told me, obviously," he said, shrugging like it was no big deal. "How else would I have known?"

I thought about it for a second, but I couldn't remember telling him. Still, he was right. How else would he know? I must've mentioned it in passing and forgotten. I've been a little all over the place lately, and it's not a massive deal anyway. I trust him.

"Yeah, I guess so. I must've forgotten," I said with a laugh. His answer made sense, but there was something... I don't know, odd about how quickly he covered it. I let it go, though. Tonight wasn't the night to overthink things, and I had no real reason to suspect him. He's bought me a TV and given me money for God's sake!

We kept talking, moving to more personal topics. I told him about how much I want to work in the music industry, how I used to dream about my own A&R company one day. He listened, really listened, which was rare. Most guys would nod along, pretending to care, but I could tell Alex was genuinely interested. It made me feel seen and heard in a way that I hadn't felt in a long time.

When dessert came, we shared a tiramisu, laughing as we fought over the last bite. He let me have it, which was sweet. I could tell he was the kind of guy who didn't mind letting me win, and I liked that about him. It wasn't a power play; it was just him being playful.

Then the bill came, and I grabbed it before he could see it, but he looked mortified. "No way, Alex. You've done enough already," I insisted, but he wasn't having it.

"Emma, no way. I asked you out so It's my treat," he said, handing the card over to the waiter with the card reader without even seeing the amount. I didn't even have a chance to get my purse out my bag

"But—"

"No buts," he cut in with that charming smile of his as the card reader beeped and spat out a curled receipt. I rolled my eyes playfully but smiled back, giving in. It was kind of nice to be taken care of for a change. I wasn't used to it, but with Alex, it felt... right. I really could get used to this.

As we got up to leave, I noticed the cool breeze as soon as we stepped outside. Without missing a beat, Alex slipped his jacket off and draped it over my shoulders. I didn't even have to ask. The gesture was so natural, so thoughtful, that it made my heart flutter. I wondered if he had pre-planned that, some sort of smooth guy move he'd seen on TV or in a film.

We walked to my car, hand in hand, talking about the night and casually making plans to meet up next weekend. I told him I'd check my work shifts, but truthfully, I already knew I wanted to see him again. It felt natural the way he held my hand, like mine was a perfect fit.

When we got to my car, I could feel the moment building between us. He was thanking me for the night, and I could tell he was trying to work up the courage to kiss me. It was sweet, really, watching him fumble for the right words, but I didn't want to wait for him to make the move. I knew what I wanted, so I grabbed his face, both hands on his cheeks, and kissed him. Hard. It wasn't the soft, tentative kiss you might expect on a first date, but it felt perfect. I wanted him to know how I felt.

When I pulled back, he looked a little stunned, and I smiled, brushing my thumb across his cheek. "Thank you, for everything," I whispered, feeling like I'd just shared something important with him, even if it was just a kiss.

I got into my car, giving him one last smile before driving off. As I pulled away, I caught a glimpse of him in the rearview mirror, standing there, looking like he was still processing what had just happened, and I couldn't stop smiling the whole way home.

This was the start of something good. I could feel it. I wanted Alex.

Alex

I can't stop thinking about her.

Since our date, it's like she's embedded herself in every corner of my mind. Every time my phone buzzes, it's her. Every notification, every ping—it's Emma. We talk non-stop now. Messaging all day, calling at night until one of us falls asleep. I wake up with a smile because I know she's the first thing I'll think about, and the last thing I'll hear before I close my eyes.

In my head, she's already my girlfriend. We haven't had "the talk" yet, but I know it's just a formality at this point. She spends her days telling me about her work, her friends, her dreams. I know more about her than I've ever known about anyone else, and she knows me. I've shared parts of myself I don't usually let people see. She gets me.

That's why, when she invited me over to her place for dinner on Friday, I knew it was going to be *the* night.

The rest of the week crawled by, but I didn't mind because I knew what was coming. Emma. Friday. Dinner. Her house. She said she'd cook for me, and that's not something you do for just anyone. Cooking for someone—it's personal. It means something.

I spent hours imagining how the night would go. Every detail played out in my head, over and over again, like a movie. I could see her in the kitchen, maybe wearing something casual and effortlessly sexy. Her hair down, like it was on our date, those soft waves falling over her shoulders. I could almost smell the food she'd be making. Something delicious, something special, just for me.

I thought about how the night would end, too. It would be late, the room dimly lit, the tension between us thick, undeniable. She'd look at me, and I'd know, without a doubt, that she was ready. She'd pull me close, whisper my name, and that would be it. The moment we became something real.

I was already hers. The idea that she might not feel the same? Impossible.

When Friday finally came, I was buzzing. My stomach was tight with anticipation, and my mind wouldn't shut up.

As I drove to her place, I kept glancing at my phone, re-reading the messages from the week. She was excited to see me too. I could feel it in the way she texted, in the little emojis, the flirty comments, the incredible pictures she sent. She wanted this as much as I did.

When I pulled up to her house with the red door, my heart pounded in my chest. Her place was small but nice, cosy. Lights were on inside, casting a warm glow through the windows. I could see the shadows of her moving around in the kitchen, setting things up.

I smiled. She was getting everything ready for me. For us.

I parked outside, and she opened the door before I could even knock. God, she looked amazing. Casual but perfect. She wore a simple white vest top and figure-hugging jeans, nothing too fancy, but it suited her so much. Her hair was down, just like I'd imagined. The scent of whatever she was cooking hit me immediately—spices and herbs, something rich.

"Hey, you," she smiled, leaning in to kiss my cheek, her touch lingering for just a second too long. Or maybe that was my imagination.

"Hey," I replied, trying to sound smooth.

She ushered me inside, and I took in her home. It was... her. The place had that lived-in feel, but neat, filled with little touches of her personality —books stacked on the coffee table, a soft blanket draped over the couch. There were photos too— some of friends, some of her family. I studied them for a second, noting the faces I'd heard about in our conversations.

I followed her to the kitchen, the smell of dinner wrapping itself around me. It was intimate, standing there in her space, watching her move between the stove and the counter. This how it was supposed to be. Just the two of us. Together. I made sure to tell her how amazing it smelled, and she looked at me with the cutest smile—maybe she was extra comfortable, being in her own house.

The dinner was perfect. She'd made some kind of pasta dish—rich, creamy, with a bit of spice. We ate at her small kitchen table, candles flickering between us, casting soft light on her face. The conversation flowed as easily as it always did, but tonight it felt different. More charged. Every word, every glance, felt like it had a weight behind it. I was leaning in, hanging on her every sentence, every laugh.

She was glowing tonight. Maybe it was the wine, maybe it was just the atmosphere, but she looked softer, more relaxed. I felt like I was watching her let her guard down, letting me in even more.

At one point, she laughed, a little too loudly, and her eyes locked with mine. God, I love that laugh.

She looked away first, breaking the tension, standing to clear the plates. I watched her, my heart beating faster, knowing the night was just beginning.

I stood up to help, grabbing the empty wine glasses as she took the plates to the sink. The kitchen was small, which meant when I moved in beside her, we were close—closer than before. The warmth of her body, the soft scent of her perfume, the way her shoulder brushed against mine—it all made my head spin.

"You don't have to help, you know," she said, her

voice light, teasing.

"I want to," I replied, and I meant it. Being near her, doing something so normal together—it felt intimate in a way I couldn't quite describe.

She smiled but didn't argue, so I stayed, rinsing the glasses while she loaded the dishwasher. It was domestic, almost like we'd done this a hundred times before. I liked the thought of that.

When she closed the dishwasher with a soft click, she turned to face me, leaning against the counter. There was a look in her eyes, something unreadable but intense.

"That was amazing," I told her. "I think you just ruined restaurant pasta for me forever."

She laughed, tilting her head. "Oh, so I set the bar too high? That was a mistake."

"Maybe. But I don't mind if you keep trying to outdo yourself."

She rolled her eyes but smiled, her cheeks slightly flushed from the wine. For a second, neither of us spoke. The air between us changed —thicker, heavier. I could hear her breathing, soft but a little uneven, matching the way my chest tightened.

This was it.

I stepped closer, slow enough to give her time to

stop me if she wanted to—but she didn't move away. Her lips parted slightly, and I could feel the warmth radiating off her skin.

"Emma," I murmured, my hand brushing against her waist. She didn't flinch. Didn't pull back. If anything, she leaned in, just a little.

Her eyes searched mine, as if she was deciding something, weighing the moment. Then, so quickly I almost didn't process it, she reached up and pulled me in.

The kiss was slow at first—soft, testing, until I felt her fingers grip the front of my shirt, pulling me closer. That was all I needed. I deepened it, my hands sliding to her lower back, pressing her against me. She tasted like wine and something sweet, something uniquely her, and I wanted more.

She sighed into my mouth, and the sound sent heat rushing through me. I could've stayed like that forever—lost in her, in this moment—but she pulled back first, just enough to catch her breath.

Her lips were swollen, her cheeks flushed, and I'd never seen anything more beautiful.

We finished the clearing up and got comfortable on the sofa where the conversation shifted to family, and I noticed a change in Emma's expression—the slight falter in her smile, the way her fingers toyed absentmindedly with the stem of her wine glass. Then, with a small breath, she told me about her dad. Kevin.

She didn't say his name with anger, but there was something else there—something heavier. She told me how he left her mum, how he had a new family now, new kids. How, once upon a time, she had been his whole world. *Daddy's little girl.* The phrase barely made it past her lips before her voice wavered, and she blinked quickly, as if trying to swallow the emotion down before it could surface.

I stayed quiet, letting her speak. She wasn't looking for advice—just someone to hear her.

Her dad had always been successful, a business owner who made sure she never went without. He'd even helped her buy her house, the one with the red door, and used to send money each month to support her. But when he started his new life, the payments stopped.

"It's not about the money," she said quickly, shaking her head, as if reading my thoughts. "It's just… he used to be there. He used to care."

I nodded, my fingers brushing hers. She was an only child—she'd been used to a certain kind of attention, a presence in her life that had suddenly disappeared. No wonder it hurt.

She told me she was still close with her mum, but

things weren't the same. Her mum had changed since the split. Sadder. Less like the woman she used to be.

I leaned in, running my fingertips gently along her arm, a quiet reassurance that I was listening. I hated seeing her like this, her guard slipping just enough to show the cracks beneath. But after a moment, she sighed, blinking away the emotion, and forced a small smile. She was ready to move on from it, and I followed her lead. I didn't want this to cast a shadow over the night.

We sat close enough that my leg pressed against hers, and she didn't pull away. The warmth of her body against mine sent a slow pulse of anticipation through me.

She started talking about a job she wanted to apply for, something that would bring her one step closer to her dream, but I struggled to focus. Her voice was soft, thoughtful, but my mind was somewhere else. My thoughts were consumed by her. By us. By tonight.

Then, just like that, it was over.

Emma glanced at her phone, breaking the moment. "Hey, it's getting late," she said, her voice gentle, almost reluctant.

My heart clenched. I didn't want to leave. Not yet. Not when everything felt so *right.* But I forced a small smile. "Yeah, I guess it is."

She smiled back, but something about it felt distant. Or maybe I was just overthinking. Had I misread things? No. I knew her. I *knew* what this was. She just needed time. She had her reasons, her past. Maybe she needed to feel safe, to feel sure.

I could wait. However long it took, I'd wait.

Because she was mine.

As I stood, she walked me to the door, stopping close—*too* close for just friends. The air between us was charged, something unspoken lingering in space around us. My pulse pounded in anticipation, but before I could say anything, before I could make a move—

She kissed me.

Soft. Quick. But enough to send a fire ripping through my chest. Then she wrapped her arms around me, pulling me into a tight embrace. I could feel her warmth, the press of her body against mine, her head resting on my chest, and for a second, I didn't breathe.

"Goodnight, Alex," she whispered, her lips curving into a small smile as she pulled away. The way she looked up at me with those incredible eyes, almost teasing me with her vulnerability.

She gave me a cute little wave as I left but I barely remembered the drive home. My mind raced, replaying every second, every touch, every look. Tonight wasn't *the* night.

But soon.

Soon, she'd be mine.

Emma

I'd been prepping all day, but I still felt nervous.

Alex was coming over for dinner. And even though we'd been talking for a while now, *this* felt different. More personal. This was my space —my little world—and I wanted everything to be perfect. Not just the food, but the atmosphere. The way he'd see me. I wanted him to feel comfortable, but also... *impressed?* I hated admitting that, even to myself.

I'd spent the morning tidying, even though my place was already fairly neat. Still, I found myself fluffing the pillows, straightening the books on the coffee table, wiping down the counters *again*. I even lit a couple of candles—not too many, just enough to make the room feel warm and intimate without looking like I'd tried too hard. Everything needed to seem effortless, natural. Which, of course, it wasn't.

Choosing what to wear had been its own battle. I wanted to look good without it seeming like I was trying too hard. In the end, I settled on a white string vest and fitted jeans—casual but flattering. The vest dipped just enough to hint at something more, without screaming for attention. And I *knew* Alex would notice. That wasn't the point, but... okay, maybe it was a little.

Dinner was easy enough to figure out. I'm not the best cook, but pasta? Pasta, I could do. I went with a spicy penne arrabbiata—something simple, but with a little *kick*. Something I'd made before, so there was no chance of messing it up. The brownies for dessert were store-bought, but that was fine. If I played it off as a joke, Alex wouldn't care. It was the thought that counted, right?

By the time he arrived, I felt good. The house smelled amazing, the table was set, and I was comfortable in my own skin.

When I opened the door and saw him standing there, I couldn't help but smile.

He looked good. More relaxed than usual. Jeans and a hoodie. Something about it felt… soft. A part of me wanted to pull it off him and wear it myself.

"Hey, you," I said, leaning in to kiss his cheek.

He smelled fresh, that familiar aftershave wrapping around me for just a second. It made my heart flutter, but I ignored it.

I could tell he was taking everything in—the candles, the scent of garlic and chili hanging in the air, the way I looked. And when his eyes lingered on me for just a moment too long, I knew I'd made the right choice with the outfit.

We small talked a little as I gave him a beer and finished serving, then we sat and ate at the small table in the kitchen rather than the dining room. It felt more intimate this way. Closer. The conversation flowed, easy and effortless, just like always. He made me laugh—he always does—and it felt good, having him here, in my space. In this little bubble of mine. He seemed much more relaxed than I expected considering he was in my house, but maybe he was only nervous in public.

The pasta turned out great—*thankfully*.

"You're lucky I didn't burn this," I teased, twirling my fork through the sauce.

"You're underselling yourself," he said, grinning. "This is great."

His voice was warm, but it was the way he looked at me that made something in my stomach twist. Like I was something *special*.

I could feel his eyes on me whenever I moved —clearing a plate, refilling his glass—and each time, a small shiver ran down my spine.

As the night wore on, our conversation shifted to the sofa, dipping into quieter topics. He asked about my family. About my dad. His new life. His new kids. I tried to keep my voice steady, but I could feel the lump forming in my throat. Alex didn't push—he just listened—but still, I felt that moment of awkwardness. That heaviness.

So, we let the conversation drift back to something lighter. And it didn't ruin the night. We shared a brownie and the last of the wine. The candles flickered, casting soft shadows against the walls, and everything felt... easy. Comfortable. Natural.

I sat next to him—not too close, but not far either.

And I could feel it. That *tension*. That unspoken thing humming between us, waiting.

At some point in our conversation, his leg

brushed against mine.

It was barely noticeable at first, just a light touch, but it sent a jolt through me. I didn't move away. In fact, I liked the warmth of his body so close to mine. But there was a part of me that wanted to let this build. To savour it. I didn't want to give the wrong impression by moving too fast, even though—if I was honest—the thought of him staying over had crossed my mind more than once.

I knew if I let him stay, things would escalate. *Fast.* And while a part of me was tempted—*very* tempted—I also wanted to be sure. This felt good, right, but I didn't want to rush into something and risk complicating things. Not that I thought I'd regret it with Alex, but... I didn't want him to get the wrong idea. I liked him too much for that.

I liked the way he was looking at me—his eyes just a little darker, more intent—but I also saw something else. A kind of expectation or maybe hope.

I glanced at the time. *Shit.* It was getting late. Maybe too late.

My heart sped up as I debated with myself. Should I ask him to stay? Should I let this happen? Give in to the moment? A thousand scenarios playing out in a matter of seconds.

But no. *Not tonight.* We needed more time.

"It's getting late," I said softly, almost regretting it the second the words left my mouth.

For a fraction of a second, I saw it—the flicker of disappointment in his face. He tried to hide it, but I caught it before he could smooth it over. My heart dipped. I *wanted* him to stay, but I needed to do this right. I smiled, hoping he'd understand.

"Yeah, I guess it is getting a bit late," he said, his voice quieter and slightly defeated now.

He stood up, and I followed him to the door, my stomach twisting. The night had been perfect, but I didn't want it to end without something he can remember. Not without a kiss, at least.

When we reached the door, I hesitated. He looked genuinely sad and part of me felt cruel, but then I remembered just because he was in my house, doesn't mean he gets to be in my bed too. Men don't get to expect that just because they were nice for an evening.

The air between us was heavy with something unspoken, so before he had the chance to overthink it all, I reached up, took his face between my hands, and pulled him in for a kiss.

It was quick—soft, but firm. Enough to tell him that I *was* into this. Into him. But I didn't let it linger.

Instead, I wrapped my arms around him, burying myself in his chest for a second longer than I probably should have, before pulling away. When I looked up, he was flushed, his breath a little uneven, and I liked that. I *really* liked that.

His hand lingered near mine, as if he didn't want to let go. Neither did I.

I watched him walk to his car, giving him a small wave as he drove off.

Then I stood there for a moment, letting the cool night air settle over me.

Tonight, had been *perfect.*

And I knew it now—Alex was the one.

~

The week after dinner with Alex felt like a blur.

It was as if everything was falling into place— or at least, that's what I kept telling myself. We'd been texting constantly, sending cute goodnight messages, little updates about our days. He checked in on me, asked how I was sleeping, made me laugh when I needed it.

It had been *so* long since someone was this attentive. *This involved.*

He wasn't officially my boyfriend, but... it was starting to feel like he was.

And I liked that.

Then, in the middle of all that, something else happened. Something I hadn't expected.

I had almost forgotten about the job application I'd sent a while back—an Artist Marketing Coordinator role at a small agency about half an hour away. I hadn't expected to hear anything. I'd *polished* my CV a little too much, exaggerated some freelance work, stretched the truth just enough to make myself look more impressive.

And then, out of the blue, I got the email.

'We're pleased to invite you for an interview next week...'

I read it three times before it sunk in.

This was a big deal. A *huge* deal. Something I could actually build a future around, something that didn't involve minimum wage and endless, soul-crushing shifts.

I had literally dreamed about this moment.

But instead of excitement, panic set in.

They wanted a character reference.

Specifically, someone I'd worked with in the

marketing or music industry. Someone I'd claimed I'd done freelance work for.

And I had no one.

That whole section of my application—the freelance work, the industry experience—was built on… well, not lies, exactly. But certainly not the whole truth.

I had written it hoping they wouldn't check.

But they clearly did.

For the next couple of days, I agonised over it, running through every possible option, every possible way to get out of this mess without blowing my shot. I couldn't back out now.

I couldn't tell them I didn't have anyone—not when I'd claimed to have all this *experience*.

And then, I thought of Alex. Perfect reliable Alex.

It was a crazy idea, but somehow,
I knew it would work.

Alex had been nothing but kind, and more than that—he was willing to help. He had already done so much for me. The TV. The money he'd slipped into my account like it was nothing. I hadn't even asked, and yet he provided, as if it were second nature for him to take care of me.

He'd do anything for me if I really needed it.

We were texting back and forth like usual, and I decided to bring it up. I was nervous, but I played it cool. I didn't want to make it seem like a huge deal, like I was asking too much. Just a simple favour. That's how I framed it.

"Hey, I got that job interview I told you about! Only thing is, they want a character reference. Someone in the industry. Do you think you could help me out? Pretend to be someone I used to work with? I never expected to hear back, and you know everyone puts that they have references available. Pleaseeeeeee, I really want this job! xxxx"

I hesitated for a moment before hitting send, my heart tapping against my ribs as I watched the screen glow in the dim light of my room. I *might* actually get this job.

A reply came almost instantly.

"Of course I will, Emma. What do you need me to say?"

I exhaled, a wave of relief washing over me. I knew he'd say yes, but seeing the words made it real. I couldn't help but smile, and not just because of his willingness to help. It was more than that.

It seems I've found my knight in shining armour. The solver of my problem.

We talked on the phone into the night, planning how we'd approach it. I could hear the excitement in his voice, the eagerness to do this for me, like it was another way to prove how much he cared. I gave him a name—Mark, a former manager at a small marketing firm called Ixon—and fed him the details he'd need in case they called him, though I hoped the letter of recommendation would be enough.

He didn't question a single thing. Not once. No hesitation.

I found myself wondering what else I could ask of him. How far I could push before he'd say no.

But I brushed the thought away just as quickly. I didn't want to think like that. I wasn't taking advantage of him… was I?

After we hung up, I lay there in the dark, staring at the ceiling, trying to silence the doubts creeping into my head.

I wasn't using him.

He wanted to help. He cared about me.

That's what relationships were supposed to be, right? Helping each other out? I'll be there for him when he needs me. I'll support him too.

I forwarded the new email address I'd created to the reference email. 'MarkConner@Ixon.com'—

knowing Alex would receive the emails when I sent him the password in the morning.

I knew he'd write a good letter, but I asked him to let me read it over before he sent it, just to make sure it was perfect.

The next morning, I sent Alex the password for the fake email account. I was up early, sipping my coffee at the kitchen counter, that strange mix of excitement, guilt and fear bubbling in my stomach. *I wasn't doing anything wrong;* I reminded myself. Everyone fudges things on their CV a little. This was no different. Besides, Alex wanted to help.

By the time we got on the phone, I'd already mapped out a rough outline for the letter in my head. I figured if I walked him through the basics, he'd take it from there. But as soon as we got into the details, I heard it—that tiny hesitation in his voice.

"I mean, what if they ask me about specific projects? Or want details about the company? I don't really know how that stuff works, Emma."

There was an uncertainty in his tone that made my stomach tighten. For a split second, I thought he might back out. *Might actually say no.*

I couldn't let that happen. This job was exactly

what I needed, especially with my reduced hours, this was the chance to finally step into the music industry.

I softened my voice, leaning into the tone I knew would calm him. "Alex, it's fine, honestly. They're not going to grill you. It's just a character reference, not a full-blown background check. Ixon was a small firm, remember? No one's going to dig that deep. Just keep it simple and confident. I trust you babe."

A pause.

I held my breath.

"I don't know..." He trailed off, wavering.

I had to push—just a little more.

"Please, Alex." I let a gentle plea slip into my voice. "You've already done so much for me, and this is just one more little thing. You *know* how much this job means to me. And I'd do the same for you in a heartbeat." I let that sit for a moment before adding, softer now, "I'm not asking for much... just your help."

That did it.

"Alright," he exhaled, giving in. "Yeah, okay. I'll do it for you."

Relief washed over me. I smiled. "You're amazing. Thank you so much, Alex."

We talked for a little longer and I made sure to keep it light, so he didn't second guess himself. I promised him I'd cook the best meal he's ever had, and even hinted at not letting him leave next time. Then I pretended I had things to do, but really, I just wanted him to start working on my recommendation letter. I mean, I did have things around the house I could do, but I had too much nervous energy to clean.

By the time Alex sent over the first draft of the letter, I already felt more in control. I'd subtly steered him back on course, and now all that was left was to make sure it was *perfect*. I opened the email on my laptop and skimmed through it.

It was... fine. But not quite enough.

I called him immediately. "It's great, but we just need to tweak a few things, okay?" I kept my tone light, casual, as if this was nothing more than a finishing touch.

"Sure, whatever you need," Alex replied, eager to please.

I guided him carefully, choosing my words. "You need to make it sound a bit more *personal*, like you really knew me well. Talk about my work ethic, how I always went above and beyond. Mention a couple of specific tasks—how I handled clients, how I managed campaigns. Even if you don't know the details, just make it *sound* good."

"Right…" Another pause. I could feel the doubt creeping back in. "But what if they ask about the clients? Or the campaigns? I don't know anything about marketing, Emma."

I took a slow breath, keeping my patience. "Alex, trust me. They won't. And even if they do, just be vague. Say something like, *Emma was an integral part of our client outreach.* Keep it general but positive. You've got this." I let out a soft laugh, like it was all so simple, so harmless. "You're overthinking it baby."

I'd noticed the pet names worked wonders when he needed a little push.

He laughed too, and I could hear the huge smile in his voice, he liked being called cute names. "Yeah, maybe I am. Okay, I'll fix it up."

"Thank you," I said, my voice warm again. "Honestly, you're saving my life."

Later that evening, the final draft landed in my inbox.

This time, it was perfect.

I smiled as I read through it, satisfied.

Subject: Character Reference for Emma

To whom it may concern,

I am writing to provide a character reference for Emma, whom I had the pleasure of working with during her time as a freelance marketing consultant at Ixon. I was Emma's direct supervisor, and during our time together, she consistently proved herself to be an invaluable asset to our team.

Emma demonstrated a remarkable ability to manage client relationships, often going above and beyond to ensure that all projects were completed to the highest standards. Her creativity and initiative were key in helping our firm grow, particularly in managing social media campaigns for several high-profile clients in the arts and entertainment industries.

Her work ethic was exemplary. Emma was not only punctual and reliable, but also incredibly driven and results focused. She frequently took on additional responsibilities, stepping in to support colleagues and ensuring that projects were delivered on time. Her positive attitude and adaptability made her a pleasure to work with, and her contributions significantly enhanced our team's overall performance.

In summary, I can confidently recommend Emma for any role within your organisation. She has proven herself to be hardworking, talented, and passionate about her work, and I have no doubt she will continue to excel in any position she takes on.

If you have any further questions, please feel free to contact me at this email address.

Sincerely,

Mark Conner

Ixon Marketing

I sat back, a quiet contentment settling over me. Everything was lined up perfectly. But then, a flicker of doubt.

Was I pushing him too much? Was I asking too much from someone who so clearly had his heart set on me?

I brushed the thought aside. This wasn't

manipulation. It was… survival. I *needed* this job, and Alex was helping. That's what partners do.

I sent him a quick thank-you text, adding a few extra x's at the end for good measure. His reply came almost instantly—his words warm, eager. "Happy to help. Proud of you for chasing your dreams."

Alex

After I hit send on the email, my hands wouldn't stop shaking. I stared at the screen, reading and re-reading the letter I'd just sent. It looked professional, polished— almost too good. Emma had made sure of that. She'd helped me tweak it until it was flawless, until it sounded like I'd known her for years as a marketing whiz.

But I hadn't.

The truth was, I didn't know the first thing about marketing, managing clients, or half the things I'd just written. If they fact-checked even a little, I'd be completely out of my depth. And yet, I couldn't say no.

Not to Emma.

Not when she asked like that, almost begged if I could *just help her*. She made it sound so simple, so harmless, and all I wanted was to be the person she could count on.

Still, the anxiety gnawed at me. I tried to shake it off, but my thoughts kept circling back to that email. What if they asked questions I couldn't answer? What if I slipped up? I wanted to do right by her, but I didn't want to screw this up.

It wasn't just her new job on the line.

It was *her trust in me*.

And that mattered more than anything.

I'd done things for her before without her knowing. But this was different.

This... she would judge me for.

A few days later, I was at work, staring at my screen, when my phone rang. The number was unfamiliar, but the moment I saw it, something inside me twisted.

I *knew*.

Even before I answered.

"Hello?" I said, stepping into the stairwell for some quiet. My pulse quickened.

"Hi, Mark, this is Jessica Matthews from Westbridge Marketing. I'm calling to verify a character reference for Emma. You provided a letter of recommendation for her, and we just have a few follow-up questions."

My heart nearly stopped.

This was it.

The moment I'd been dreading.

"Of course," I said, forcing my voice to stay steady. The lie was already forming on my tongue. "What would you like to know?"

Jessica's tone remained polite, professional. "Could you tell me more about Emma's role at Ixon? Specifically, the kinds of clients she worked with and the contributions she made to your marketing strategies?"

I swallowed hard, trying to remember the things Emma had coached me on. *Keep it vague. Talk about social media campaigns and clients. Nobody will ask too much.*

Yet here they were.

Asking for details I didn't have.

"Emma was a real asset to the team," I began, feeling the words stumble out of my mouth. "She handled a lot of client communication. Social media campaigns were kind of her specialty. She was great at driving engagement, especially for our local clients in the arts and entertainment sectors."

A drop of sweat rolled down the back of my neck.

Was I saying too much? Not enough? My mind raced, but I couldn't let the hesitation show.

Jessica didn't seem to notice. "That's great to hear. Could you give me an example of a campaign she led? Something that stood out to you?"

My chest tightened.

An example.

This was where it could all fall apart.

"Well, one campaign that really stood out was for a local music festival," I said, grasping at the first thing that came to mind. "Emma took the lead on that one. She developed a strategy to increase ticket sales through social media outreach and partnerships with local influencers and businesses. It was a huge success. We saw engagement rise by... uh, about 50%."

I had no idea where I pulled that number from, but it seemed to do the trick.

Jessica hummed approvingly. "And would you say Emma was comfortable working independently, or did she rely more on team support and collaboration?"

I forced myself to breathe. "Oh, she's definitely independent. Always took initiative, looking for ways to improve things without much oversight. But she was also a great team player when it came to bigger projects—often took younger staff under her wing."

A pause. A long pause..

Then—

"Thank you so much for your time, Mr. Conner," Jessica finally said. "We appreciate the insight. Have a great day."

"You too," I replied, forcing a smile into my voice. "Feel free to reach out if you have any more questions."

The moment I hung up, the relief hit me all at once.

Followed swiftly by pride.

I'd gotten through it.

I'd made it up on the spot, just like Emma had told me I could.

I'd lied.

And not just a small, harmless lie.

I'd fabricated an entire *history* for Emma, spinning it out of thin air.

I did it for her.

I told myself I had no choice.

Emma *needed* me.

She trusted me to help her get this job, and I couldn't let her down. Not after everything she'd shared with me—how much she'd opened up.

I *had* to be there for her.

No matter what.

That night, when I called Emma to tell her how the call had gone, I could hear the excitement in her voice before she even spoke.

"They asked a lot of questions," I told her, trying to keep my tone light. "But I think I handled it. I told them about the music festival campaign you 'ran.' They seemed impressed."

"You're amazing, Alex," she said, warmth spilling into every word. "I knew you'd do it perfectly."

Her praise felt so good.

Knowing I'd made her *happy*.

I'd do anything for her— literally anything she needed.

Besides, I'd done worse than lie for a job.

Emma

I stared at the email, the bold "Congratulations!" blinking up at me like a promise I'd been waiting for. Westbridge Marketing wanted me. A real job—a real future—all thanks to Alex.

He had no idea how much I needed this.

I leaned back in my chair, biting my lip as the reality of it settled in. Satisfaction curled in my chest, warm and thrilling. Everything was falling into place.

And tonight, I'd tighten my hold on Alex.

Another simple dinner. A home-cooked meal. Nothing extravagant, nothing flashy. I *knew* how to play this part—modest, sweet, grateful Emma. It was important to keep him in the right headspace, to remind him that he was my hero, the one person I could *trust*.

But tonight, I was going to take things further.

I wanted him to stay.

I wanted to show him he'd *earned* that intimacy.

I moved through the kitchen, chopping vegetables for the stir-fry, already picturing how the night would go. Alex, sitting across from me, watching me with that dopey, love-drunk expression. The way his breath would hitch when I leaned in close. How his hands might shake when I whispered that I'd been *thinking* about him.

It wouldn't be hard to make him believe it. He was already hanging on my every word.

But.

There was something else.

A shadow in the back of my mind. A pull I hadn't completely shaken.

Bradley.

I hadn't seen him in weeks. He'd been quiet—too quiet—but I knew it wouldn't last. It never did. I figured he was laying low after his run-in with the police, but Bradley never stayed out of my life for long. Eventually, he'd show up at my door, drunk or high, demanding to talk, to fight. Maybe both.

Not this time though.

This time, I'd *control* the situation. I *had* to. I still didn't feel like I'd had my revenge for what he'd done—for storming into my house, for breaking my TV, for every sick game he ever played with me.

I know I should let sleeping dogs lie and just get on with my life.

Yet…

My fingers hovered over my phone, my pulse thrumming as an old, familiar heat coiled inside me.

Bradley and I had always burned *hot*. Explosive. Passionate. Messy. The kind of connection that made you feel like you were on fire even when you were drowning. He was *bad for me*, but that didn't stop me from craving the pull—the way he could infuriate me and ignite me in the same breath.

I could still hear his voice in my head. *"You're mine, Em. You'll always be mine."*

I should have hated him for that. I should have erased him completely.

But I didn't.

I couldn't.

Because I *knew* how to play him.

And knowing I had Alex meant, now I could.

I typed out the message quickly, my fingers steady, my heart anything but.

"Hey Brad, hope you're doing okay. Maybe we can meet up soon and talk? I just needed some time to think."

I stared at the words, the bait carefully laid, before silencing my phone and setting it aside. He wouldn't reply instantly—he'd make me wait. He always did.

But he *would* reply.

And when he did, I'd be the one calling the shots.

I was setting the table when my phone shook and hummed.

Alex.

"On my way. Can't wait to see you! P.S. I'm very hungry!"

I stared at the screen for a moment, feeling a thrill rush through me.

He thought he was coming over for a thank-you dinner. A nice evening.

But I had so much more planned.

I needed him in love with me. *Completely.* Mind, body, and soul. I needed him to feel like he was the only one who mattered.

And Bradley?

Well…

The wheels were in motion to deal with him.

The doorbell rang.

I took one last glance in the hallway mirror, tilting my head slightly. *Simple dress. Soft makeup. Hair down.* Effortless. Or at least, it needed to *look* that way. Like I hadn't planned this. Like I wasn't thinking ten steps ahead.

I took a slow breath and opened the door.

Alex stood there, gripping a bottle of wine like it was some kind of peace offering. His eyes lit up the moment he saw me, his shoulders relaxing. "Hey," he said, that shy smile already curling at his lips.

Predictable.

"Hey yourself," I murmured, stepping aside to let him in. "You didn't have to bring wine."

He shrugged, rubbing the back of his neck. "I just wanted to bring something, you know… to thank you for inviting me."

I shut the door behind him, letting my fingers graze his arm as I did. Subtle. "You're sweet," I said, watching the way his chest rose slightly at the compliment. "I should be the one thanking *you*—I couldn't have gotten the job without you."

His whole face lit up. *There it is.* That flicker of pride, the rush of validation.

He wanted to believe it. He *needed* to.

We sat down to dinner, and I played my role effortlessly. I asked him about his day, listened with just the right amount of focus, let him feel like I *saw* him. When I laughed, I let it linger. When I refilled his glass, my fingers brushed his. Each moment was crafted, each touch deliberate.

And it was working.

I watched the way his eyes moved over me, the way his smile softened, like he couldn't quite believe I was sitting here with him, sharing the same air, the same space.

By the time we finished eating, the shift was palpable.

He was leaning in more now. His voice lower, warmer. His hand brushed against mine more often, his fingers lingering in a way they wouldn't have before. I refilled his glass one last time, tracing the rim with my fingertip as I handed it to him.

I let the silence stretch, just enough to make him feel it.

"You know," I said softly, watching the way his fingers curled around the stem of his glass, "I've been thinking about this for a while."

His head lifted, his eyes flicking to mine. "What do you mean?"

I stood slowly, circling the table, my movements unhurried, unrushed.

"I mean," I murmured, leaning down, my lips so close to his ear that I could feel his breath hitch, "I've been thinking about *you*."

He went still, his fingers tensing around his glass. I ran my fingertips over his shoulder, tracing lightly down his arm, feeling the way he stiffened beneath my touch.

"You've been so good to me, Alex," I whispered, letting my lips graze the shell of his ear. "And I think it's time I showed you how much that means to me."

He turned slightly, his eyes locking onto mine, dark with something uncertain. There was conflict there—desire battling restraint, excitement laced with hesitation.

Good.

I needed him to hesitate.

Because that's where the power was.

His breath was uneven now, his fingers twitching like he didn't quite know what to do with them. He wanted to make the first move, but he was scared to. Too unsure. Too nice.

I took his hand, guiding him to his feet. He followed easily, his grip warm but hesitant, tension coiled in his fingers.

"Are you sure?" he asked, voice barely above a whisper.

I smiled, tilting my chin up slightly, letting my lips brush against his in the softest of kisses. Just enough to pull him deeper, to make him *feel* the answer before I even spoke it.

"One hundred percent, yes."

As we walked down the hall toward my bedroom, I glanced over my shoulder. The front door was locked, the house was quiet, and everything was falling into place.

Bradley was out of the picture. For now.

But Alex... I was just getting started with him.

Alex

Her lips were soft, addictive, moving against mine with a slow, deliberate rhythm. Every brush of her mouth, every shift of her body against me, sent heat curling through my veins. It was intoxicating, the way she kissed—not rushed or desperate, but controlled, like she knew exactly what she was doing to me.

And fuck, she did.

My heart pounded as she led me down the hall, her fingers threaded through mine, warm and certain. I followed without question, completely under her spell, barely aware of anything but the way she felt, the way she looked at me—like I was the only thing in the world that mattered.

Inside her bedroom, the air thickened.

The dim glow of the lamp cast long, lazy shadows across the walls, the light flickering over the delicate things that made this room *hers*—the neatly stacked books, the forgotten sweater draped over a chair, the faint scent of her perfume clinging to the air. It was overwhelming, completely her, and now I was *inside* it, being pulled deeper with every glance, every breath.

Emma turned to me, eyes dark with passion, something that made my stomach tighten and my pulse hammer. She reached for me, fingertips ghosting along my arm before trailing down, slow and deliberate, until they found my hand.

I exhaled sharply.

She felt it. Smiled.

And then she kissed me again.

This time, there was no hesitation, no soft buildup—just heat, raw and consuming, as her lips moved with more hunger, more intent. She pressed closer, her body moulding against mine, and I couldn't stop myself from gripping her waist, pulling her tighter, needing her nearer.

She tasted like wine and something sweeter, something uniquely her, and I was already addicted.

I barely realised we were moving until the backs of my knees hit the bed. Emma didn't stop. She pushed me down, following me, straddling my hips like it was the most natural thing in the world.

And maybe it was.

Maybe this was exactly where we were always meant to end up.

Her hands found the buttons of my shirt, undoing them one by one, her touch featherlight but scorching. I helped her, barely able to keep my fingers steady, my need for her so sharp it was almost painful. She slid the fabric off my shoulders, her eyes roaming my skin with a hunger that made my breath hitch.

Then her hands were on me.

Fingertips tracing over my chest, across my stomach, mapping me like she wanted to commit every inch of me to memory. My skin burned beneath her touch, every nerve sparking to life, and when she dipped her head, pressing hot, open-mouthed kisses along my collarbone, my restraint frayed completely.

I flipped her beneath me in one movement, swallowing the gasp that escaped her lips.

She met my urgency with her own, fingers sinking into my hair, tugging just hard enough to send a shiver down my spine. I groaned against her throat, kissing, tasting, nipping at the delicate skin there, drinking in the quiet little sounds she made as I moved lower.

Her nails raked down my back. My hands slid under her shirt, teasing up the warm, bare skin of her waist before pulling the fabric over her head.

And fuck.

She was stunning.

Breathtaking.

The sight of her—flushed, lips parted, chest rising and falling in quick, shallow breaths—was enough to steal whatever control I had left.

I leaned down, brushing my lips across her delicate shoulder, trailing lower, drinking in every reaction, every tremble, every hitched breath. My hands explored her, learning the shape of her, the softness of her skin on my fingertips. She arched beneath me, pressing closer, pulling me in, and it wasn't enough. It would *never* be enough.

I needed her.

And she needed me.

What happened after that was a blur of heat and motion, of tangled sheets and whispered names, of bodies coming together in a slow, deliberate rhythm that built, higher and higher, until everything shattered in the most incredible way.

It wasn't just physical.

It wasn't just lust.

It was something more—something I couldn't name, but felt in every kiss, every breath, every way she let me in. She wasn't just giving me her body; she was giving me *her*, and I wanted to cherish it, to prove to her that she meant more to me than she could ever imagine.

And for the first time in my life, I felt whole.

Afterward, we lay tangled in each other, the world outside forgotten. Her head rested on my chest, her fingers tracing absent patterns against my skin, and I closed my eyes, trying to slow the frantic beating of my heart.

I had no idea what tomorrow would bring.

But for tonight?

She was mine.

I whispered her name, my voice raw, stripped bare. She stirred against me, her body warm and soft beneath the sheets, her hand still resting on my chest. When she finally looked up, her eyes were heavy-lidded, her lashes fluttering as if she were caught in the hazy space between sleep and wakefulness.

I swallowed hard, my throat tight. I knew I

shouldn't say it—not yet. Not when the weight of this moment still lingered between us, fragile as glass. But the words pressed against my ribs, clawing their way free before I could stop them.

"I love you."

The silence that followed was unbearable.

Her lips parted slightly, but no words came. No sharp intake of breath, no trembling exhale —just stillness. For the briefest second, I saw something flicker in her expression, something fleeting, unreadable.

And then it was gone.

My pulse pounded against my skin, my chest constricting as the realisation hit me like a slow, sinking weight.

She wasn't going to say it back.

I forced myself to keep breathing, to keep still, even as the sharp sting of rejection twisted deep into my ribs. Maybe she needed time. Maybe she wasn't ready. Maybe she just— Maybe she never would be.

Her fingers skimmed lightly over my skin, tracing slow, hypnotic circles over my chest. It should have been soothing, reassuring, but it wasn't. It felt like a placeholder, like she was giving me just enough to keep me there but not enough to give me what I really wanted.

What I needed.

Her voice was soft, almost hesitant. "Alex…"

I held my breath.

"I… I really appreciate you"

That was it. That was all she gave me.

Not 'I love you.' Not even a whisper of it.

Just a few empty words that landed between us like stones, sinking deep, heavy and unmoving. And yet, she said them so gently, so sincerely, as if she thought they'd be enough to patch over the crack she'd just carved through me.

I told myself I shouldn't be disappointed. That this was still new, but that meant something. That her warmth, her presence, the way she clung to me just moments ago—none of that was a lie.

But I couldn't shake the hollow ache in my chest, the gnawing doubt curling through my stomach like smoke.

I forced a smile, brushing a loose strand of hair from her face, tucking it behind her ear. "I'm here for you Emma."

She smiled back, but it didn't quite reach her eyes.

Something inside me tightened.

I held onto her for a while, held onto the moment like I could make it mean something more than it did. I ran my fingers along her spine, memorising the way she felt beneath my touch. I buried my face against her hair, inhaling the faint, lingering scent of vanilla and warmth, trying to burn it into my senses.

Trying to convince myself that this was enough.

But the room felt different now. The bed felt colder, the space between us stretching wider, an invisible wall forming where there had been none before.

I stayed until I heard her breathing even out, slow and steady, her body relaxing into sleep. And even then, I hesitated, watching her in the dim light, memorising every curve, every shadow, as if this might be the last time.

Carefully, I slid out from beneath the sheets, moving slowly so I wouldn't wake her. The air felt cooler against my bare skin as I reached for my clothes, pulling them on one piece at a time, feeling the weight of the night pressing against me.

At the door, I paused.

I glanced back at her one last time.

She looked peaceful, curled up beneath the covers, her lips slightly parted, her hair a tangled halo against the pillow. So close, yet so distant.

My heart clenched painfully in my chest.

I had told her I loved her.

And she hadn't said it back.

I closed the door softly behind me, stepping out into the stillness of the night, and for the first time, I let myself feel it.

The quiet devastation of wanting someone more than they wanted me.

I told myself it didn't matter. That maybe she just needed more time. That love wasn't something you could force. Not when she's had her bad experiences with it. I could try to justify it to myself, but deep down, I knew the truth.

Maybe she would never love me the way I loved her.

And maybe... maybe I'd already given her too much.

Emma

When I kissed him, I made sure it felt real—slow, deliberate, like I was giving him everything he craved. His hands roamed my back, pulling me closer with that same quiet desperation I'd come to recognise and enjoy. He needed this. Needed me. And I let him. I melted into him just enough, let my breath hitch at just the right moment, let my fingers tremble slightly as I ran them through his hair. I knew what he wanted—what he needed me to be—and I gave it to him effortlessly.

Because that was the trick, wasn't it?

To make it feel real.

And in a way, maybe it was. I wasn't cold, not entirely. I liked the way his touch lingered, the way he looked at me like I was his whole world. There was something intoxicating about knowing I had that power, that he would do anything to keep me close. And that's exactly where I needed him. Close. Loyal. Mine.

As I pushed him toward the bed, I could feel his hesitation—brief, uncertain—but I smoothed it away with a look, a touch, a soft murmur against his skin. His walls crumbled so easily under the right pressure, and I knew just how to apply it.

When I straddled him, I moved with precision, slow and deliberate, keeping my eyes on his, watching the way he responded to every brush of my fingers. His breath hitched when I traced my nails down his chest, and I smiled, letting him believe it was nothing but instinct.

I helped him remove his shirt, my fingertips ghosting over his skin like I was memorising him. Because that was the thing about Alex—he didn't just want me, he wanted to be everything to me. He wanted to be needed. And I was happy to let him believe he was.

I wasn't faking it. I wasn't cruel. But I never let go completely the way he did. Even as our bodies moved together, even as my breath mixed with his, there was always a part of me that remained just slightly out of reach. It was necessary. If I let myself fall too deeply into this, I'd lose sight of what mattered.

This was more than just us. More than just a night tangled in sheets and whispered words. This was about securing his devotion, reinforcing everything I'd spent so long building between us.

I let my head rest against his chest afterward, listening to the rhythm of his heartbeat as it slowed. His arm tightened around me, protective, possessive, like he thought he was keeping me safe. I let him believe it. I let my fingers trace lazy patterns over his skin, as if I had nothing else on my mind but him.

And for a moment—just a moment—I felt something shift.

The way he delicately stroked my face, like I was under his protection, I could feel him looking at me like he would kill for me.

Bradley gave me raw passion, but Alex, he gave me that warm feeling that only genuine love can give.

But I couldn't get caught up in this—not the way he was. I couldn't let myself fall for completely yet. This had to stay controlled, precise. I had to keep my focus. Because as much as I might have enjoyed the warmth of his arms around me, the safety of his touch, I wasn't going to be completely vulnerable for him yet. I made that mistake before and it only hurt me.

This was about keeping him where I needed him until I knew for sure.

And tonight, had done exactly that.

Then, finally, just as my rationalising thought process ended, he gave me the words I'd been waiting to hear.

"I love you."

I concealed a smile, resting my hand over his

heart.

Perfect.

Alex

The next morning, I woke up to sunlight streaming through the curtains of my small apartment, but something felt different. That moment from last night—the moment I told her I loved her, and she didn't say it back—was stuck in my head like a song I couldn't turn off.

I told myself it wasn't a big deal. Maybe she just wasn't ready to say those words yet. Emma had been through a lot with Bradley—the way he treated her, the way he tore her down. I couldn't expect her to open up overnight. It wasn't fair for expect that.

And yet, no matter how much I tried to rationalise it, a hollow ache settled in my chest. It wasn't just that she didn't say it back. It was the way she smiled instead, the way her fingers brushed my arm like she was soothing a child rather than answering me.

I forced myself to focus on the good parts of the night. How close we'd been. How she kissed me like she meant it. How she felt on top of me. How we felt together. How, in those moments, I felt like the only person in the world that mattered to her.

Every time we spoke since, every time I sent her a text, I found myself listening for something unspoken, watching for a shift I couldn't quite put my finger on. I wanted to believe nothing had changed, that I was just overthinking, but the more I tried to ignore it, the more it gnawed at me.

I decided I wasn't going to ask her about it. Not yet. Emma had been through hell with Bradley, and it made sense that she'd be hesitant. Maybe she just needed time to trust that this—us—was real. Maybe she wasn't ready to let someone in like that again.

And I could wait.

I had to.

But even as I told myself that, the doubts crept in.

We kept talking to each other over the next week, and at first, everything felt normal. She'd reply to my texts with the same warmth, the same playful teasing that had made me fall for her in the first place. But then, other times, she'd take hours to respond, and when she did, her messages were short, distant. Lacking warmth.

I told myself it was nothing. She'd just started her new job at Westbridge Marketing—of course, she was busy.

But the thoughts kept coming.

Why hadn't she said it back?

Was it because she didn't feel the same? Or because she was scared to?

When she cancelled our Friday night plans because she was too tired, I told myself she was just exhausted from work. But the thought slipped in anyway—was she really tired, or did she just not want to see me? When she didn't reply to my messages right away, I'd stare at my phone, wondering if she was pulling away. But I never asked. Never pushed. The last thing I wanted was to pressure her, to make her feel like she owed me something.

So, I stayed quiet.

Sitting at my desk at work, I caught myself staring at my phone again. My fingers hovered over the keyboard, trying to think of something to say. Something casual. Something that wouldn't make it seem like I was waiting for reassurance.

"Hey, how's your day going?"

I typed it out. Deleted it. It sounded too desperate.

"Thinking about you, hope you're okay."

Worse.

I finally settled on something simple: "Hope work's not too stressful today. Miss you."

I hesitated before sending it, feeling that familiar tension in my chest. I hated how much I cared about her response; how much I needed it. How her reply could dictate my mood for an entire day.

A few minutes later, my phone buzzed. My heart leapt as I unlocked it.

"Thanks, just swamped with emails today. Miss you too. x"

I exhaled, relief flooding through me. It was fine. Everything was fine. She missed me. She wasn't pulling away. I was just overthinking it.

But still…

One kiss.

I kept telling myself I wouldn't bring up that night. I couldn't. If I pushed her too soon, if I pressured her, I might ruin everything. I had to be patient. I had to let her come to me when she was ready.

But each day that passed without hearing those words from her made the hole inside me grow a little bigger.

And I didn't know how much longer I could ignore it.

Because of the cancelled Friday plans, we had rearranged to meet at her place again Saturday night.

I told myself I was fine, that this was just another night like any other. But as I stood outside her door, my hand hovering before I finally knocked, I couldn't ignore the nerves twisting in my stomach.

The door opened, and there she was—Emma. That familiar, bright smile curved on her lips, warm and effortless, just like always. But behind her eyes, something flickered. Fleeting. Hard to pin down.

"Hey," she said, stepping aside to let me in. "Sorry the place is a bit of a mess. I've been all over the place with work."

"It's fine," I said, brushing it off as I stepped

inside. "I don't mind."

The scent of her—soft vanilla and something faintly floral—wrapped around me, familiar and grounding. But as much as I wanted to sink into the comfort of being here, of being with her, something felt... off.

We sat on the couch, and for a while, everything felt normal. She talked about her job, about the project she was working on, her voice smooth and animated as she gestured absentmindedly. I nodded, chimed in when I was supposed to, but it was hard to focus. My mind kept looping back to that moment.

That night.

The words I'd said. The words she hadn't.

I wasn't going to bring it up. I'd promised myself I wouldn't. But the longer we sat there, the more that knot in my chest tightened, winding itself into something unbearable.

And then, before I could stop myself—

"Emma, about the other night..."

The words hung in the air between us, fragile and uncertain.

She looked at me, her expression soft, but there was a wariness there, a carefulness in the way she held my gaze. "What about it?"

I swallowed, wishing I could take it back, but it was too late now.

"I just…" My throat felt tight. "I know I said I love you. And I don't want to make you feel uncomfortable or anything, but…" I exhaled slowly. "You didn't say it back."

For a split second, something passed through her eyes. Guilt? Hesitation? I couldn't tell. Whatever it was, it vanished too quickly to be sure.

"Alex," she said softly, reaching for my hand. Her fingers were warm against mine, her grip gentle. "I care about you. I really do. But I've been through a lot—you know that. I don't want to rush things or say something before I'm ready."

I nodded, forcing a smile even as my chest ached. "Yeah, I get that. I just… I wanted to make sure you're okay. That we're okay."

She smiled, and for a moment, I let myself believe it. But there was something in it—something distant, something hollow.

"I'm okay," she said. "I promise."

I wanted to believe her. I really did. But as I looked at her, at the way she was so effortlessly slipping past this moment, that hollow feeling inside me only deepened.

I couldn't shake the feeling that I was losing her.

How? Why? I can't let this happen.

Emma

I knew the moment he walked through the door that something was off.

He smiled—sweet, earnest, the way he always did—but it didn't reach his eyes. He was trying to play it cool, trying to act like nothing was wrong. But Alex was never good at pretending. Not with me. That was one of the things I liked about him. He was easy to read. Easy to manage. Almost endearing—almost.

But I knew what was coming.

And I wasn't looking forward to it.

The night we spent together had been good. More than good. It had gone exactly how I wanted it to —kept him hooked, fed him just enough to make sure he'd stay close. He was predictable that way. The way he looked at me, the way he wanted more but was too careful to push too hard. I could feel it building, the way a storm gathers in the distance before it finally breaks.

And then, he'd said it.

I love you.

I'd felt it coming, creeping closer with every touch, every lingering glance. I hadn't stopped it, hadn't tried to steer things in a different direction. Why would I? It was inevitable. But what I hadn't expected was how much it bothered him when I didn't say it back.

I think he thought I didn't notice. That I hadn't seen that flicker of hurt in his eyes when all I did was smile, when I didn't give him what he was hoping for.

But I saw it.

I saw it, and I let it happen.

Because what was I supposed to do? Lie? Tell him what he wanted to hear? No. That would've been worse. That would have made things messy. And I don't do messy.

The truth was, I didn't love him. Not yet. Maybe not ever. Love wasn't something I gave away easily. Not after Bradley. Not after everything I'd been through. I'd been careful, deliberate in the way I handled Alex. He was useful, and I wasn't ready to lose him. But love? No. That wasn't part of the plan.

Still, I could feel his eyes on me, searching,

waiting for something. He wanted reassurance, wanted to hear those words from me. And I wasn't ready to give them to him.

We talked for a while, mostly about work—how Westbridge Marketing was keeping me on my toes, how I was trying to settle into the new role —but I could feel the tension building. He wasn't really listening. Not to any of it.

His mind was somewhere else.

And I knew exactly where.

It was only a matter of time before he cracked.

"Emma, about the other night…"

His voice was soft, hesitant. I could hear the nerves creeping in, and for a brief moment, I wanted to roll my eyes. But I didn't. Instead, I turned to him, my expression carefully measured—sweet, concerned, perfectly calibrated.

"What about it?" I asked, even though I already knew.

He hesitated. I saw the way his throat worked, like he was debating whether or not to go through with it. For a second, I thought he might back down. But then, he took a breath and said it.

"I just… I know I said I love you. And… you didn't say it back."

There it was.

The insecurity. The vulnerability. The desperate need for validation.

I could almost *feel* him bracing for my response, waiting for me to tell him what he wanted to hear, hoping that maybe I'd say it now, just to ease his mind.

But I wasn't going to.

Instead, I reached for his hand, letting my fingers curl around his—warm, reassuring.

"Alex," I said softly, keeping my voice low, gentle. "I care about you. I really do. But I've been through a lot—you know that. I don't want to rush things or say something before I'm ready."

I watched him carefully, reading his every micro-expression. His face softened, but there it was again—that flicker of disappointment, barely hidden beneath the surface. He nodded, forcing a smile, and I squeezed his hand just a little. Just enough to make him *feel* like everything was okay.

"Yeah, I get that," he said, voice barely above a whisper. "I just... I wanted to make sure you're okay. That we're okay."

I smiled back, soft and reassuring, the way I knew he needed me to.

He smiled back, but I could tell it wasn't the same. There was hesitation behind it—quiet, careful. A little smile that didn't quite reach his eyes. He was still worried. Still unsure.

And I liked that.

There's something reassuring about a man who isn't completely comfortable. It means he's still trying. Still looking for ways to prove himself.

That's where I needed Alex to be.

He didn't scare me like Bradley did. Not even close. Alex was soft in all the right ways—sweet, dependable, the kind of man who tries too hard not to mess things up. The kind who will wait as long as it takes, just for a chance.

But that was exactly why I couldn't say it back. Not now.

He needed to stay in that space—hooked but uncertain. Close, but never quite sure if he had me. That neediness? It gave me space to breathe. Space to steer things where I needed them to go.

He didn't say it again. But the way he looked at me—it was all there. He wanted me to love him back. To reassure him that this was real, that we were real. But life doesn't work like that. Not mine, anyway.

I wasn't built for fairy tales. I had other

priorities. Other truths hanging over me.

So, I smiled. Held his hand a little longer than I needed to. Let the silence sit between us like something gentle. Something safe. He didn't push. He never would.

He'd wait for me.

And I'd make sure he always had to.

The rest of the evening played out like a strange kind of normal.

We curled up on the sofa, half-watching something on TV we'd both forget by morning. We talked in quiet tones—about work, about silly memories, about nothing really. And even with the laughter and soft glances, there was a tension beneath it all. A kind of invisible line we didn't cross.

When it got late, he stood slowly, like he was waiting for me to say *stay*. But I didn't.

I walked him to the door, still barefoot, wrapping my arms around myself as if I were cold.

"Thanks for tonight," he said, almost whispering it.

I nodded. "Yeah, it's been nice."

He leaned in and kissed me—soft and uncertain.

Searching for something in my lips that I wasn't quite ready to give.

Then he pulled back and smiled that half-smile again.

"I'll text you when I get in."

I nodded once more. "Okay."

And just like that, he was gone.

The door clicked shut behind him, and I stood there for a moment in the quiet, staring at the empty space where he'd been.

Alex

The next day, I really tried—but I couldn't stop thinking about it.

The way she'd said she cared about me… but didn't say she loved me. I told myself it was fine. That I was being overdramatic. That she'd opened up more than she ever had before.

But the silence where *I love you* should have been —it echoed. It clung to me.

I tried to push it out of my head, but it kept creeping back in, gnawing at the edges of every quiet moment. She cared. She really did. But why couldn't she just *say it*?

I reminded myself that she had her reasons. Her past. Her pain. I couldn't expect her to throw her whole heart at me overnight. I needed to be patient. She was worth waiting for.

Still... something about the way she held me before I left. That long, quiet pause at the door. Her eyes had looked soft. But unreadable. Like she was both inviting me in and holding me at arm's length all at once.

Work helped, briefly. Gave me something to focus on. But every time my phone buzzed, I'd jump—hoping it was her. When it wasn't, the knot would twist tighter in my stomach. When it was... it would all melt away, just for a second. Like she had some kind of switch inside me, and all she had to do was flick it.

I kept telling myself I was doing everything right. I didn't push her. I gave her space. I never made her explain herself. I played the long game, because she was worth it.

But part of me was still wondering—was she pulling away? Or was I just being paranoid?

That's when I realised... I had to do more.

Something real. Something bold. I had to show her that she could trust me completely. That I wasn't going anywhere.

She needed to know I was hers. And she was mine.

It wasn't long before the opportunity came up.

Emma

He really was a good person. Loyal, soft in the right places, even noble in that annoying, self-sacrificing kind of way.

But I needed him more desperate. A little less sure of us. A little more *willing*.

That's when the idea started to take shape. It started like a whisper—one of those fleeting little thoughts you usually ignore. But I didn't. I let it linger. I *fed* it.

He'd already lied for me. Helped me twist the truth. Fabricated a whole story just to get me through the door at work.

But what else would he do... if I asked?

That's how I'd find out.

Since I messaged Bradley, he'd been texting again. Dropping his usual slime into my inbox—old habits, never dying. I hadn't replied. I didn't need to. He just needed to know I'd thought about him for half a second. That was always enough to pull him back in.

Now, I could use that. I could *twist* that.

That weekend, I went out for coffee with Alex—some quiet café neither of us had been to before. Just a lazy Saturday morning thing. I sipped my latte and leaned into him, just enough for warmth, just enough for comfort.

And then I let it drop.

"I've been hearing from Bradley again," I said softly, like I almost didn't want to admit it. "He's been texting me."

Alex's arm stiffened where it rested around my waist. His whole body tensed, like he was bracing for impact.

"I didn't want to worry you," I added, glancing down at my cup, "but I'm not really sure what to do about it."

There it was—the way his jaw clenched. That subtle shift in his breathing.

He was protective. Always had been. And I *loved* that about him.

"What?" His voice dropped—low, tight, dangerous. "Why is he still bothering you? Why didn't you tell me?"

I exhaled slowly, already preparing the look—the one I knew would melt the edge from his anger just enough to keep him on a leash. Vulnerable, wide-eyed, a perfect blend of strength and softness. "I didn't want to stress you out," I murmured, brushing my fingers through my hair like I was trying to stay calm. "You've been so good to me. I didn't want to drag you into my mess. I thought I could handle it."

He didn't speak. Not right away. But the silence between us wasn't empty—it was heavy, charged with a storm I'd summoned with a single confession. I could feel it building in him. His body was still, but his energy wasn't.

"You don't have to handle it alone, Emma," he finally said, his voice low and urgent, like the words were being carved out of him. "You shouldn't have to. I'm here for you. Always."

I turned to him slowly, tracing a line along his jaw with a touch that was deliberate, slow, intimate. "I know," I whispered. "I just... I don't want to make things worse."

He caught my hand in his like he was anchoring me—or maybe himself—and held it tight enough to hurt. "He's not going to get away with this. I'll take care of it."

That was what I wanted. Not just the words, but the conviction behind them. I had him.

I didn't ask how he planned to 'take care of it.' I didn't need to. I knew the seed had been planted, and I wasn't about to interrupt it while it grew. Instead, I leaned into him, letting my body sink against his chest, breathing in his scent, letting him wrap himself around me like armour.

We didn't talk about it again that day.

But I knew part of his mind had already left the room. Hopefully, it was somewhere dark— plotting, planning.

Alex

The rage didn't just simmer—it roared.

It sat just behind my ribs like a furnace, heat rising with every breath I took. Bradley. Still bothering her. Still making her feel afraid, unsafe. I pictured his face, smug and untouchable, like he thought no one could stop him.

He was wrong.

Emma needed someone who wouldn't just say the right things but *do* them. Someone who would protect her, even if that meant crossing lines no one else dared approach.

That someone was me.

That night, after we'd stopped talking and she'd fallen asleep oblivious, like she had no idea the fire she'd just stoked, I lay awake staring at my ceiling. My eyes traced the outline of cracks in the plaster like they were forming a map—a path leading directly to him.

I'd already intervened once. Quietly. Strategically. She didn't know about that time, and she didn't need to. I set him up; I helped her land that job when things were falling apart.

But this... this needed more. This required something bigger. Something final.

I started thinking in layers—how I'd find him, where he went, who he still spoke to. I ran through options like a checklist, slowly building out the perfect strategy. I didn't know what I was truly capable of until I began imagining it clearly —step by step.

As the days passed, the blueprint in my mind sharpened. I needed leverage. Or better yet... a way to make him disappear.

And if I could do that for her—if I could remove him completely—maybe she'd finally see how much I loved her. Maybe then, she'd say it back.

Maybe then, she'd be mine.

Emma

I t was working.

I saw it in the way his eyes followed me with that haunted intensity, like I was something holy he was meant to protect. I watched it simmer in the clenched set of his jaw whenever I mentioned Bradley's name. The cracks in his calm were showing, widening, fracturing.

He was already wrapped around my finger, but now... now he was coiling tighter. Completely mine.

Over the next few days, I let the tension build like a slow-burning wick. I gave him just enough —small pieces of carefully curated fear. A few late-night texts. A screenshot of a missed call. A voicemail I "accidentally" played loud enough for him to hear across the room.

And when I left one of Bradley's more aggressive messages open on my phone—just long enough for Alex to "find it" while we were out—I saw the explosion before it even came. His expression twisted into something unrecognisable, primal. His hands curled into fists. His voice dropped to something dangerous and unfiltered.

Perfect.

He was spiralling, and I was holding the thread.

Part of me was impressed. The depth of his passion, the absolute fixation—it was intense. His fury, his need to protect me, to *own* the situation—it was thrilling. I could feel the power of it humming through him like electricity, and I let it flow through me too.

But this was only the beginning.

If I wanted Alex to be truly useful—*irrevocably* useful—he needed to go further. I needed him to cross a line so sharp there'd be no coming back. Something he couldn't undo. Something that would *bind* him to me, completely.

And I knew exactly how to get him there.

Alex

The rage didn't just simmer inside me—it surged, breathed. A living, venomous thing that wrapped itself around every thought I had, whispering violence in the quiet corners of my mind. It was constant now, throbbing beneath my skin, sitting in the pit of my chest like a second heartbeat. Bradley. The name alone triggered something feral in me. No matter how many times I forced myself to smile through the day, to wrap an arm around Emma and pretend the world was fine—the nights betrayed me.

That's when it returned. In the silence. In the

shadows.

I'd already gone further for her than she'd ever know. But this? This wasn't about damage control. This was a final act. A declaration. A warning carved into flesh and fear. I needed him gone—not scared, not shaken—*gone.*

I wasn't going to play games this time.

There was no hesitation when the plan began to take shape. I hunted for him like a ghost in the background, eyes locked on his movements. Found the shitty little bar he still clung to, like it gave him some sort of identity. Tracked him back to his flat. I'd already ruined that job, those friends, and now I'd dismantle what little he had left.

This had to be precise. Invisible. Emma couldn't be touched by any of it—not the fallout, not the questions. But when it was done... when the dust settled... she'd know.

She'd finally see that everything I did was for her, because of her. Every act. Every sin.

And maybe then she'd look at me with something more than softness. Maybe she'd see the depth of it all. The weight of my devotion.

Maybe she'd finally say the words I'd been dying to hear.

The next few days passed in a blur of shadows and headlights. Every spare second, I was out there—tailing him, studying him, waiting. Always waiting. I barely slept. Couldn't. Not with my mind racing in the dark beside her.

I'd lie there, arms around Emma, her breath slow and steady against my chest, and I'd stare into the ceiling, mapping it out. Wanting to whisper it all to her. To tell her how close I was to fixing this. To tell her that soon, he wouldn't be a problem. That soon, we could be *free.*

But she wouldn't understand. Not yet.

Once it was done, though—once I'd ended it— everything would change.

It had to.

Emma

I t was almost too perfect.

Alex had become a storm I could summon with nothing more than a whisper. I didn't even have to do much anymore—just leave a breadcrumb here, a suggestion there—and he'd spiral, desperate to prove something that didn't even need proving.

He didn't know he was already mine.

Watching him unravel was intoxicating. The way he burned for me, the way he swallowed down his rage during the day, only for it to bleed out behind his eyes at night—it was beautiful. Dangerous. Addictive.

He thought he was hiding it, that I couldn't see the fire building. But I'd lit the match.

The Bradley messages were my masterpiece. Crafted just right—enough tension, enough doubt. I'd send one just before he came over, then delete it before he could see the full thread. Leave the notification hanging there like a secret caught mid-breath. I'd catch the way he'd spot it, the way his whole body would tighten, jaw clenched so hard I thought his teeth might crack.

He never said a word. But I knew. I could feel the violence blooming beneath his skin.

And that's exactly what I wanted.

I didn't need him rational. I needed him reckless. Consumed.

Every crumb I dropped fed the thing growing inside him. The hero complex, the need to protect me—it was evolving. Turning dark.

Twisting.

I made casual comments—maybe I thought I saw Bradley near my work, maybe he messaged something weird. Alex would freeze every time, that little muscle in his neck twitching like a live wire. He was coming undone, and he didn't even realise I was holding the thread.

He thought he was the one keeping me safe.

But it was me. It was always me.

I had to be careful not to overplay it. Maintain the soft concern, the innocence. "You don't have to do anything, Alex." That's all it took. Because when I said *don't*—he heard *do*.

It was thrilling, watching the transformation. The sweet man I met was still in there somewhere, but he was buried beneath something heavier now. Something raw.

And I needed that version of him.

The one who didn't hesitate.

The one who'd break the world for me.

The one who'd never come back from what he was about to do.

Alex

The rain had thickened, the kind of downpour that blurred the world and muffled its sound. Heavy drops thudded against the concrete as I stood cloaked in shadow, watching him—Bradley—stagger out of the bar like a man who had no idea what kind of night he was walking into.

He was drunk. More than usual.

I could see it in the way he fumbled with his lighter, flicking the flame just shy of his cigarette over and over, cursing under his breath. His head lolled, his movements clumsy, his senses dulled.

Perfect.

The car park was deserted, apart from the soft orange glow of the streetlamps reflecting off slick asphalt. It was late. No witnesses. Just me. Him. And the rain.

He didn't notice me, of course. Bradley never

noticed anything that didn't serve him. That was his weakness—too arrogant to see danger coming until it was already on top of him.

Tonight, I was that danger.

I moved silently between the rows of cars, my footsteps masked by the storm, the hood of my jacket pulled tight over my head. My pulse pounded in my ears, each beat louder than the last. Every instinct in me screamed to stop, to turn around—but I couldn't.

Gone was the meek and mild Alex. Emma needed me. And I would do whatever it took.

He finally got the cigarette lit, took a long drag, then exhaled into the rain, the smoke curling like a ghost between us. For a moment—just a second —I hesitated. But then I saw her face. I heard her voice. The tremble when she told me how unsafe he made her feel. How he kept turning up. Kept messaging. Kept crossing lines.

That pushed me over the edge.

I closed the last few feet like a shadow. He must have sensed something because he turned, sluggish and slow, just as I grabbed him by the back of his jacket and spun him around. His eyes widened. Then narrowed with recognition.

"What the fuck do you think you're doing?" he slurred, the alcohol thick in his voice as he tried to shove me off.

Too late.

My rage surged, and I slammed him into the side of a parked car. The impact echoed through the lot, his cigarette flying from his fingers and sizzling into a puddle. The glowing tip died with a hiss.

"Stay the fuck away from Emma," I growled, my voice low, coiled tight with fury. "This is your only warning."

His head lolled back, and he laughed—dry and sharp. That same twisted grin I'd seen a hundred times in photos and videos.

"Emma?" he scoffed. "All this for her?" His voice dropped, venomous. "You really think she's yours? She'll use you and toss you aside like the rest of us. She's good at that."

The words hit harder than I expected. A quiet crack down the centre of my thoughts. But I didn't flinch. I couldn't. He didn't get to speak about her like that.

He shoved me weakly, trying to regain balance, but I was already back on him. I drove him harder against the car this time, the sound of the impact swallowed by thunder overhead.

My fists clenched.

"Don't talk about her," I spat, my vision tunnelling. "You don't know *anything* about her."

He laughed again—that same awful, guttural sound that made my skin crawl.
"Oh, I know more than you think, mate. You think you're special?"

The rage rose like a tide, sudden and blinding.
Before I even registered the motion, my fist shot forward and slammed into his face with a brutal crunch.

Bradley reeled, his head whipping sideways. For a heartbeat, everything went still. The rain drummed harder around us, drowning out the ragged sound of my breathing. The moon vanished behind thick, brooding clouds—like even it refused to witness what came next.

Then he straightened.

He dragged a sleeve across his nose, smearing the blood, and spat on the ground.
"That all you got?" he slurred, eyes burning with a cocktail of booze and fury.

I didn't think—I just reacted.
The second punch landed clean, a savage crack against his jaw. His body twisted with the force of it, and his feet slipped on the slick pavement. He staggered, arms flailing for balance.

But the alcohol had already robbed him of that luxury.

He went down hard.

It all moved in slow motion—the way his skull collided with the concrete edge of the curb.
The dull thud.
The snap.
And then silence.

He collapsed like a puppet with cut strings.

Blood bloomed beneath his head in an instant, vivid and obscene against the rain-darkened concrete.
A glistening pool, catching the glow of the lonely streetlamp like a ruby dropped in a gutter.

My stomach turned. My breath caught in my throat.

I couldn't move.
Couldn't think.
I just stared at him—at the blood spreading, thick and steady, seeping into the cracks of the pavement.

He wasn't moving.

He wasn't...

Shit.

I staggered back, heart crashing against my ribs

like it wanted out. My hands were shaking. I hadn't meant to hit him like that.
I didn't mean for this.

I dropped to my knees beside him, hovering, frozen. Should I check him? Should I... touch him?

No. No, I can't.

His skin was already pale, the rain washing over his face, mixing with blood that wouldn't stop coming—from the gash at the side of his head where bone met curb.

"Bradley?" I whispered, my voice a dry rasp. "Bradley, wake up. Come on... wake up."

Nothing.

His chest didn't rise.
His half-lidded eyes stared skyward, blank and unblinking.

No.

This wasn't how it was supposed to go.
I just wanted to scare him—to rattle him. A warning. Something to make him back off.

Not this. Not—

Shit. Shit. Shit.

I pushed to my feet, the whole world tilted. My thoughts were a chaotic blur.

I had to go. Now.

I forced myself backward, away from him. From the blood. From those vacant eyes.

And then I turned—and I ran.

The rain lashed at me, slicing through my soaked clothes as I sprinted across the car park, lungs burning, chest heaving.
I didn't look back. Couldn't, not until I made it home.

All I knew was the thundering in my ears, the pounding of my heart, and the terrible, deafening truth echoing in my skull.

Bradley was dead.

I'd killed him.

And I had no idea what the hell I was supposed to do next.

Emma

I scrolled through my phone mindlessly, sipping on my coffee. The morning was quiet, the usual rain tapping softly against the window. Just another ordinary day—or so I thought.

A notification popped up on my Facebook feed, the kind of thing I usually ignored, but this one had a headline that caught my eye: "Man Found Dead in Car Park Outside Local Bar—Suspected MURDER."

I paused, my thumb hovering over the screen. The article mentioned a bar, one I recognised. Bradley's bar. I frowned but quickly pushed the thought aside. No. It couldn't be him. It was just some random drunk who'd gotten into a fight or had an accident. Bradley was always getting into scraps, but he'd never get himself killed.

Still, the nagging feeling lingered as I clicked on the article, skimming through the details. The body had been found late last night, soaked in blood, in the rain... and there was no suspect in custody. No name mentioned yet, just a vague description of the victim and a comment about police urging witnesses to come forward.

I felt a knot tighten in my stomach, my mind racing. The timing, the location—it all fit. But no. There was no way Alex would have done that. He wasn't capable of that level of violence. He wasn't a killer.

I set the phone down, trying to shake off the creeping unease. I glanced over at the clock, realising it was already late. Alex would probably be up by now. Should I ask him? Maybe he'd seen something on the news, maybe he could reassure me it wasn't him.

The news article stayed open on my screen as I got ready for the day, the words blurring together as I moved about the flat. No matter what I did—whether brushing my hair or straightening my clothes—I couldn't shake that sinking feeling in my gut. My phone buzzed on the counter, and I glanced at it, half-hoping it was Alex. Or even Bradley

But it wasn't.

Instead, a second article appeared in my feed, this one more direct: "Body Identified as Local Resident Bradley Thomas, Police Investigating."

The room seemed to close in on me, the edges of my vision tightening as I stared at the screen. Bradley. Dead. I swallowed hard, trying to make sense of it all, but it was too late. The truth was already there, staring me in the face, unavoidable.

Alex *must* have done it.

There was no question now, no doubt. I could feel it deep in my bones. The same possessiveness, the same protective obsession that had made me feel secure—had made me feel powerful—was now the very thing that had made him a murderer.

I sat down on the edge of the sofa, phone still clutched in my hand, a cold sweat forming at the base of my neck. Bradley was dead, and Alex had killed him.

The knock on my door broke the silence, startling me out of my thoughts. I quickly composed myself, standing up and heading towards it, I found myself staring into the familiar eyes of my friend, Jess, her face pale and drawn. She held up her phone, her eyes wide. "Emma, have you seen this? It's all over Facebook... Bradley's dead. They found him outside that bar. You know the one."

I blinked, letting the shock register on my face as naturally as I could, even though my insides were twisting. I had to play this right.

"What?" I whispered, my voice cracking just enough to sound believable. "No... Are you sure it's him?"

Jess nodded, her fingers trembling as she scrolled through the article, showing me the same post I'd already just seen. I let my hand fly to my mouth, covering the gasp that escaped. "Oh my God... I... I can't believe this."

She stepped inside, eyes wide with worry, her hand resting on my arm. "I knew he was a dick, but dead? Who would've done that to him?"

I shook my head, my heart pounding in my chest. "I don't know," I murmured, my voice sounding small, hollow. "I can't believe it. I haven't talked to him in a while now."

I felt the familiar weight of guilt settle in, but I pushed it down. Now wasn't the time to feel sorry for Bradley. He'd gotten what was coming to him. What he deserved. The only thing that mattered now was that no one ever linked this back to Alex.

"I need a minute," I muttered, stepping away from Jess and retreating into the kitchen. I could feel the adrenaline kicking in, my brain already calculating the next steps, already plotting how I'd play this.

I grabbed my phone and typed out a text to Alex, keeping it light. Casual. Innocent.

"Hey, have you seen the news? Something crazy happened last night at that bar... xx"

I hit send, then placed the phone face-down on the counter. My fingers were still trembling, but I forced a steady breath. Stay calm. Stay separate. Let the shock feel mutual. Manufactured disbelief was safer than silence.

The screen buzzed.

"No, what happened? Are you okay?"

I didn't hesitate—too much time would look suspicious.

"It's Bradley. He's... dead. They think it was an assault or something. I don't know... It's all over Facebook. I'm okay, just shocked xxx"

Short. Vague. Just enough emotion to feel real, but not enough to raise suspicion. Let *him* connect the dots. Let him sweat. I needed him unsure, dependent, vulnerable. I needed him to trust me now more than ever.

Another buzz.

"Oh my God. I didn't know. That's crazy."

I read it twice. The words were simple, but I could feel the weight behind them. That little flicker of panic, the way his sentences got shorter, tighter. He was scared.

Good.

I let out a long breath, letting the tension drain from my face. Not relief—just calculated calm. Alex was playing it safe, pretending like nothing happened. That was fine. I could play that game too. But I needed him to confess eventually, to crumble under the guilt. Only then could I help him. Only then would I know how much control I really had.

I turned toward the living room, where Jess was curled up on the sofa, phone in hand. Her brow was furrowed, her eyes wide and glossy. She didn't look away from the screen as I sat beside her.

Without a word, I reached out and rested my hand gently on her knee. My expression softened, carefully curated. Enough sadness to be believable. Enough detachment to feel safe.

"I can't believe it," I said, voice low. "He could be a nightmare, but... dead? It's just horrible."

"Do they know who did it?" I asked, like I didn't already know exactly who did it.

She shook her head, "Not yet. I guess... I guess the police are still figuring it out."

Jess leaned into me slightly, and I let her. Played the role of the supportive friend. The shocked bystander. The shocked ex-girlfriend.

But my mind wasn't on Jess. It was on Alex.

If he slipped, even once—if he confessed to anyone but me—I wouldn't be able to protect him. He had to come to me. He had to *need* me. That was the only way this worked.

I reached for my cup of tea, sipping it slowly, my eyes fixed on the muted TV screen showing a photo of Bradley under the headline:

LOCAL MAN KILLED IN LATE-NIGHT ATTACK – POLICE SEEK WITNESSES

They'd start digging soon. CCTV, witnesses, timelines. But I wasn't worried.

Alex would crack before the cops got close. He always did.

And when he did?

I'd be waiting.

Alex

The rain hadn't stopped for even a minute, and the storm inside me wasn't dying down anytime soon either. Every second since that moment felt like a hammer pounding against my skull, relentless and unyielding. I couldn't sleep. I couldn't eat. My thoughts spun like throwing knives, slicing through every attempt at normality. Bradley was dead.

And I was the one who'd killed him.

His name was everywhere now—headlines, social media, whispered conversations at the corner shop. Every time I saw it; the reality sank deeper into my bones. This wasn't just some bad dream. There was no reset button. No do-over.

At first, I tried to pretend. To act like life could still go on. I told myself it was for Emma—that I'd done it to protect her. That lie almost worked. Almost. But guilt has claws. It doesn't scratch politely; it burrows, digs deep, and poisons everything it touches. Every time my phone went off, I'd flinch like I'd been shot.

And it wasn't just paranoia anymore.

I sat on my laptop scrolling articles and social media's, all talking about it. CCTV footage had surfaced and been circulated online. A super fuzzy grainy clip of me walking into the car park. The rain had blurred most of the image, but not enough for me to hide behind it. I could see the shape of *my* body, the intent in *my* stride. The camera luckily didn't catch anything that happened after, at least not that had been released, but that almost made it worse. It left just enough space for suspicion to bloom.

It felt like a noose tightening around my neck, one inch at a time.

I couldn't carry this alone. I needed Emma. I needed her more than I ever had. I had to go to her.

Her house was warm when she opened the door, the contrast jarring against the cold feeling in my soul. She looked at me—really looked—and I could see the concern in her eyes. She knew. Not the specifics, maybe, but enough that in one look, I knew. She knew.

"Alex," she said softly, stepping aside. "What's going on?"

I couldn't speak. I stood there, soaked through, fists clenched so tightly they ached. My hands wouldn't stop shaking. I felt like I was holding a thousand volts of electricity, and one wrong word would make me explode.

She gently closed the door behind me, her hand finding my arm, steadying me, guiding me to the sofa. "Talk to me," she whispered. "What happened?"

I sat down hard, elbows on my knees, my head in my hands. The air felt heavy, like it was pressing down on me. My throat was tight, my heart hammering.

"I killed him," I finally managed, my voice barely above a whisper. "I didn't mean to. I swear, Emma, I didn't mean to. It just—happened."

I waited for the recoil. The fear. The disgust. But none of it came.

She knelt in front of me instead, her hands gently finding mine, her eyes searching my face.

"Tell me everything," she said, calm and measured, as if I'd just told her I'd had a bad day—not that I'd taken someone's life.

So, I told her. All of it. The setup with the coke.

The confrontation. The moment Bradley's smug face pushed me too far. The way his head cracked against the curb like a dropped watermelon. The way I froze. Panicked. Ran.

I poured it all out. Every detail. Every thought. It came like a flood. And when it was over, when I had nothing left to give, I just sat there, hollowed out and shaking.

She didn't cry. She didn't flinch. Instead, she squeezed my hands and leaned closer.

"You did it for me," she whispered. "To protect me."

I nodded slowly, the weight of it all still sitting on my chest. "He wouldn't leave you alone. I couldn't let him keep hurting you."

She leaned in, her lips grazing my ear, her voice barely a breath. "Thank you, Alex. You have no idea what that means to me."

Something about the way she said it made my skin crawl—but I pushed the feeling down. I wanted to feel peace, closure, gratitude. But instead, I felt… off. Like I'd just handed over a piece of myself and she'd pocketed it with a smile.

And then she kissed me.

Soft. Intentional. Grateful.

Before I knew what was happening, she was guiding me towards the bedroom. I didn't resist. I let myself be led, my brain still foggy, my body acting on instinct. Her hands moved to my jeans, unbuttoning them with quiet urgency.

"I need you," she whispered. "Let me show you how much you mean to me."

A part of me wanted to stop. Just for a second. To process. To breathe.

But then her mouth found mine again, and that whisper in the back of my mind—the one that said this was all wrong—went silent.

The guilt disappeared for a moment, buried under the weight of her touch, her breath, the way she pulled me close like I was her salvation. The world melted away. There was no investigation, no dead body, no headlines. Just her. Just now.

And for that brief sliver of time, I let myself believe that maybe I *was* the hero. Her hero.

When it was over, we lay tangled in each other, sweat cooling on our skin. My mind buzzed with a thousand unanswered questions, but my body was calm, spent. She curled into my side like nothing had happened. Like we were just a normal couple, ending a long day with sex and whispered words.

"I'm a murderer," I said, my voice low, broken. "Emma... I don't know how to live with that."

She lifted her head, her eyes meeting mine with eerie stillness. "No, you're not. You're *my* hero. You did what needed to be done. Bradley can't hurt me anymore. You saved me and I will forever be grateful to you Alex."

She called me her *hero*. That felt like her words were like honey over broken glass. Sweet. Comforting. But sharp underneath.

I wanted to believe her. I *needed* to.

Still, part of me wondered why she was so calm. Why she was so quick to forgive. Wasn't this meant to change something between us?

Shouldn't it have?

But she kissed my chest, her fingers drawing circles over my skin, and said, "I knew I could count on you, Alex. I do *love* you."

And just like that, I didn't care anymore.

She loved me.

She was grateful.

She was mine.

And I'd do it all again if she asked me to.

Emma

As I lay beside him, watching him sleep, a slow, satisfying warmth unfurled in my chest. He was mine now — truly, completely mine.

I'd always wondered if he had it in him, if he'd ever go *that* far. And now I knew. He'd done it — he'd actually killed for me. Crossed that invisible line.

And the best part? He believed it was his choice. His decision. His act of protection and devotion.

He didn't realise he'd passed the ultimate test — but that was fine. He didn't need to know.

I shifted slightly, brushing a strand of hair from his damp forehead as his eyes fluttered open. Still fogged with sleep, still vulnerable. "Morning," he mumbled, his voice hoarse. "What time is it?"

There was hesitation beneath his words — that flicker of guilt still clinging to him like smoke. I'd seen it before, after he told me. It would linger for a while. But I knew how to soothe it. I knew exactly what to say, how to look at him, how to touch him to make it disappear.

"How're you feeling?" I asked softly, letting my fingers trace slow spirals down his arm.

He turned his head, staring at the ceiling for a moment before answering. "I... I don't know. Still trying to make sense of everything."

I reached for his hand, lacing my fingers through his, squeezing it gently. "That's normal, Alex. What you did... it wasn't easy. But it was the right thing."

His lips pressed into a thin line. That same guilt, creeping back. "But I killed him, Emma. I *killed* someone."

I tilted his face towards mine, letting my thumb trail lightly along the curve of his jaw, anchoring his gaze to mine. "You *protected* me," I said, my voice firm but tender. "Bradley wasn't going to stop. You know that. He was a threat. And now... he's gone. You did what needed to be done. For me, for us. And I love you for it."

His eyes searched mine, desperate for reassurance, for permission to stop drowning in it.

I leaned in, pressing a kiss to his forehead, then to his lips. "Thank you," I whispered, letting every syllable drip with sincerity. "You've given me a safety I've never known before."

He exhaled shakily, the tension in his shoulders beginning to unwind beneath my touch. He wanted to believe it — that this was love, that everything he'd done had been worth it.

That's exactly what I needed him to believe.

"You did it for me," I murmured, drawing closer, letting my breath dance against his ear. "And I know it's hard right now, but I'm here. We'll carry this secret together."

My voice softened to a whisper, like a promise wrapped in silk.

Alex

After I left, her words echoed through my head all morning, soaking into every corner of my thoughts.
"You did it for me, and I love you for it."

She said it like it was simple — like it was *true*.

And in those quiet moments, with her arms wrapped around me and her voice soft against my skin, I *almost* believed it.

The rest of the day passed in a daze. Everything felt off — distant, disconnected, like I was moving underwater. Work was a joke. I couldn't focus. Every sound seemed too loud, every passing glance from a coworker prickled under my skin like needles.

It was like they *knew*.

Like they could see it — branded across my face. *Murderer.*

But Emma's voice grounded me. Her words echoed like a tether in the storm. *She needed me.* I had protected her. I'd stepped up. And as wrong as it all felt... there was something else creeping in.

Relief.

And worse — *pride.*

That evening, I ended up at her flat again. I didn't even realise I was heading there until I was already on her doorstep. My body just moved without me.

She opened the door before I knocked, like she'd been waiting, like she *knew* I'd come. She pulled me in with both arms, held me like I was the centre of her world.

It felt good.

Safe.

But beneath that safety, something twisted inside me — something I didn't want to look at too closely.

I pulled back slightly, eyes locking onto hers. I needed to *know*.

"Emma," I said slowly, "do you really think it was worth it? What I did?"

She didn't hesitate. Her hands came up to my face, fingers brushing softly along my jaw. Her eyes didn't flinch.

"Alex," she said, steady as ever, "you gave me my life back. My freedom. My safety. I could never thank you enough for that."

Her words sank into me like warm water, easing

something tight and painful in my chest.

She was safe because of me.
She was free because of me.

That had always been the goal, hadn't it? From the beginning, I just wanted her to be okay. To feel protected. To be mine. And now, she *was.*

She leaned in, her breath brushing against my cheek.

"There's no one else I could ever trust like this," she whispered. "No one who would ever go so far for me."

Something shifted.

The knot inside me loosened.

Right and wrong didn't matter anymore. The line I'd crossed — it was too far behind me now.

All that mattered was her.

I was hers.
She was mine.

And as I drifted into sleep beside her, I knew with total certainty:
I'd do *anything* she asked. Anything.

-

I woke early the next morning, my mind already buzzing before my feet hit the floor. I slipped out of bed and left without waking her, needing space, air — *something*.

But nothing helped.

My head felt thick, like it was packed with noise and static. Every time my phone buzzed, my stomach twisted. Every glance from a coworker felt weighted, suspicious.

They know.

I kept telling myself it was just in my head. That no one could know. The police didn't have enough — they couldn't.

But even as I repeated it, I knew it didn't matter.

The truth wasn't just something I'd buried — it was *in* me now.

I kept hearing Bradley's voice, those final moments spinning in a constant, looping reel. The way he laughed. The way he *didn't* laugh when he hit the ground.

That *thud.*

Crystal clear.

Over and over.

Emma had been quiet today. A few texts. Casual things.
How's your day?
Don't stress. I'm here for you.

But they felt empty, like Band-Aids over bullet wounds.

I couldn't stop wondering — now that she'd had time to think, did she feel differently? Did she regret anything? Did *she* see me differently now?

I couldn't take it anymore.

After work, I didn't even text her. I just went.

I needed her.

To see her face.
To hear her voice.
To find that fragile calm only *she* could give me.

Emma

I wasn't surprised when I heard the knock.

Alex had been coming apart at the seams since that night, unravelling one quiet panic at a time. I'd expected this sooner or later — the weight of what he'd done wouldn't sit still. It never does.

I glanced at my phone before answering the door — a news alert still open, the headline bold: **POLICE APPEAL FOR WITNESSES IN CITY CENTRE DEATH INVESTIGATION.**

I turned the screen face-down.

When I opened the door, there he was — soaked through, rain dripping from his hair, his face pale and drawn like something hollowed out. His eyes carried that distant, haunted look again. The same one I'd seen when he first told me.

Poor broken Alex.

He looked like a man haunted by ghosts — ghosts I'd conjured and wrapped around him like chains.

"Hey," I said softly, stepping aside. "Come in. You're soaked."

He walked past me without a word, head down, shoulders hunched like he was bracing for some invisible blow. I closed the door quietly and followed him into the living room.

He dropped onto the sofa, his hands clutching his face like he was trying to hold it together.

"I can't do this," he muttered. His voice cracked under the weight of it.

"Do what?" I asked gently, perching beside him, close enough to touch but not smother.

"This... lying, hiding." His voice shook. "I can't stop thinking about it. What if someone saw me? What if I get arrested, Emma? What happens to us then?"

Us.

Always thinking of us. That's what made him perfect.

I placed my hand on his knee, grounding him, easing the rising tide in his chest. "Alex, listen to me. You're okay. You've done nothing that can be traced. You're safe."

"But what if—"

"Shh." My voice firmed, still soft, but cutting through his panic like a thread of steel. "You're spiralling, baby. It's just your mind running in circles. You've been under so much pressure. You're not thinking clearly. But I am. And I *know* you're safe."

Alex

Her hand on my knee was the only thing anchoring me to the moment.

I felt like I was slipping, like I was on the edge of something dark and endless, and only she could pull me back. She always knew what to say. Her calm steadiness made the chaos inside me feel... manageable.

But even in that comfort, something unsettled me.

Why wasn't she more afraid?

Why wasn't *she* panicking?

"Emma... what if they figure it out?" I asked, my voice low. "What if someone saw me that night?"

"They won't," she said calmly, not a flicker of fear in her voice. "I've seen the news. They're grasping at straws, Alex. There's no footage clear enough to identify anything. You said that yourself."

I tried to shake the doubt from my head, but it clung like damp clothes.

She leaned in, her fingers brushing my jaw, tilting my face until I had no choice but to meet her eyes.

"You did what you had to do," she said. "You protected me. And now it's *my* turn to protect you. Do you trust me?"

I hesitated, just for a second.

But in her eyes, I saw certainty. Warmth. Control.

And I needed that more than anything.

"Yes," I whispered.

Her lips curled into a slow, gentle smile.

"Good," she breathed, then leaned in and kissed me — slow, intentional, like a seal of reassurance. Her fingers tangled in my hair, pulling me close. And just like that, the fear dulled.

She knew how to silence it.

She was everything. My sanctuary. My absolution.

When she pulled away, she rested her forehead against mine, her breath warm.

"I need you strong, Alex," she whispered. "For me. Can you do that?"

I nodded, swallowing the last of my doubt. "Yeah. I can do that."

I *had* to be strong.

It's why she loves me.

Emma

He was so easy to control when he was like this — frayed at the edges, desperate for comfort, for direction.

All it took was the right words, a soft touch, a gentle promise whispered into the silence. He needed reassurance like oxygen. And when he was in this state — fragile, anxious, emotionally stripped bare — I could guide him anywhere.

But now, with the investigation heating up, simplicity wouldn't be enough. I had to be precise. Tactical. One wrong move from Alex and everything would unravel. He wasn't stupid, but guilt was making him unpredictable — and panic always made people messy.

I leaned back into the cushions, letting him settle against me, his head heavy on my shoulder. His breathing had slowed, his muscles loosening inch by inch as I stroked his hair. He thought this was comfort — intimacy.

But it was strategy.

He needed me.

And I needed him too — just not in the way he believed.

In all honesty, Bradley had been the test. A brutal, necessary threshold. I had to know how far Alex would go; how much he'd give if I asked.

And now I knew.

He would kill for me.

And that made him invaluable. He did more than I ever expected, and I know it was technically an accident, but *he* went there, right? *He* approached Bradley, right? He knew the potential and *he* did it anyway.

Still, I couldn't let him fall apart, not when it would affect me. He had to stay sharp, calm, composed — at least on the surface. He had to believe the worst was behind us, that he was safe now.

So, I softened my voice and broke the silence, careful, gentle.

"I've been thinking."

His head lifted slightly, his voice a quiet murmur. "About what?"

"About what the police might be looking for."

I felt the way his body tensed beside me, like a spring pulled too tight. His eyes found mine, searching for something—hope, maybe.

"What do you mean?"

"Don't worry," I said quickly, my fingers slipping through his hair in slow, soothing strokes. "It's nothing serious. Just... precautions. I think we should cover our tracks a bit more. Get rid of anything that could tie you to that night. Just to be safe."

The anxiety flared again — I could feel it in the way he shifted, in the shallow hitch of his breath.

"Like what?"

I kept my tone breezy, casual, like we were talking about laundry, not evidence. "The clothes you wore. And your shoes. They might have trace evidence. Mud, fibres. It's probably nothing, but it's how people get caught in those shows, right? Little details."

He went still for a moment. I watched the thoughts churn behind his eyes.

Then, slowly, he nodded. "Yeah... yeah, that makes sense."

Yes, it does.

I leaned in and kissed his temple, letting my voice warm with just the right amount of tenderness. "I'll help you. We'll take care of it together."

He didn't notice the flicker of excitement in my voice.

Alex

Emma was calm. Too calm.

She moved and spoke with purpose. She sent me home and told me to come back with everything I wore that night, even my underwear. I didn't question her, didn't hesitate, just did what she said. When I came back, she was sat casually watching TV like it was a normal day. She took my black bag of guilt-ridden clothes and disappeared into the kitchen.

She made it all seem so easy.

As if she wasn't holding the evidence that could bury us both.

"There," she said when she came back into the living room, flashing me a smile like it was just a household chore. "One less thing to worry about baby."

I tried to smile back, but my lips barely moved. My throat was dry.

My hands wouldn't stop shaking.

I shoved them into my pockets, hoping she wouldn't notice — but of course she did. She noticed everything.

"I'll take care of this," she added, her voice breezy, effortless. "You don't need to think about it anymore."

I pathetically nodded, my tongue heavy, words stuck somewhere between fear and surrender. I didn't ask where she planned to take it. I didn't ask how or when either. A part of me didn't want to know.

Ignorance was safer.

She stepped closer, so close I could smell the soft trace of her perfume — familiar now, something warm and sweet that clung to the air like a memory. Her hand slid up to my face, her palm resting gently against my cheek. Her thumb stroked my skin once, twice.

"See?" she whispered. "It's all under control. We're safe."

And for a moment — just a moment — I believed her.

The pressure in my chest loosened. The heat behind my eyes faded. She had that effect on me, like her touch could turn down the volume on everything screaming inside my head.

But it was still there.

The guilt.

Emma must've seen the fear flicker behind my eyes, because she leaned in slowly, her breath warm against my skin, her lips brushing mine like a promise.

"You've done so much for me," she murmured, her words curling around my spine. "Let me take care of you now."

I kissed her back, needing her more than I wanted to admit — needing the stillness she gave me, the illusion that everything was fine. That I hadn't destroyed a life. That I wasn't coming undone.

She was my anchor the sea. My compass in the wilderness.

The only thing that felt real in a world that was starting to tilt sideways.

Emma

He was starting to crack.

Watching him hand over those clothes — that symbolic offering of trust, guilt, and desperation — it was exhilarating. I didn't feel bad saying this, but he was mine now. In every way that mattered.

Still, I had to keep him steady. A man unravelling wasn't useful. If he spiraled too soon, did something reckless, said something stupid... it could all come crashing down. And I wasn't about to let that happen.

I took his clothes into the kitchen then returned to him on the sofa. He hadn't moved. Still hunched forward, elbows on knees, eyes locked on the floor like it held some hidden answer that might save him.

"Alex," I said softly, easing down beside him. I slipped my arm through his, my touch gentle but firm, anchoring him back to me. "You're overthinking again."

He sighed, tension radiating off him. "I just... I don't know how you're so calm about all this. It's like it doesn't even faze you."

I let out a breathy laugh — not mocking, just enough to feel real. He was right, of course. It didn't faze me. Not in the way it should. But he couldn't know that.

"You think I'm calm?" I asked, tilting my head. "Alex, I'm terrified. But if I fall apart, what happens to us?"

He looked at me then — really looked — his eyes wide, raw, pleading for something steady to hold onto. That was the thing about Alex: beneath the guilt and fear, there was a longing to be led. He needed someone to tell him what to do, what to feel, who to be.

And I was more than happy to be that someone.

I reached up, brushing my fingers through his hair, letting them trail to the back of his neck where I let them rest. "You're not alone in this," I said softly. "I promise you. I'm right here. We're in this together, no matter what."

He nodded slowly, still unsure, still carrying that weight.

But that was fine. Doubt could be softened.

He'd come around.

He always did.

Alex

Her words helped. They always did.

But the fear never really left. It clung to me, like smoke in my lungs, heavy and suffocating.

It wasn't just about what I'd done — it was about

what it meant.

I'd killed a man. For her.

And she didn't seem afraid of that.

No... that wasn't fair. She cared — I knew she did. But not in the way I'd expected. She wasn't horrified or even shaken. There was no trembling, no shame.

If anything... she seemed proud.

That should've scared me. Maybe it did, somewhere deep down. But mostly, it comforted me.
But that comfort also made me feel sick.

What did that say about me? About *us*?

"I don't know how you're so strong," I muttered, dragging a hand through my hair. It felt greasy, damp from the rain earlier — or maybe just from the panic still clinging to my skin.

"I'm strong because I have to be," she said, her voice calm, unwavering. "And because I owe it to you. After everything you've done for me."

That hit me harder than I expected.

She didn't hate me. She didn't fear me.
She *believed* in me.
After what I'd done... she still looked at me like I was worth something.

And that made the guilt twist in a different way.

"I just want to make sure you're safe," I said, my voice cracking at the edges. It was the truth — the only one I still trusted.

She leaned in and kissed my temple, slow and deliberate. A gesture so tender it almost undid me.

"I am," she whispered. "Because of you."

Her words wrapped around me like warmth in winter — fragile but real. For a moment, the storm quieted, the world narrowed to her touch, her breath, her presence.

She was everything and as long as I have her, I can survive anything.

Six Months Later

Alex

Six months had passed, but sometimes it felt like it had all happened yesterday. The sharpness of that night had dulled around the edges, like a bruise slowly fading—but the ache never left.

The investigation into Bradley's death had fizzled out, just like Emma said it would. The police didn't have enough evidence, and after a few weeks of knocking on the same doors and chasing the same shadows, they moved on. No more questions. No more nights spent jumping at every knock or waking in a sweat with my heart racing.

But the weight of it? That stayed. I know what why did.

Emma had been my anchor through all of it. She always knew exactly what to say, exactly how to soothe the panic that threatened to pull me under. Her words, her touch, even just the way she looked at me—it grounded me when everything else felt like it was falling apart.

She was perfect. In every way.

And now, more than ever, I depended on her.

I wasn't sure when it started, but somewhere along the way, I'd stopped going home. My room felt cold now, lifeless. I spent nearly all my time at hers. Her little house with the red door, once unfamiliar, had become something else entirely. It was our world now. A sanctuary. A place where the past didn't haunt every corner—at least not out loud.

Being with her wasn't just comforting. It was *necessary.*

With Emma, I could breathe again. Like the heaviness in my chest finally eased when she was near. Like what I'd done didn't matter as long as she was beside me. She made it feel right.

Our relationship had settled into something normal—or at least, a version of normal we could live with. We didn't talk about that night unless I brought it up, and even then, she never lingered. Just quiet reassurances: *You did the right thing. You saved me.* And maybe I needed to hear that more than I wanted to admit.

The guilt still lingered. It gnawed at the edges of my mind when things got too quiet. Sometimes I'd catch myself zoning out, staring at nothing, just... replaying it. The way his body went still. The silence after.

But Emma made it easier to push those thoughts aside. Her warmth. Her belief in me. Her love.

And the truth is, I do love her. Maybe it didn't look like the kind of love people put in films or books, but it was real. She was everything I ever needed: supportive, understanding, beautiful, and pure.

She gave me a purpose.

She gave it all meaning.

And if I had to go back—if I had to make that choice again.
I'd still choose her. I still do it all.
Every time.

Emma

Six long months had passed, and life had settled into a rhythm I could control. The chaos of that night, the investigation, the fear—it had all quieted into background noise. Just as I knew it would.

The police had nothing. No forensics, no witnesses who could place Alex at the scene. They'd asked their questions, knocked on the usual doors, but eventually, like most systems built on red tape and protocol, they gave up.

Alex had unravelled in those early days. But I'd kept him steady. I'd held his hand through the guilt, whispered away his fears, fed him just enough reassurance to keep him from breaking.

And slowly, gently, I tightened the knot that held us together.

He lived here now, more or less. My home— once just a place of solitude—had become *ours*. A sanctuary. A haven. A place where I could soothe and tether him in equal measure.

He still had his moments.

Sometimes I'd find him staring blankly at nothing, his mind caught in that dark loop of guilt and regret. But I was always there, a calming presence, ready with a touch to his arm, a kiss to his cheek, a soft "You did the right thing."

And he needed that. He *needed me*.

What we had now—it wasn't ordinary, but it was beautiful in its own way. He was devoted, entirely. He clung to me like I was the last steady thing in a world that no longer made sense. And I rewarded him, carefully. A smile here. A night curled up in bed. A whispered "I love you" when his eyes filled with that look—the one that said he didn't know who he was without me.

He'd do anything for me. I'd proven that. And I wasn't about to let that go to waste.

But the past six months hadn't only been about Alex. They'd been about preparation. Strategy.

Because soon, I'd have to deal with something far bigger.

My father.

I hadn't told Alex much about him—just fragments, shadowy hints. The kind of truths that sit quietly in the corners of a room, too heavy to look at directly. Alex didn't need to know it all. Not yet. He wouldn't understand.

But he would. Eventually.

My father was the original architect of my pain. A man who believed control was love, silence was loyalty, and obedience was the only acceptable form of affection. He'd never hit me. That wasn't his style. But what he did was worse. A slow erosion of self.

I'd learned early to hide what I felt. To smile when I was scared. To nod when I wanted to scream.

But I wasn't that girl anymore.

And if he tried to come back into my life—when he *inevitably* did—he'd find that I wasn't scared of him. Not anymore.

Because now I had Alex.

He was mine—in body, in heart, in mind. And when the time came, he would do what needed to be done. Just like before.

For now, though, I played the part. The loving girlfriend. The soft-spoken comfort in a storm that had long passed. I made our life seem simple, serene. I made Alex believe we were healing.

I glanced over at him, watching the way his brow furrowed as he read something on his phone. He looked so focused, so vulnerable in that quiet way he had.

He didn't know it, but he was already part of a much bigger plan.

The past was behind us.
But the future?
The future was mine to shape—
And his hands would help mould it.

Alex

I was at her place again—like usual. The small house had quietly become my home, its silence and softness a welcome contrast to the noise that still simmered somewhere inside me.

It was the kind of place where nothing bad could reach us. Or at least that's how it felt when I was there—warm, cocooned, suspended in a version of life where guilt didn't sink its teeth in quite as deep.

Emma was in the kitchen, humming softly to herself as she made tea. I watched her from the sofa, the way she moved with this effortless grace, like she was untouched by the things that haunted me.

"Tea?" she called, glancing over her shoulder, her soft smile catching me off guard the way it always did. It was the kind of smile that made you forget why you'd ever been afraid in the first place.

"Yeah, please," I said, leaning back into the cushions, letting the hum of the kettle and the scent of her fill the space between my thoughts.

She came back with two mugs, setting one in front of me before curling beside me on the couch. Her leg pressed lightly against mine. That little touch—it grounded me. Pulled me back.

Moments like this made everything feel *almost* normal. Like we were just a regular couple with nothing but weekend plans to worry about.

"I was thinking," she said, her voice light but carefully measured, "we should take a trip. Get out of here for a bit."

I turned to look at her. There was something in her tone— like it was rehearsed.

"A trip?" I echoed. "Yeah? Where were you thinking?"

She shrugged and took a sip of tea. "Somewhere quiet. Somewhere we can just... breathe. Forget for a while."

Her words dropped into my chest like a stone. Heavy, but somehow soothing.

"Yeah," I said. "That sounds good."

I didn't ask *why*. I didn't need to. I trusted her. But something felt strange.

So, we sat like that for a while, in the kind of silence that didn't need filling. It was easy with her. It always had been.

And then, out of nowhere, she said something that changed everything.

"You know," she murmured, almost like an afterthought, "my dad's not the easiest person to be around."

The shift in tone was subtle, but immediate.

I turned to her, frowning slightly. "Your dad? You've never really talked about him before."

She sighed, her gaze flickering toward the window, somewhere far away. "There's not much to say. He's... complicated. Let's just say he wasn't exactly Father of the Year."

Bitterness laced her voice, sharper than anything I'd ever heard from her. It felt like I'd touched something raw, something she'd buried and ignored.

I didn't push. I never did.

Emma would tell me what she wanted, when she was ready. I respected that.

But still—her words lingered long after the conversation ended.

The investigation into Bradley's death had faded

into the past. Our life had smoothed into something resembling peace. But clearly, there were still shadows in the corners. Quiet ones.

And I was beginning to realise that whatever ghosts haunted me…

Emma's might be worse.

I loved her. I needed her. And maybe that was exactly why I didn't notice the darker side to her. But part of me knew there were pieces of her story I hadn't been given yet.

And as much as I feared what those missing pieces might reveal…

I wasn't going anywhere.
Not now.
Not ever.

Emma

I t had been a long time since I let myself think about my father.

For years, I'd kept the memories locked away —like fragile, rotting boxes stored in the attic of my mind, sealed shut to stop the stench from leaking into the present. But lately, it felt like someone had crept up there and pried them open, and now the past was spilling out —uninvited, impossible to ignore. But with Alex here, I didn't want to ignore them anymore.

He had always been a looming figure. A presence that cast shadows long after he left the room. He wasn't cruel in the way some fathers are—not outwardly—but he wielded power like a blade, disguised beneath tailored suits and expensive watches.

Growing up, he was the provider. The man who made sure we never wanted for anything. Holidays abroad, a private education, money that seemed endless. But it all came with invisible strings—unspoken expectations, quiet threats, emotional withdrawal masquerading as control. And I clung to it. I clung to him.

Until the affair.

I was barely out of university when I found the messages. Blatant, grotesque messages, hidden in plain sight on his phone. A trail of betrayal stretching back *years.* He'd been cheating on Mum the entire time—lying, gaslighting, living two lives.

I remembered the confrontation. How my voice shook but didn't break. How I'd cornered him in the study, the truth between us like blood on the floor.

He didn't deny it.

He hated being told what to do—and I had forced him to confess, to unravel everything in front of mum.

It destroyed her.

And it destroyed us.

The divorce came fast, a destructive legal break with a very messy emotional aftermath. Mum walked away with a settlement that looked good on paper, but I saw the way she unravelled behind closed doors. The weight of humiliation, the sharp sting of knowing you were replaceable. The brutal truth that she never mattered, she was there to cook and clean for him really.

And me? I was cut off like a dead limb.

He blamed me. Not the infidelity, not his lies. *Me.*

I had taken control from him, and men like my father don't forgive that kind of disobedience.

I rebuilt my life without him. Piece by painful piece. I learned to live without the cushion of his money, without the illusion of his approval. And I told myself I'd moved on. That I was free of him.

But then the letter came.

It arrived like any other post—disguised in a cream envelope, the kind used for wedding invitations, or thank-you notes. But the embossed logo on the back stopped me cold.

His solicitor.

At first, I thought it was a mistake. Something meant for Mum, or one of his endless business associates. But when I opened it, my stomach turned to ice.

An appointment.

Two weeks from now. A meeting to *discuss revisions to his will.*

I read the words over and over, until the meaning blurred, then sharpened with cruel clarity.

He was rewriting me out of his legacy.

For most of my life, his money had been his only language of love. He couldn't say he was proud. He couldn't hug. But he could set up trust funds.

He could make promises about the future, about taking care of us *one day*.

Now, with his new wife—decades younger, designer-clad, always camera-ready—and their two perfect children, I was being erased.

Replaced.

Forgotten.

I hadn't spoken to him in a few years. The occasional forced birthday text or cold, one-line email were all that remained of our relationship. He had moved on. Built a shiny, hollow new world.

And I was expected to quietly disappear.

But I *never* thought that he would cut me out in death, I always thought that this was his way of teaching me hard life lessons but when his time came, he would look after me in the end. Apparently not.

The appointment was in two weeks. That was how long I had to stop him from cutting me out completely.

I stood in the middle of the living room, clutching the letter in my hand so tightly the paper crumpled at the edges.

This wasn't about greed. It never was. This was about *justice.*

I had been loyal. I had protected our family, told the truth when it mattered. And he had punished me for it.

Not this time.

My mind spun through possibilities; through names I hadn't spoken aloud in years. Favors I'd tucked away like spare keys. I didn't need his money to fight—I needed information.

The letter didn't say what the changes were. Only that they were coming. But I had contacts. People who still moved in his world. People who would help me.

I would find out what he was planning.

My hands were trembling—not with fear, but with resolve. This time, I would be the one in control.

The sound of the door opening pulled me back.

Alex stepped in, his eyes finding mine instantly. "Hey," he said gently. "You okay babe? You look stressed."

I forced the edges of a smile and walked toward him, slipping into his arms like I belonged there. Like nothing had changed.

"I'm fine," I murmured, resting my head against his chest.

"You sure?" he asked, pressing a soft kiss to my temple.

"Yeah," I whispered. "I'm sure."

I wouldn't lie to him.
But he didn't need to know yet.

Not until I had a plan.

For now, I would keep him close—safe from what was coming.

The letter sat on the coffee table like a loaded gun —silent, still, but dangerous in its implications. I didn't need to read it again. Every word was branded into my memory, seared into my brain.

My father—the man who once orchestrated my life with meticulous precision—was planning to erase me from it entirely.

Two weeks. That's all I had before his meeting with the solicitor. And right now, I had nothing. No leverage. No strategy. Just a slow-burning fire in my chest and a mind that wouldn't stop racing.

He had the money, the power, and the connections. He had the public image of a doting patriarch and the private reality of a man who traded his daughter for a prettier façade. A new wife. Two new children. His perfect second act.

But I wasn't a footnote. I wasn't going to vanish so he could playhouse with my replacements.

Not this time.

Alex had been doing better recently. The shadows that once clung to him had started to loosen their grip. The nightmares were less frequent, the paranoia quieter. The police had moved on from Bradley's death, just as I knew they would. No evidence. No witnesses. Just a messy, unanswered tragedy filed away and forgotten. We were free of it.

But while he found his way back to the surface, I was beginning to drown again. I needed to bring Alex into the picture, but I needed to do it the right way. I didn't want to manipulate him; he needed to choose to help me.

I scrolled through my phone, ignoring the tightness in my chest, until I found the name I needed. *Paul.* A relic from my old life. He used to be one of my father's closest friends—before the divorce. Paul was friends with my mum growing up and didn't approve of how my dad treated her. It helped that he'd always had a soft spot for me too.

The phone rang twice before he picked up. "Emma?" His voice was surprised, cautious.

"Paul. It's been a long time."

We didn't dance around the pleasantries for long. I explained enough to pique his interest, laying on the emotion just enough to get his sympathy. I kept it vague, aware that Alex was curiously listening to me mentioning my dad. Paul listened intensely. And then, he agreed.

He told me that he still had some contacts— loose threads in my father's tightly woven world. He'd tug them and see what unravelled, but he couldn't make any promises.

It wasn't much. But it was something.

I ended the call and set the phone down and took a deep breath.

Alex was watching me; I could feel him. His expression softening the moment I turned, and our eyes met. "You've been quiet," he said, sitting beside me. "Everything okay?"

I forced a smile, leaning into him slightly. "Just… thinking."

He studied me, those dark eyes gentle now instead of haunted. Ready to be my hero. Again. "You sure?" he probed.

I nodded. "Yeah. I'm sure."

But I wasn't. Not yet. Not until I had something solid. Something to I could make a plan from. I would have to wait and see what, if anything

Paul could find out. For now, I just needed to keep Alex close, and aware that there was something going on. Suspended and ready to protect me.

The next few days passed in a slow crawl of anxiety and strategy. Paul came through—bits and pieces at first. My father's new wife was the one pushing for the changes. She wanted it all tied up, secure, clean. I was the leftover— the inconvenient reminder of a life my father no longer wanted to acknowledge.

She saw me as a threat.

The information came in fragments, but together it told a clear story: the meeting wasn't just a legal formality—it was an execution. One that would cut me out of everything. Not just financially, but symbolically. Erased from the narrative. Deleted.

I spent hours pacing the house, whispering ideas to myself like prayers. Nothing seemed good enough—until it did.

It wasn't about stopping the meeting. It was about shifting the power. Reminding my father who I really was. Who he'd made me become.

But I couldn't do it alone.

That night, I sat Alex down. The air between us was thick with the unsaid.

"I need your help," I said.

He didn't hesitate. "Of course. Anything." Like he'd been expecting it, but if I did everything right, he would be.

I looked into his eyes—the same ones that once brimmed with guilt, with fear. Now they were steady. Trusting. Fiercely loyal. Ready to act.

I told him everything. About the letter. The new wife. The whispers of betrayal and inheritance. I laid it bare, the way you do when someone has already seen you at your darkest.

"This isn't just about the money," I said. "It's about what I'm owed. What he's stolen from me over and over again. And I won't let him take anything else."

Alex's jaw tensed. "What do you need me to do?"

I paused, letting the moment settle between us.

"I need you to help me stop him. I need to make sure he *feels* it. That he knows I'm not gone. I'm not quiet. I'm not erased. That he can't just cut me out."

He reached for my hand, his grip strong, grounding. "I'm with you. Whatever it takes."

A chill moved through me—not of fear, but anticipation. This was more than a plan now. It was a declaration.

My father thought he'd won. That I was just a scar he could cover with a cleaner version of his life.

But he forgot one thing.

Scars don't vanish. They deepen. Harden.

And I'd learned from the best.

This time, *I* was in control.

Alex

Six months.

That's how long it had been since that night in the car park. Since I stood over Bradley's lifeless body, soaked to the bone, heart thundering in my chest, hands shaking as the rain washed his blood toward the gutter.

The memory was still there—burned into the back of my mind like an afterimage I couldn't blink away—but it didn't haunt me the way it once did. Not like in those first few weeks, when I could barely breathe for the weight of it. Back then, every quiet second felt like a trap. Every knock at the door, every passing siren made my stomach twist. I was sure it was the police. That they knew. That they were coming.

But they never did.

And Emma—Emma was everything. My calm in the chaos, my compass in the dark. While I unravelled, she stayed solid. When I spiralled, she held me. When the fear gripped me so tightly, I couldn't move, she was the steady hand pulling me back to shore.

She never flinched. Never looked at me with judgment or fear. Just those steady eyes, full of certainty. *We're safe,* she told me, over and over. *They have nothing.* And eventually, I started to believe her.

She made it all feel survivable.

And slowly, piece by piece, the terror started to loosen its grip.

The investigation fizzled out, just like Emma said it would. No arrests. No follow-ups. No late-night phone calls or early morning door knocks. It was as if the world had decided to forget about Bradley altogether.

And I let it.

Because Emma helped me bury the guilt deep enough that I could breathe again.

We'd found a rhythm since then—a fragile kind of peace. Some mornings, I even woke up without that tight knot in my stomach. I could make tea, read the paper, sit beside Emma on the sofa and feel... normal. Or as close to normal as I'd ever been.

I still thought about it. I always would. But it didn't devour me anymore.

And that was because of her.

She knew when I needed space, when I needed distraction, and when I needed her arms around me like a shield. She never once made me feel like a monster. Only human.

And God help me—I did love her. Fiercely. Obsessively, even.

That night had bound us together in a way nothing else could. And now, six months on, I felt strong again. Whole. Not healed, maybe, but functioning. Present. Like myself.

I owed that to Emma.

I was sitting on the sofa in her living room,

cradling a mug of tea as the rain whispered against the windows. The world outside was grey and blurred, softened by the downpour, and inside, everything felt still. Safe.

From the kitchen, I heard Emma humming to herself as she prepared dinner, her voice low and melodic. The kind of sound that made a house feel like home.

I watched her move—confident, focused, graceful. She was so composed, even now. And I found myself wondering if she ever thought about that night. If the weight of it followed her the way it still hovered over me.

She didn't show it, if it did.

She caught me watching her and smiled, that soft, easy smile that always managed to quiet the noise in my head.

"Dinner's almost ready," she said lightly, as though this was any other evening.

I stood, stretching slightly. "Need a hand?"

She shook her head, eyes playful. "You just relax. I've got this."

I leaned against the counter, watching her stir something on the stove. There was something hypnotic about these little routines—the quiet domesticity we'd created out of the wreckage.

For the first time in a long time, I felt like I had something worth holding on to. It's almost like we needed it all to happen the way it did to come together.

"You've been amazing," I said, the words slipping out before I had time to question them.

She turned slightly; brow lifted in surprise. "What brought that on?"

I shrugged. "Just... thinking. About everything. How much you've helped me. I don't think I'd have made it without you."

She stepped toward me, placing a hand gently on my chest. "You're stronger than you think."

I covered her hand with mine. "Only because of *you*."

Her eyes searched mine for a long moment, then she said, softly, "We got through it together."

I kissed her then. Not out of passion, but out of quiet gratitude. Out of a love forged in silence and blood. Whatever we were now—whatever we'd become—it had survived the worst of storms.

The next few days passed like that. Quiet. Ordinary. A rhythm of shared space and small comforts.

But then Emma mentioned the letter.

It seemed like nothing at first. Just a vague comment about her father. Something legal. Something irritating.

But by that evening, I could tell it was more than that.

She sat me down after dinner, her expression unreadable, the calm replaced by something sharper. Focused. Controlled. And underneath it, I could feel the storm brewing.

"I need your help," she said quietly.

My stomach clenched. "Anything," I said without hesitation.

And I meant it.

She told me everything—about her father, his new family, the solicitor's letter, the looming meeting. Her voice didn't shake, but the emotion in it was unmistakable. It wasn't just about inheritance. It was about betrayal. About being erased.

"This isn't about the money," she said, eyes locked on mine. "It's about everything he's taken. Everything he's still trying to take."

Her words lit something in me. Rage, maybe. Loyalty. That protective fire that only Emma could spark.

"What do you need me to do?" I asked, my voice low.

She didn't hesitate. "Help me stop him. Make sure he doesn't win."

I reached for her hand. "I'm with you. Whatever it takes."

She nodded once, her fingers tightening around mine. And just like that, I was in. All in.

This was a different kind of battle. Not like that night in the car park—quick, chaotic, reactive. This was calculated. Measured.

And I was ready.

Because Emma had saved me from drowning in the aftermath of that night.

Now it was my turn to save her.

~

The night pressed in around me, heavy and damp as I crouched beneath the window of the cabin style office in the middle of a construction yard owned by Emma's father. My breath came shallow, barely there, as I strained to listen.

Inside, I could hear him was pacing, his voice a harsh slash across the stillness of the night.

"No, I told you already," he snapped. "I'm handling it. Just trust me—for once."

The words landed sharp, jagged. I couldn't hear the reply—just the low murmur of a woman's voice on loudspeaker, muffled through the thick glass. His wife. The tension in his tone told me enough. It wasn't a conversation—it was a collision. Anger ricocheted off the walls.

"I'm sorting everything," he said, his voice rising. "The house, the money—what more do you want from me? I said I'd take care of you and the kids and I'm doing it. I can't just click my fingers but trust me, I am doing it."

The knot in my stomach tightened. This wasn't business. This was personal.

There was a long pause, a chair scraping sharply against the hardwood floor. The phone slammed down. Silence followed. A breath held too long.

And then footsteps and the door opening.

I shrank lower, heart hammering in my chest. Emma's father stepped out, his face hard and set, jaw clenched tight like he was biting back more than just frustration. He didn't look left or right. Didn't even pause. He stalked to his car, slammed the door, and disappeared into the night.

I waited, counting slow seconds before reaching for my phone. The cold had seeped into my bones, but I didn't notice it—not really. My focus was locked on the voice that answered on the other end.

"He's gone," I whispered. "Arguing with his wife. Sounded bad."

There was a beat of silence. Then Emma's voice, calm but precise.

"Did you catch anything useful?"

"Not much. But he's rattled. Whatever this is— it's personal and she seems to be a big part of it."

Another pause. Then her tone shifted—cool, clear, certain. "Follow him, please Alex. I want to know where he's going."

So, I did. Luckily traffic was fairly light, and I caught up to him with ease.

The car sliced through the wet streets, the rain now a steady drizzle that smeared across the windshield in slow, ghostly streaks. I kept my distance, two, sometimes three cars behind. His driving was fast, purposeful. No hesitation. He knew exactly where he was going.

Twenty minutes passed. Then, without warning, he turned into a narrow side street. The houses were large, but old, faded. Quiet. Lined with trees that creaked in the wind and left heavy shadows on the road.

I parked two houses down, engine off, headlights extinguished. He got out of the car, glancing once at the house before heading straight for the porch. A light flicked on and, the door opened before he even knocked.

A woman stood there.

Younger than I expected. Casual. Barefoot. She smiled like she'd been waiting all night.

He leaned in, whispered something close to her ear. His hand brushed the small of her back. She laughed. Then they disappeared inside.

The door closed softly behind them.

I sat there, the truth thick in my chest. He couldn't stop. Even now—with a new life, a new wife—he was still the same man. Still hiding. Still lying.

My phone shook in my hand, Emma's name flashed across the screen.

"What's happening?" she asked.

I swallowed. "He's at another house. It's not hers. He's with someone else. Another woman."

A pause. Then, softly, a laugh—dry, bitter, unsurprised.

"Of course he is."

I could almost hear her mind moving, gears grinding into place.

"Stay there," she said. "Keep eyes on him. I want everything."

I waited. The rain fell harder, beating down in steady rhythms as the minutes dragged into an hour. The windows of the house glowed softly, shadows flitting behind the curtains, I didn't need to see more. The truth was already written between the cracks.

When he finally left, he did so quietly—looking around first, as though shame still had some grip on him. Then he was gone again, swallowed by the night.

I called her as soon as he turned the corner. "He's gone."

Her breath was steady and almost calculating. "Good. Come back. We need to talk."

She was already pacing when I stepped into the house. The living room hummed with a new energy—focused, electric. She wasn't shaken. She was sharp. Alive. Strategising.

"This is exactly what we needed," she said,

turning to face me. "He's doing it again; he really can't help himself. Another woman, another lie. It's a pattern. One we can use."

I nodded, adrenaline from my successful surveillance mission still humming beneath my skin. "What's the play then babe?"

Her smile was slow. Measured. Dangerous. "We build a case. Pictures. Dates. Times. Enough to make him sweat. We don't even have to confront him—not unless we want to. A quiet warning might be all it takes."

She stepped closer, eyes catching the light, burning with purpose.

"This gives us power, Alex. He won't risk losing everything. Not over another affair."

The way she said it—cold, calculated—it sent a chill through me. But I didn't flinch. I didn't question her.

I admired her. I even found this passionate yet somewhat dark side of her attractive. The glint in her eye, the vibrations she moved with. Like we both shared a small part of ourselves with the dark side.

"I'll get whatever you need," I said. And I meant it.

She reached up, her hand soft on my cheek. Her

voice dropped to a whisper.

"I knew I could count on you."

Emma

The thrill of the night still lingered in the air, thick and electric, like the final pulse of a storm that hadn't quite passed. I watched Alex from across the room. He sat on the edge of the sofa, elbows resting on his knees, his gaze fixed somewhere far away. He was lost in the details—replaying everything, obsessing over the way it had all unfolded.

I knew him well enough to read the patterns. The way his jaw flexed when he was holding something in or over thinking things.

My father's infidelity hadn't shocked me. It was inevitable. Men like him always needed more—more control, more power, more affection they didn't deserve. But this time, I had leverage. Real leverage. And Alex had given it to me, like a gift he didn't even realise he was wrapping. I needed to thank him and pull him just that bit tighter for what was to come. To cement his loyalty to me.

I leaned against the doorframe, letting the silence coil between us like smoke. "You did good tonight baby," I said softly, each word precise, designed to slide under his skin.

His head turned, eyes meeting mine. There was a flicker of something raw—pride, loyalty, a hint of satisfaction. "I just want to help you," he murmured. "I hate what he's done to you."

I crossed the room slowly, letting each step land with quiet intention. "And you *are* helping," I said, sinking down beside him. My leg pressed against his, the heat of his body a live wire against mine. "More than you know."

My hand came to rest on his thigh, fingers curling slightly. I felt the tension ripple through him, then ease as I leaned in. "You're amazing, Alex," I breathed, letting my lips brush his neck. "I couldn't do this without you."

He turned, his eyes searching mine, full of need. The kind of need that begged for direction. For permission. I gave it to him in the form of a kiss—slow, deep, almost reverent. His hands slid around my waist, pulling me closer until there was nothing between us but heat and skin and unsaid things.

I pulled back just enough to look at him, letting the moment stretch, holding him there in that delicate pause. Then, without breaking eye contact, I slipped to my knees in front of him.

His breath hitched.

My hands slid along his thighs, moving with purpose but not haste. I traced slow, deliberate patterns, watching the tension knot in his jaw, the breath catches in his chest. I leaned in, my voice a hushed promise.

"You've done everything I've asked," I whispered. "Now let me show you what that means to me."

His lips parted but no words came. Just the softest sound—half gasp, half surrender—as he leaned back into the cushions, his eyes locked on mine. He was mine in that moment. All of him. Heart, body, loyalty.

I let my hands roam higher, my touch feather-light, teasing him with the ache of anticipation. His fingers curled around the edge of the sofa, holding himself steady as I leaned in closer, soft, almost playful, a breath away from what he wanted.

Every movement I made was intentional. Measured. Dominant in its tenderness. I could feel the way he trembled under the surface, the way he was trying so hard to be still.

I looked up at him, and the way he stared down at me—eyes wide, lips parted, breath shallow—was almost enough to make me smile.

Almost.

I took my time. Not out of kindness, but control. I wanted him to feel everything. To burn for it. To remember this moment as the one where he gave me all of him without even realising it. My fingers traced the outline of his waistband, slow and deliberate, before slipping beneath it.

He gasped as I touched him, his hips jerking slightly, breath unravelling with a raw, whispered moan. I leaned in, finally taking him in my mouth with excruciating slowness, teasing every inch, every reaction.

He was utterly silent at first—except for the quietest sounds of need, the softest curses beneath his breath. His hands hovered in the air, unsure whether to touch me, to hold on, or to give in completely.

Eventually, I felt his fingers thread gently into my hair, a quiet plea rather than a command. His movements were tentative, like he was afraid I might disappear.

I kept going, slowly, letting the pleasure drag out, letting it curl through him like a drug. He was close—I could feel it in the way his thighs trembled, the way he whispered my name like it meant salvation.

I pulled back at the last second, just long enough

to look up at him again. "Not yet," I said softly, licking my lips. "I want to feel all of you. I want it to last."

And then I took him in again, deeper this time, more urgent. His head fell back, a groan escaping his lips as his control slipped through his fingers. I could feel how close he was, how much he was trying to hold on, to be good, to stay in this moment with me.

When he finally finished, it was with a broken, whispered cry of my name, his hands tightening in my hair, his whole body shuddering as he gave himself over to it.

I held him there, drawing out every second, letting him feel the full weight of what I'd given him—and what he'd just given me.

When it was over, I pulled back slowly, resting my head on his thigh as he tried to catch his breath. He looked down at me like I was everything.

And I smiled.

Because I had him now.

Alex

The next few days blurred together in a constant haze of stakeouts and silence. Every night, I was back in that same spot —parked under the shadow of a leafless tree, the camera resting like a weapon in my lap, the lens aimed at the house that had become my nightly obsession.

Emma's plan was simple in theory: gather enough evidence to corner her father and make him pay. But it never felt that straightforward when I was sitting in the dark, watching through glass, cataloguing his movements like prey under surveillance. While she was at home on the sofa, checking in every ten minutes. I couldn't be annoyed as I'd rather I was out here in the dark than her.

This wasn't just about catching a cheating

husband. This was deeper. I could feel it every time I looked at Emma—this was about power, about unearthing something buried long ago. Her father hadn't just betrayed his marriage. He had fractured her life.

One night, he arrived again, just like she said he would. He stood on the porch, hesitation painting every line of his body. He didn't knock right away—just lingered, scanning the street like he could feel me out there, watching.

I lifted the camera and clicked a few times. Another piece of the puzzle. Another thread ready to unravel.

The door opened. She welcomed him with a smile and open arms. I snapped a couple more shot as they slipped inside and disappeared.

My phone vibrated in my lap. I didn't need to look to know who it was.

"Anything?" Emma's voice was soft but precise—like a scalpel.

"He's inside," I murmured. "He had a bag, looks like he's staying the night."

A pause. Then, "Good. We're almost there."

Emma

T he air in the living room was still, thick with the hum of tension and the quiet whir of the printer spitting out the batch of photos. I moved slowly, deliberately, placing each printed image on the table in a neat line like evidence in a courtroom.

Alex had done well. Better than I expected. Every frame he captured added weight to my arsenal. My father, caught mid-act—careless, smug, so sure of his untouchable place in the world.

That confidence was going to be his downfall.

I traced the edge of one of the images with a manicured fingernail. The house. The woman. The angle of his shoulders as he slipped through the door. Guilt had a posture. And I knew it intimately.

Behind me, from the kitchen, Alex appeared. I didn't turn. I heard the change in his breathing before he even crossed the room—tight with anticipation, with loyalty. With pride.

He stepped beside me, eyes scanning the table.

"We've got enough," I said quietly. "It's time to confront him."

His jaw flexed. "How do you want to do it?"

I looked up at him, my expression calm, confident. "We need to set the stage first."

His brow furrowed just slightly, but he didn't push. That's what I liked about him. He didn't challenge me. He followed.

"Just tell me what you need," he said.

I reached out and took his hand—warm, steady. So easy to hold. So easy to guide.

"I need you by my side," I said, voice low. "We're going to finish this together."

The walls were closing in around him. He just didn't know it yet.

The photos were damning—but not enough. Not for a man like my father. He'd twist the truth, discredit the evidence, charm his way out like he always did. I needed something permanent. Unforgivable.

Something that would destroy the facade he had built.

I sat back and stared at the photos again, each one a fragment of the truth. Each one sharpening the blade I was going to use.

"Any updates?" He said, his voice full of eagerness.

I didn't look up. "We're close. The photos are good, but we need more."

He came around the table, frown tugging at his mouth. "More? Like what?"

"Proof," I said, lifting my eyes to his. "Something that leaves no room for escape. Financials. Emails. Something that ties him to her. Irrefutably. I know he'll be paying her to stay quiet and not cause a scene, it's what he did with his replacement for mum."

He nodded slowly, tension tightening his shoulders. "How do we get that?"

I reached for his arm and pulled him down beside me, letting my touch linger. "We break into his office."

His body stiffened beside me. I watched it ripple through him—a flicker of fear.

I leaned closer, lips brushing the shell of his ear. "Alex, this is the last piece. Once we have it, he's finished. He'll never hurt *me* again."

He swallowed hard, still silent.

"I wouldn't ask if it wasn't important," I whispered. "You've already risked so much for me. But this is how we end it—for good."

I pulled back just enough to meet his eyes. I let my guard drop, just slightly. Let him see something that resembled fear, even if it was crafted.

"I need you, Alex," I said softly. "I can't do this without you."

There was a pause. A breath. Then he nodded. "Okay. Tell me what I need to do."

I smiled and cradled his face in my hands like he was the most precious thing in the world.

"I knew I could count on you."

That night, as Alex slept beside me, I lay still in the dark, eyes fixed on the ceiling, wide awake. My mind wasn't restless—it was razor sharp, alive with anticipation. Every piece of the puzzle was falling into place, sliding smoothly into position like well-oiled machine parts.

I thought about my father—about the way he twisted control into something that looked like love. The way he used money as a leash, keeping us obedient, tethered, always just close enough to beg. I thought about my mother, hollowed out by years of playing house under his rule, and how I'd had to become the adult in the room long before I ever should have.

He didn't deserve to win. Not this time.

And Alex... sweet, loyal Alex. He was more than my partner. He was my insurance. My shield. My weapon. My father would never touch me—not while Alex was willing to burn the world down just to keep me safe.

I smiled to myself, the shadows in the room no longer pressing in, but opening up—like a stage, ready for its final scene.

Tomorrow, we'd take the next step.
Tomorrow, we'd break into my father's world and steal back all the evidence we'd need.
And this time, there'd be no coming back.

Alex

T he plan was simple talking about it. In reality, it felt like standing on the edge of something irreversible and once again, illegal.

I stood outside the building, looking up at its darkened windows, my heart thudding in my chest. Emma had walked me through every detail, every contingency. Her voice had been calm, deliberate. Like she was ordering groceries. But now that I was here, standing in the silence, it all felt... different.

I looked back at the car parked down the street. Emma's silhouette was still visible behind the wheel, backlit by the dashboard glow. She didn't move—just watched. Waiting. Her stillness steadied me.

I took a breath and braced myself for alarms, but Paul's intel had been solid. The access code clicked the lock open with a quiet, mechanical sound that somehow echoed through the night.

Inside, the building felt cavernous. Empty. Every footstep seemed louder than the last. I kept low, stayed focused. This wasn't a smash-and-grab. It was surgical. Clean.

"Third floor," Emma had said earlier, her fingers lightly brushing mine as she outlined the steps. "His office is at the end of the hall. Left desk drawer. It's locked, but you'll get it open. That's where the real power is."

She'd smiled as she said it, like she already knew how this would end.

The office door creaked open, just as she'd said. Floor-to-ceiling windows let in fractured city light, slicing across a minimalist yet luxury space that screamed of wealth. The desk sat dead centre, perfect in its arrangement.

I went straight to the drawer. It took seconds to pick. Inside: a row of files, a black leather-bound notebook, and a slim USB drive tucked neatly in the corner.

I set everything on the desk, snapping photos as I went. The files looked like routine contracts— until they didn't. Names didn't match. Numbers floated. Strange transactions hiding in plain sight, or ghost transactions as Emma told me.

Then I opened the notebook.

Its pages were packed with dates, codes, acronyms. Some familiar. Most not. But halfway through, I found them—rows of transactions. Large sums wired to untraceable accounts. Offshore names. Obscure references.

A chill ran down my spine. Emma had warned me her father paid people off. Silenced threats. Bought loyalty. Was this more of the same?

I didn't pause to ask, I photographed the files. Took the notebook, pocketed the USB, and carefully returned the rest before heading for the stairs.

I'm not sure why I cleaned up, when he'd noticed his notepad and USB missing instantly.

The descent felt longer than the climb, but when I finally slipped out into the cool night, I exhaled hard, lungs aching. Emma's car was still waiting. Still and calm. Just like her.

I slid into the passenger seat, shut the door, and handed her the bag.

Her eyes didn't leave mine. "Well?"

"I got it," I said quietly. "Files. A notebook. A USB. There's… a lot in there."

She took the bag from me gently, her fingers brushing mine. That same touch that had comforted me a hundred times. Only now, it felt more like control than comfort.

"You did good, Alex," she said, flipping through the notebook. Her lips curved—not into a smile, exactly. Something smaller. Sharper. "This is exactly what we needed."

I hesitated. "Emma… there's something in there. Transactions. Big ones. And a repeated name— initials. A.J. Ring any bells?"

She paused for just a heartbeat too long. Then the smile returned— the reassuring smile that normally told me everything was fine.

"It could be anyone. My father's been laundering money for decades. I wouldn't be surprised if half of London's underworld has initials in that book."

It sounded rehearsed. Too easy. But I let it go.

She turned fully toward me, one hand resting on my knee. "You're amazing, you know that?"

"I just want to help," I said, quieter now. "To make this right. For you."

"And you are," she whispered, her voice like silk over glass. "You're everything I need, Alex."

She leaned in and kissed me—soft at first, then deep, like she was claiming me all over again. I felt myself melt into her touch, my doubts dissolving in the heat of her mouth.

When she finally pulled away, her eyes sparkled with something unreadable. Something dangerous.

"Let's go home," she said.

And I followed.

Of course I did.

Emma

The morning after Alex came back with the notebook and USB drive, I sat alone in the kitchen, a steaming cup of tea cradled in both hands, its warmth seeping into my palms. The house was silent, still cocooned in early light. Alex was upstairs, likely sprawled across the bed, lost in the kind of heavy sleep that only follows adrenaline and blind trust. I thanked him again the night before, in the only way he seemed to truly understand and appreciate.

The notebook was open in front of me, its pages fanned out across the table like a map of decay—transfers, names, codes, and the initials I couldn't stop staring at: A.J.

I tapped my finger against the paper, once, twice. The sound was soft, rhythmic, deliberate. I knew exactly who A.J. was. I had always known. But I wasn't ready to let Alex in on that part of the story. Not yet. Maybe not ever. Unless I had to, I didn't want to scare him.

A smile curled slowly at the corner of my lips —small, private, a secret blooming in the quiet. This wasn't just about exposing my father. This was about dismantling him, brick by brick, until there was nothing left but the hollow man beneath the suits and the smirk. I could feel the control shifting. With every new piece of evidence, every thread of corruption unearthed, I was reclaiming the power he had stolen from me and mum.

And Alex.

Sweet Alex. He was more than just a weapon in this. He was the safety net beneath my high wire, the eager accomplice who would do anything I asked—out of love, out of desperation, out of need. That kind of devotion was rare.

I heard footsteps on the stairs, then the soft creak of the hallway floorboards. A moment later, Alex appeared in the doorway, rubbing sleep from his eyes, his T-shirt rumpled, hair still mussed. He looked so endearingly dishevelled it almost made me feel bad for drawing him into my world.

Almost.

He glanced at the spread of documents on the table and gave a sheepish smile.
"Still going through it?"

I nodded, keeping my expression tired but hopeful. "There's so much here," I murmured, letting a faint edge of overwhelm creep into my voice. "It's hard to know where to start, but… it's good. It's really good."

He poured himself coffee, then sat beside me, close enough that his leg brushed against mine. His presence was grounding, like a tether—but he didn't realise *he* was tethered to *me.*

"What's the next step?" he asked, his voice low, cautious.

I hesitated, not because I lacked a plan, but because I needed him to believe it was *our* plan.

"I think…" I leaned back slightly, letting out a breath, my fingers absently tracing the edge of the notebook, "we need to build pressure first. If we confront him outright, he'll bury it."

Alex's brows pulled together. "So, what do we do?"

"We make him sweat," I said, my voice calm, confident. "Anonymous. Untraceable. A couple of photos sent to his private email—something that makes it clear he's being watched. Just enough to unnerve him."

Alex nodded slowly, taking it in. He wanted to help. Needed to help.
"And then what?"

"Then we watch," I said softly, meeting his eyes. "We wait for him to panic. Men like my father don't deal well with paranoia."

I closed the notebook; the sound of the cover

snapping shut like the end of a chapter.

Alex reached out and took my hand, his grip warm and earnest. "Whatever you need. I'm with you."

I offered a gentle smile, one that masked so much more beneath the surface. "I know you are babe."

And I did. I knew he'd follow me into the dark, without question.

Alex

The logic was sound. The plan made sense. And yet, as I watched Emma talk through it—her voice calm, her gaze bright with something I hadn't seen before—I felt something twist in my chest.

She was... excited by it all?

I couldn't put my finger on it. Maybe it was the way her eyes gleamed when she spoke about rattling him, about *watching him fall apart*. There was something too steady in her hands, too much ease in her control.

"Are you sure it's the right move?" I asked carefully, trying to keep my voice even.

She didn't hesitate. Her expression softened with practiced precision as she reached across the table, her fingers curling over mine. "Alex, trust me. He's not the kind of man who listens to reason. If we want to make him take us seriously, we need to shake him first."

Her touch was warm. Reassuring. Her eyes held mine like I was the only thing anchoring her.
"You've been amazing so far—don't start doubting yourself now."

Something in me relaxed. I nodded. "Okay. Let's do it."

The first email was deliberately bare: a single photo of her father outside Sophie's house. No message. No subject. Just silence and implication.

Emma had already set up the anonymous account. Her fingers didn't waver on the keyboard. She was methodical. Calm. Focused.

I watched her hit *send*, and a rush of adrenaline surged through me.

Then we waited.

The minutes passed like hours, thick and slow.

When just over an hour later, her laptop pinged, and her inbox refreshed to show a single email.

"Who is this? What do you want?"

Emma's smile was small, but it carried weight. "He's already panicking."

She didn't type a reply. Not right away. Instead, she leaned back in her chair, her expression unreadable.

"Let's let him stew," she murmured, almost to herself. Her tone had a faint playfulness to it—like a cat toying with a trapped bird.

Emma

T he next forty-eight hours unfolded like a perfectly rehearsed play.

Two more emails. Two more cracks in the mask he'd spent a lifetime maintaining.

The second email showed him on Sophie's porch again but closer this time, more incriminating. Yeah, I'd found *her* on Facebook, it's amazing what a reverse Google search can do.

The third contained an excerpt from the notebook: a transaction code and a sum of money that tied him directly to her.

His replies came faster, his composure slipping with everyone.

"Leave me alone."
"You have no idea what you're doing."
"Stop this, or you'll regret it."

I savoured each one.

The threats didn't scare me. They confirmed it was working. The more unbalanced he became, the more careless his decisions would be. The more likely he would be to crumble.

Alex had grown quieter since we started. I noticed it—the way he lingered by the window a little longer, still loyal, but something inside him was shifting. Like he wanted to act and be fix everything immediately.

I didn't let it show that I noticed. Instead, I gave him things to do—small, manageable, always just enough to keep him involved but too occupied to think too hard.

"You're incredible," I told him one night as we drafted the next message. "I don't know what I'd do without you."

He smiled—soft, shy, like a boy who'd just been told he was special. His eyes flickered with something warm, something proud.

It was so easy. He thrived on praise.

The final email was short. Cold. Targeted like a blade pressed just below the ribs.

"We know about Sophie. And we know what she costs you. Keep ignoring us, and the photos won't just go to your wife.. they'll go everywhere."

I read it once. Then again. Then hit send.

I leaned back, exhaling slowly, letting the moment settle. The silence that followed was delicious. Anticipatory. I could almost see his reaction in my mind: the clenched jaw, the barely restrained fury, the way he'd check every lock in his house twice that night.

Across from me, Alex sat stiff and watchful, like he was bracing for a storm he wasn't sure he wanted to be part of.

"That's going to push him over the edge," he said quietly.

I met his eyes. Steady. Cool. "That's the point."

His gaze lingered on mine, searching. For what, I didn't know. Maybe he didn't either.

I reached out and took his hand again. My thumb brushed gently over his knuckles.

"You're doing amazing, Alex," I said, letting my voice go soft. "I couldn't do this without you."

His smile was faint, almost reluctant—but the tension in his shoulders eased.

That was all I needed.

Alex

The days passed in a blur of tension and unreadable silences. Each new email Emma sent raised the stakes, dragging us deeper.

Her father's responses had shifted. The arrogance was still there, but it was slipping, cracked at the edges.

"What do you want? Money? Is that what this is about?"
"This will ruin you more than it ruins me. Think carefully about your next move."

I read each message with a pit in my stomach,

but Emma... she read them like they were weather reports. No emotion. No hesitation. Just quiet, clinical analysis. She was focused in a way that unsettled me—calm, poised, like every line of his panic only confirmed what she already knew.

It was one of those late nights, the kind that felt weighted with unsaid things, when I finally asked the question that had been gnawing at me.

"What happens if he doesn't give in?" My voice came out lower than I intended, like saying it aloud might make it real.

She glanced at me, her features softening just enough to pass for vulnerability. "He will," she said with quiet confidence. "He has to. His entire life is built on lies and appearances. If the truth comes out, he loses everything."

I wanted to believe her. God, I *needed* to believe her. She always had this way of making you feel like she'd already worked everything out. Like she was ten steps ahead.

But part of me—some stubborn, whispering instinct—couldn't shake the feeling that this was spiralling beyond us. And that maybe Emma didn't want to stop it.

Emma

I could feel the worry radiating from Alex like heat off a flame. He didn't say much, but I could see it—in the way he rubbed his hands together, the way he hovered behind me like he was waiting for something to go wrong.

But I didn't address it. He didn't need clarity. He needed purpose.

And I had given him that.

This wasn't about money. It never had been. This was about *him*—the man who had dictated my life with rules, silence, and fear. The man who made me small every time I tried to grow.

Now it was my turn. And I wasn't going to let guilt or second thoughts steal it from me.

I watched Alex leaning over the laptop, his brow furrowed as he re-read the latest response. So sweet. So willing. So unaware of how deep we were in.

But he'd learn. Eventually.

The emails were working. Each reply from my father carried the weight of unravelling control.

I could feel the tension in his words, like he was grasping for a foothold on a cliff that was already crumbling.

And then, like the final move in a perfectly played game, my phone buzzed.

I picked it up, already knowing what it would say.

"Meet me. Name your price, but this ends now."

A slow, satisfied smile curved across my lips.

"It's happening," I said, glancing up at Alex. "He's ready to talk."

Alex

Emma's excitement was unmistakable, and for a second, it even stirred something in me—a flicker of victory. But beneath it, deeper, something darker churned.

This was it. The moment we'd been working toward. The moment it all turned.

"Where?" I asked, leaning in, trying to keep my voice steady.

"He didn't say," she replied, her eyes dancing with anticipation. "But that doesn't matter. We'll control where this happens. Somewhere quiet. Neutral. Somewhere *we* decide."

There was something different in her now —sharper, more driven. It wasn't just about exposing him. There was something personal, something deeper, in her tone that made the hairs on the back of my neck rise.

"You're sure this is the right move?" I asked, quieter this time.

She turned to me, softening like she always did when I wavered. Her eyes were wide, open, warm. "Alex, I know it's intense. But this is the only way. He *has* to be stopped. And we're the only ones who can do it."

Her hand slid into mine, her fingers curling between mine with perfect familiarity. That one gesture—so small—calmed me more than I wanted to admit.

"I need you with me," she whispered. "We're so

close. Don't let fear ruin this."

I held her gaze for a moment longer, and then I nodded. Her words wrapped around me like armour, like a promise.

"I'm with you. Always."

But as I said it, a quiet voice in the back of my mind whispered a different truth.

I didn't know where this would end. I only knew we'd already crossed too many lines to go back.

Emma

The meeting wasn't going to happen right away. That would've been too easy. I wanted him to stew. Let the panic build. Let his thoughts twist and turn in the dark, like rats clawing at the inside of a cage.

In the meantime, I began laying the groundwork. Every move had to be precise. I scouted possible locations—places far enough from surveillance and curious strangers, but not so remote that we'd be trapped if things went sideways. An abandoned warehouse. A gated car park near the edge of the industrial district. A vacant office floor I had access to through an old friend. Every option had pros and cons, and I weighed them obsessively, preparing for a conversation that could turn dangerous at any moment.

But preparation wasn't just about place. It was about people. Specifically, Alex.

He needed to be ready. Alert. Sharper than he'd ever been. So, I coached him. Rehearsed every possible scenario until he could answer instinctively. What to say. When to stay silent. How to act.

"You're the reason we've gotten this far," I told him one night as we sat cross-legged on the living room floor, a notepad open between us, pages filled with scribbled notes and contingency plans.

"I couldn't do this without you."

He met my gaze, unwavering. "I just want to protect you, Emma. To make sure you're safe."

"And you are," I said, letting my hand drift gently across his cheek, pausing just long enough for the weight of the moment to settle between us. "I don't know what I'd do without you."

That part wasn't a lie.

I closed the laptop gently, my fingers lingering against the lid like I could still feel the weight of the message inside.

"Meet me. Name your price, but this ends now."

It should have brought relief. A conclusion. The closing act. But instead, the words vibrated with something else—threat wrapped in civility. An ending, yes. But whose?

I knew my father too well. He didn't negotiate unless he was certain of the outcome. He didn't ask for meetings unless he'd already planned the ending. If he was willing to face me in person, it wasn't because he wanted peace.

He'd bring something. Not lawyers. Not bribes. Something darker. Something... final.

That's when it clicked.

A detail from the notebook—a name, or rather, an absence of one. Two letters. A.J. I had skimmed over it before, assuming it was some accountant or partner in one of his shadow companies. But now, those letters glared back at me like a neon warning.

I shot up from the chair, the legs scraping against the hardwood with a sharp screech. Alex looked up from the sofa, his brow furrowed with concern.

"Everything okay?" he asked, voice low, measured, the way he always sounded when he was worried but trying not to show it.

I didn't answer at first. My mind was racing. Memories, connections, consequences— snapping into place like puzzle pieces I had been too afraid to examine before. I've heard of 'A.J' before, when I was younger.

A.J. wasn't an accountant. He wasn't a partner.

He was a *cleaner*.

The kind of man my father called when money wasn't enough.

When something—or someone—needed to disappear.

I wondered for a moment if I'd made a mistake not telling him who it is. He is preparing to go to war with an unknown enemy who is actually his daughter.

Alex

T he air in the room changed.

One minute, Emma had been in control, composed, talking through strategy with that steely calm that always made me feel like everything was going to be okay. And now... something had shifted.

Her energy had gone still, like the calm just before a storm breaks.

"Emma?" I stood up, crossing the room slowly, careful not to startle whatever thought had just grabbed her by the throat.

She turned toward me; her eyes locked on something far away.

"I know who A.J. is," she said quietly, like she was admitting it to herself as much as to me. "I'd assumed it was some shadowy financial figure, maybe someone who managed dirty money."

But Emma's face told me otherwise.

"Who is he?" I asked, stepping closer, even though part of me didn't want to know.

She hesitated; her jaw set in that rigid way it did when she was under pressure, I'd first noticed it in the coffee shop when Bradely interrupted her working day.

"He's... a fixer," she said finally. "The kind of man my father calls when a problem can't be paid off or buried with paperwork. I remember it from when I was a kid. He's known him forever."

My stomach turned. A fixer. The implication settled in my chest like a slab of ice.

"What kind of problems?" I asked, already bracing for the answer.

Her eyes dropped to the floor, and when she spoke again, her voice was barely more than a whisper.

"People. Businesses. Threats. Anything that stands in his way, I guess. Whatever is needed by my dad." She looked back up at me, her face darker now, laced with something I hadn't seen before—fear, maybe. "If A.J. is involved, this meeting isn't just a negotiation."

She paused.

"It's a trap."

Emma

The room was thick with tension as I watched Alex process what I'd just told him. His brow furrowed, hands curling into fists at his sides. He wanted to protect me—that much was clear—but I could see the flicker of doubt in his eyes, the weight of what this meant pressing down on him.

I stepped closer, resting my hand lightly on his arm. "Alex, listen to me. We need to be ready. If he's bringing A.J. into this, we can't go in unprepared."

He nodded slowly, his jaw tight. "What do you want to do?"

I squeezed his arm, letting a soft smile play on my lips. "We make sure he doesn't have the upper hand. We control the narrative. We go in with everything—photos, emails, the notebook—and make it clear that if he tries anything, it's all going public."

"And if that doesn't work?" Alex asked, his voice quieter now.

I tilted my head, gaze steady. "Then we make sure we're one step ahead."

He didn't know it yet, but I had something else. Something that would shift the balance of power in our favour if it all went wrong.

Alex

Emma's confidence was magnetic, pulling me in even as my instincts screamed this was dangerous—more dangerous than anything we'd done so far.

But I couldn't argue with her logic. If her father was bringing in someone like A.J., we had to be prepared for the worst. I had to protect her.

"Do you think he knows it's us?" I asked, breaking the heavy silence.

Emma shook her head. "No. Not yet. He's too focused on covering his tracks to figure out who's behind the emails. But if A.J. is involved it's because he's taking the threat very seriously."

Her words sent a shiver down my spine, but I pushed the fear aside. "So, what do we do next?"

"We tighten the screws," she said, sharp and

decisive. "One more email. Something that makes it clear we're not bluffing. Then we set the time and place for the meeting."

Her plan was clear. Methodical. Terrifyingly risky. But I nodded. I'd follow her into the fire.

Emma

The final email was perfect—short, pointed, designed to shake him.

"We know about A.J. We know what he does. If you try to pull something, everything goes public. We're not afraid of him, and we're not afraid of you. This ends now."

I hit send. The tension in the room didn't lift. Alex sat silently beside me, and though he didn't say much, I felt the unease pouring off him.

Good. I needed him sharp. On edge. Ready to act.

The reply came faster than I expected.

"Fine. Tell me where. Tell me when. Tell me how much. But don't push me any further."

I leaned back in my seat, a slow smile spreading across my face.

"It's time," I said, looking over at Alex.

He nodded, jaw set. "Where are we going to meet him?"

I considered my options. Somewhere private, somewhere we could control the environment. Somewhere he couldn't predict.

"There's an industrial lot on the edge of town," I said finally. "Empty, quiet, no cameras. It's perfect. I've been already."

Alex hesitated, then nodded decisively. "Okay. Let's do this."

The moment Alex said, "Let's do this," something inside me shifted. It wasn't just the plan, or the growing sense of control I had over everything—it was him. The way he looked at me. So sure. So devoted. So completely *mine*.

He didn't know it, but that loyalty turned me on more than anything else ever had. I liked him before. But I'd never *wanted* him—not like this. Not until I knew he was willing to burn the whole world down for me.

"Alex," I said, my voice low, slicing through the

quiet. He turned to me, eyes softening.

"Yeah?"

I didn't answer. I stood in front of him slowly, my hands resting lightly on his shoulders. I felt the tension there; the weight he carried for me.

"You're incredible," I whispered, letting my fingers trail down the length of his arms, then back up to his neck.

His brow furrowed, uncertain. "I'm just trying to help you, Emma."

"You're doing more than that," I murmured. "You're everything I need."

And then I kissed him.

At first it was soft, slow—something tentative and full of promise. But that didn't last.

It grew.

His hands found my waist and gripped tight, pulling me closer. I straddled him, sinking into his lap, my knees pressing against the cushions as I rocked forward. I could feel the sharp catch of his breath on my neck, the tremble in his hands.

I pulled his shirt over his head, dragging my fingers across his chest as I exposed him. I didn't rush. This wasn't a moment to race through—it was one to consume.

I wanted him to *feel* what he meant to me. What he was giving up. Who he belonged to now.

My top slipped away with a stretch and a smile. He stared, wide-eyed, like he was seeing me for the first time, but I didn't give him the space to speak. I leaned into him, skin against skin, my lips pressing down his jawline, down his throat, across his chest.

He whispered my name like a prayer and a warning all at once.

"Emma..."

I pulled back just enough to meet his gaze, my thighs tightening around his hips. My voice was steady, sultry, in complete control.

"You don't have to say a word. Let me show you."

We moved as one, hips grinding, breaths tangled. I rocked against him slowly, deliberately, feeling his strength give way to surrender. His hands roamed my body like he was learning it from scratch, like memorising it might save him.

He kissed me like I was salvation.

And I gave him exactly what he needed—power, passion, *me*.

When it was over, we didn't speak. We lay tangled on the sofa, my body draped over his, his arms clinging to me like he couldn't bear to let go.

I rested my head against his chest, the steady rhythm of his heartbeat grounding me.

"I love you, Alex," I said softly, the words warm and quiet.

His arms tightened. He kissed the top of my head.

"I love you too, Emma."

I smiled against his skin.

For now, we were perfect.

Tomorrow, we'd burn everything—together.

Alex

The morning light crept through the curtains, casting long shadows across the room. I blinked against the brightness, my body sore in a way that felt good—earned. Last night replayed in fragments: Emma's touch, her kiss, the way we moved together like the rest of the world didn't exist.

It felt like a blur—like I'd been consumed by her, body and soul.

For the first time in days, the tension that had knotted itself into my chest had loosened. She had that effect on me—pulling me back into the moment, making everything outside of us feel distant. Irrelevant.

I descended the stairs, groggy but content, and found her in the kitchen. She was already dressed, her hair loose around her shoulders, pouring two mugs of coffee like she'd been up for hours. Calm. Collected. Focused. Like always.

"Good morning," I said, rubbing the sleep from my eyes.

She glanced over her shoulder, lips curling into a faint smile. "Morning, babe. I made coffee."

I joined her at the counter, accepting the mug she handed me. The warmth grounded me.

"Did you sleep well?" she asked casually, leaning back against the worktop.

"Yeah," I said with a slow nod, a small smile tugging at my mouth. "Better than I have in a long time."

She returned the smile, but her eyes drifted to her phone. A flicker of something sharper passed through her.

"Good. We've got a long day ahead of us."

She waited until we'd finished our coffee before picking up her phone. The mood shifted instantly—the air in the room turning heavier, more clinical. She tapped out a message with sharp precision.

"There," she said, setting the phone down. "I've told him. 8 p.m. at the warehouse."

Her voice was steady. Certain. "It's perfect. Quiet. Private. No cameras. He'll feel exposed but won't risk making a scene. It gives *us* control."

I nodded, the weight settling on my shoulders again. The warehouse lot she mentioned was an abandoned industrial estate on the edge of town. Cracked concrete, rusted metal fences—no one went there anymore.

"What if he brings someone?" I asked. "What if he brings A.J.?"

Her eyes flicked to mine. Cold, calculating. "He won't. Not yet. He'll want to see who he's dealing with first."

I exhaled slowly. "And if he does?"

Her hand found mine, squeezing it gently. "Then we handle it. Together."

The day dragged.

Emma kept herself busy—scrolling through work emails, reviewing the notebook again, checking and rechecking the files and photos. Her laser focus was oddly calming, even as it made the knot in my chest twist tighter.

But I couldn't sit still. I paced the living room, thoughts spiralling in all directions. What would he say? What would he do? What would *Emma* do if it all went wrong?

By late afternoon, I needed air. I told her I was heading out for a walk. She didn't try to stop me —just nodded and went back to what she was doing. She knew I'd come back to her before showtime.

The streets were quiet, the hum of distant cars blending with the rustle of wind in the trees. I walked aimlessly, hands buried deep in my pockets, mind racing.

We'd come so far. Too far to turn back now. But as the hours crept closer to 8 p.m., doubt edged in.

Not about Emma. Never about her.

But about me.

Would I be enough if things got ugly? Would I

be able to keep her safe? I'd followed her this far—every step, every risk—because I loved her. Because she made me feel like I mattered. Like I was capable, but what if I wasn't?

I stopped at a quiet park, sitting on a bench as the sun dipped behind the trees. I let the silence press in around me, tried to breathe through the nerves.

This wasn't about me. It never was. It was about *her*. About keeping her safe. About giving her the life she deserved. The life *we* deserved.

I pulled out my phone, flicking through the photos. From the first image she'd sent me on Noted, to the last one we took together in her house. Every picture told the story of how far we'd come.

She'd helped me become more than I thought I could be. And now, I'd give everything to protect her. I am the man I am, because of her.

When I got back, the house was quiet. Emma sat at the kitchen table, her phone in hand, eyes scanning the screen.

She looked up when I walked in. Her face softened.

"Feeling better baby?" God, I love when she calls me that.

I nodded, dropping my jacket on the back of the chair. "Yeah. Just needed some air."

She stood and crossed the room in two strides, her hands resting on my shoulders.

"We've got this, Alex," she said gently. "It feels big, but we've planned for everything. And we're doing it *together*."

I nodded again, her words rooting something solid in me.

"Go shower and get ready," she said, stepping back. "We leave in an hour." I didn't question it; I did need to freshen up.

The water was piping hot and steaming, washing some of the tension from my skin.

By the time I stepped out, I felt clearer. Sharper. More like the man she needed me to be.

When I came downstairs, she was already waiting—dark jeans, leather jacket, her hair pulled back into a sleek ponytail. Her presence filled the room. Commanding. Untouchable.

And stunningly sexy.

"Ready?" she asked, locking her eyes onto mine. There was a fire in them. She believed in this. She believed in *me*.

"Ready," I said, and this time, I meant it.

We stepped out into the cool evening, the sun dipping below the rooftops.

This was it.

The drive was quiet, the low hum of the engine filling the space between us like static. Streetlights slipped across the windscreen in flashes of amber and gold, casting fleeting shadows across Emma's face. Her focus was razor-sharp, eyes fixed on the road ahead, jaw tight with determination. She didn't speak. She didn't need to. The silence was already loud enough—The plans were set and there was no going back now.

We were five minutes out. Five minutes from the riskiest situation I've ever been in. Five minutes before I could need to defend Emma.

Again.

My pulse throbbed behind my ribs like a warning drumbeat. The closer we got, the heavier everything felt—like gravity itself had thickened around us. We weren't just driving to a meeting. We were heading straight into the unknown.

Then, just before the turnoff, Emma eased the car onto the gravel shoulder, tyres crunching to a stop beneath us. She slipped the gear into park but left the engine idling, headlights casting eerie shadows into the trees ahead.

She turned toward me slowly, deliberately, her profile melting into full view.

"Alex," she said, her voice calm—too calm. There was a steel edge under it now, one I hadn't heard before.

I shifted in my seat, instantly alert. "What is it?"

Without answering, she reached over and popped open the glovebox. Her fingers moved with eerie precision, no hesitation. When she drew her hand back out, the air between us shifted.

My breath hitched.

A gun.

Cold, matte black. Compact. Familiar in design, alien in her hands.

I stared at it, throat closing, the rest of the world blurring at the edges. "Where the hell did you get that?"

Her eyes flicked down to it, brushing a thumb lightly along the barrel like it was something sacred—or dangerous. "I've had it since I was seventeen."

My head jerked back. "Seventeen?"

She gave the smallest nod, her expression unreadable. "My dad had a collection—locked cabinets, bragging rights. I took this one. I didn't even know why at the time. Maybe it made me feel safe. Maybe it was just rebellion." Her voice was far away for a second, caught in memory. "The guy who ran his gun club… one of his staff got arrested for theft. That's who took the fall. My dad covered it up fast, swept it under the rug like everything else. All to protect his name."

My stomach coiled as I stared at the weapon in her hand. "And you've had this the whole time?"

Again, just a nod. No shame. No apology.

I couldn't look away. The gun sat like a curse between us—silent, waiting, heavy with history. "Why are you showing me this now?"

She didn't blink. "Because I want you to take it."

Everything in me recoiled. "Emma, no—"

"Alex," she cut in, her tone sharpening like a blade. "This isn't a plan to use it. It's insurance. Just in case. I don't think it'll leave your pocket. But if something goes wrong… if my father—or if A.J.—try anything…"

She let the rest hang, but I could see the end of that sentence in her eyes. *If they try to kill us.*

I clenched my hands against my thighs, nausea

rising like bile. I wasn't built for this. I never wanted to be. But now, that choice felt long gone.

"I don't know about this," I said, voice low and raw. "This isn't who I am."

Emma leaned in closer, her voice softening but her eyes locking on to mine with burning intensity. "I know exactly who you are. You're the man who's fought beside me, walked into darkness for me, held me when I couldn't breathe. This isn't about becoming something you're not. It's about making sure we walk away from tonight. Both of us. To live our lives, together."

She reached for my hand, pressed the cool weight of the weapon into my palm.

"It's just a precaution," she whispered. "That's all."

The gun rested in my hand like a secret I hadn't asked for—metal and threat, all bound together.

I didn't nod. Didn't speak.

But I didn't hand it back, either.

Emma

I saw it in his eyes—the hesitation. The tightness in his jaw, the flicker of doubt as his gaze settled on the gun. He was scared. And how could I blame him? But this wasn't about fear. This was about survival.

"Alex," I said softly, reaching for his hand, letting my fingers brush against his. "I wouldn't ask if it wasn't necessary. You won't have to use it—you probably won't even touch it once we're there. But knowing it's close… it keeps us safe. It gives us a guarantee."

His eyes met mine, searching. For what, I wasn't entirely sure—reassurance, maybe. Trust. I gave it to him, offering him the calm I'd rehearsed, the steadiness I knew he needed to see in me.

"I need you," I whispered. "You're everything to me. I can't do this alone."

His shoulders slumped slightly, the tension draining from him in slow surrender. He nodded.

"Okay," he murmured, his voice thin and quiet. "I'll take it. But I'm not using it unless—"

"You won't have to," I interrupted gently, cutting off the thought before it could take shape. "It's just a precaution. That's all."

Alex

The gun felt foreign in my hands, the weight of it wrong, like I was holding something that didn't belong to me. Cold metal, smooth grip—it should have comforted me, but it didn't. It unsettled me.

"Does it even work?" I asked, my voice cracking slightly.

"It works," she said, flatly. No doubt. No room for questioning.

I stared at the weapon, my thumb tracing its edge like I was trying to read it with my skin. Every part of me wanted to put it down. To tell her no. To say we didn't need to stoop to this. But then I saw his face in my mind—her father—and even Bradley, and everything we'd already done. Everything I'd already done.

And then I saw Emma.

Her laugh. Her smile. The way she looked at me like I was her world.

I accepted what I was prepared to do. For her. I slid the gun into my jacket, the weight of it dragging me down, settling against my ribs like a secret too heavy to carry. And maybe—just maybe—I liked how it felt. It's very hard to deny the life taking metal power you hold in your hand.

"Let's get this over with," I said, the edge in my voice sharper now.

Emma's lips lifted into a small, pleased smile. "That's my Alex."

She turned the key in the ignition, and the car rumbled to life. The warehouse waited ahead of us.

And so did her father.

The gun pressed against my ribs like a warning,

cold and constant. Emma, beside me, was the picture of calm. Hands steady on the wheel. Eyes fixed forward. Her body relaxed, like we were headed to a dinner party instead of a confrontation that could flip our lives upside down.

I watched her from the corner of my eye, trying to see through the surface. Looking for nerves, a crack in her façade—something human. But there was nothing. She was a statue carved from quiet rage and cool control.

"You okay?" she asked suddenly, not looking at me. Like she could feel me trying to read her.

I nodded, even though my fingers were clenched against the edge of the seat. "Yeah. Fine."

She reached out, her hand landing on my knee, warm and grounding. "We'll be fine, Alex. You just have to trust me."

"I do." And I meant it. But that didn't untie the knot in my stomach.

The industrial estate loomed like a forgotten ruin—abandoned, cracked concrete and rusting fences, lit by flickering orange streetlamps that cast long, sharp shadows. Emma pulled into a darkened corner and killed the engine.

"He'll be here soon," she said, eyes on the clock. 7:45 p.m.

My palms were slick with sweat. Even the silence felt thick—like the world was holding its breath.

Emma reached into her bag and pulled out the notebook and USB drive, placing them carefully on the dashboard like artefacts in a ritual.

"This is everything," she murmured, more to herself than to me.

Time stretched. Every sound around us felt louder—the low hum of distant traffic, the whisper of wind rattling the fence, the faint creak of metal in the night.

Then headlights pierced the darkness.

My body tensed as the sleek black car pulled in. It moved with quiet authority, gravel crunching beneath its tyres. It came to a smooth stop just metres away. The driver's door opened.

And there he was.

Her father.

He stepped into the wash of his own headlights, casting long shadows across the lot. Impeccably dressed—dark tailored suit, polished shoes. Every inch of him screamed control.

He stood there, unmoving, eyes sweeping over the lot. Then he saw us.

"Stay here," Emma said firmly, her hand

brushing my arm.

"What?" I turned to her, the tension sharpening my voice.

"I'll handle the opening. Let him think I came alone. He'll drop his guard. When I signal, you come out."

"Emma—"

"Trust me." Her eyes locked onto mine, fierce and unwavering. "I've got this."

Reluctantly, I nodded. My fingers brushed the cold weight in my jacket as she opened the door and stepped into the night.

Emma

The night air was biting, sharp against my skin. I walked toward him, each step deliberate, boots crunching over gravel. He stood motionless, watching me with that same calculated calm he'd always worn like armour. He was watching me with an almost non-expression.

"Emma," he said dryly. "Still so theatrical I see."

I gave a slight smile. "Hello, Dad."

His gaze drifted past me, scanning the shadows. "Are you alone?"

"For now," I said casually.

He sighed, pulling a hand from his pocket to rub his temple. "You've been busy. The emails. The photos. This little performance. What exactly do you want?"

"What I'm owed."

He laughed, bitter and sharp. "What you think you're owed, you mean. And what is that, exactly?"

"Everything," I replied, my voice hardening. "You've taken enough from me. From Mum. You don't get to erase me like I was just some... inconvenience."

His face tightened. "You have no idea what you're getting into."

"Oh, I know exactly," I said, stepping closer. "And I'm done being polite. You fix this—give me what's mine—or everything goes public. The files. The deals. The lies. All of it."

Alex

From the car, I watched. Their voices were low but sharp, like blades slicing through the silence. Emma didn't waver. She was a force—calm, direct, dangerous in her own right. But her father's stance, the subtle shifts in his weight, set me on edge. There was something coiled beneath his exterior.

Then she turned, casually brushing her hair behind her ear.

The signal.

I stepped out of the car, each step heavier than the last. The gun pressed into my side like a secret I wasn't ready to keep. Her father's eyes found me instantly.

"And this is?" he said coldly.

"Alex," Emma said. "The man who helped me gather everything."

His eyes snapped back to her, and I saw it—the flicker of rage behind his calm.

"You shouldn't have brought someone else into this," he warned, his voice low, threatening.

"No," Emma said, standing beside me. "The mistake was thinking you could control me forever."

He stepped forward, hands still in his pockets, his tone almost amused. "You think you've won. But you don't understand how this works."

Emma's smile was a weapon. "That's where you're wrong. You're not untouchable."

The air was alive with something electric. This wasn't a conversation. It was war.

But then... his smile shifted. It was colder now, crueller. His eyes flicked briefly to me.

"You have no idea who you're dealing with," he said quietly.

And I didn't want to but, I believed him.

Emma

I didn't flinch. Not when he stepped closer. Not when his venom started dripping from every word.

He'd always been like this—testing the limits of what people could bear, probing for weakness and disguising cruelty as concern. And now he was turning it on Alex, hoping to shift the balance. But I saw it for what it was: desperation, cloaked in superiority.

"You really think you can twist this, don't you?" I said, my voice low and steady, laced with warning. "You've been manipulating people your whole life, Dad. But this time, it won't work. Not with him. Not with me."

He glanced at me again, cool and unbothered, but I caught the flicker—something between recognition and contempt. He knew he'd hit a nerve. But I wasn't the same girl he'd silenced for all those years. I wasn't a child now.

I turned to Alex then, met his eyes. I could see the crack forming in him—the way doubt tried to creep in, clawing at the edges of everything we'd built. My father's words were poison, and Alex... Alex had been through too much already. He didn't deserve to carry this too.

I stepped between them, subtly placing myself in the line of fire, and my father's smirk faltered again.

"You want to talk about lies?" I said softly, dangerously. "Let's start with yours. Let's talk about the offshore accounts. Let's talk about

Sophie. About Mum. About the night I was thirteen and found the first cheque you paid to make someone disappear."

His mouth opened slightly—just slightly—and that was all I needed.

"I know who A.J. is," I continued. "I know what you have him do. And if you think I won't burn everything down to make the world see what you are, you don't know me half as well as you think. I am your daughter remember, Dad."

Alex

The cold settled in my chest as her father's words echoed in my ears. His voice was smooth, assured, like a man who'd played this game too many times to be rattled. And still, as I looked at Emma, standing between us like a blade forged in fire, I realised something I hadn't admitted to myself before.

She wasn't just the woman I loved.

She was dangerous.

But not to me.

And maybe that's why I didn't back away. Even as my fingers brushed against the hidden weight in my coat pocket, even as the urge to pull her away —to protect her—burned through me, I stayed still.

Because she wasn't fragile. She wasn't broken.

She was righteous fury wrapped in silk.

I met her father's gaze. "You're right," I said, my voice level. "I don't know everything. But I know enough now. And I believe her."

The look he gave me in return was pure disdain— like he was watching a puny insignificant pawn refuse to be moved.

Emma's fingers found mine behind her back, a small, grounding touch. And in that moment, all the fear I'd carried, all the doubt, melted into resolve.

Whatever happened next—we were doing it together.

Emma

I didn't blink. I didn't breathe either, but Dad couldn't see that.

Even as A.J. stepped into the light like a ghost —silent, looming, unreadable—I kept my eyes locked on my father. My pulse thudded against my throat, but I didn't let it show. Couldn't.

This was the moment he'd been baiting me toward all along.

"You always bring backup when you feel cornered?" I said, my tone sharp, biting through the stillness.

My father's smile widened, smug and arrogant. "I bring certainty," he replied. "Something you've never had much of."

I wanted to spit at his feet. Instead, I squared my shoulders.

"This isn't certainty," I said coolly, nodding toward A.J., who still stood motionless, watching like a hawk. "This is fear, disguised as insurance. And it's not going to work."

His eyes narrowed. "No, sweetheart. This is called experience. You don't walk into war without soldiers."

"And you don't bluff in front of someone who's already lost everything," I said, stepping closer. "You think this scares me? You think *he* scares me?"

A.J. tilted his head slightly, almost curious, but said nothing. His silence made it worse—made him feel like a coiled spring, waiting for permission to snap.

I could feel Alex behind me, tense, uncertain. I didn't dare look at him. Not yet. If I broke eye contact with my father now, even for a second, I'd give him an inch. And men like him only needed an inch to take everything.

But my voice didn't shake. "You brought muscle, fine. But I brought proof. And you know what that means. One call, one file drop, and your world goes up in flames."

For a moment, it was quiet again—so quiet I could hear the buzz of the streetlight overhead, the faint shifting of gravel under A.J.'s boots as he subtly adjusted his stance.

My father's smirk faltered just slightly. Enough to make my breath hitch—but I didn't let that show either.

Alex

My hand rested near the pocket where the insurance sat like a stone against my hip.

I didn't want to use it.

But I also didn't want Emma to face this alone. I couldn't let her.

A.J.'s eyes flicked to me, calculating. He didn't posture. Didn't move. Just... watched. That made it worse. There was something clinical about it —like he'd already mapped out everyone's weak points and was just waiting for the command to pull everything apart.

"Emma," I murmured, barely loud enough for her to hear.

But she didn't turn. She stood like stone, her words razor-sharp and untouchable. There was no fear in her voice, just resolve. And pride—God, so much pride.

I didn't know what A.J. was capable of, not really.

But I knew what Emma was capable of.

And if this came down to a choice between stepping back and standing by her side—

There was no choice.

I shifted forward slightly, just enough to let them know I wasn't going anywhere. That if he made one wrong move, I'd be ready. Not because I wanted to be violent. But because I wouldn't let anyone touch her.

Not ever.

Emma

He didn't get it. He never got it.

Even now, with the shadows long and cold and his fixer standing ten feet away like a loaded gun, my father still thought this was about fear. About bluffing. About me being a scared little girl with a chip on her shoulder and a handful of shaky threats.

But this wasn't fear.

This was *clarity*.

"You're wrong," I said flatly, my eyes locked on his. "I've never been more in control."

His smirk twitched, just a flicker, but I caught it —and I knew. The way his jaw tensed, the way his hand twitched just slightly in his pocket—he wasn't as calm as he pretended. He never was. He was only powerful when everyone around him *believed* he was.

And right now, I didn't believe him.

"I'm not here to beg," I said. "And I'm not here to bluff. I'm here because I *can* ruin you. Because you built your entire life on a lie and now, you're watching it crack."

"Emma," A.J. said, quieter, more focused, more precise, like a warning slipping under the conversation. "You've made your point. But if you push this, if you *really* push this... no one walks away clean."

My eyes didn't leave my father. "That's fine," I said. "As long as you bleed first."

Alex

I didn't even realise my hand was on the gun until my fingertips brushed the grip again, grounding me in the moment.

A.J. wasn't bluffing. He didn't need to. He was the kind of man who didn't *talk* violence—he *delivered* it.

But Emma...

She didn't move. She didn't flinch.

I'd seen her brave before. I'd seen her angry, cold, sharp—but this was something else. This was a woman with fire in her throat and ice in her veins. Her voice didn't shake. Her stare didn't waver. She was everything I believed in, standing in the middle of a war zone with nothing but her will to protect her. And me.

"You think this is going to work?" her father said suddenly, his voice louder now, snapping through the tension like a whip, clearly agitated by his daughter now. "You think you're going to blackmail me and walk away?"

"You're not the victim here," Emma said. "You don't get to act like you're the one being attacked. You put yourself here. You brought A.J. for backup, because even you knew you couldn't control this."

His jaw tightened. "I brought A.J. to end it, Emma. Then find you stood here."

Emma stepped forward—just once—and it was the most dangerous thing I'd ever seen.

"No," she said. "You brought him because you're terrified and your guilty."

The air cracked between them, charged with something electric—volatile. One wrong move, one raised voice, one twitch—and it would all blow.

A.J. moved fast—faster than any of us expected. One second, he was a shadow standing still in the night, and the next, he surged forward, closing the space between them like a striking viper. His hand clamped around Emma's arm, jerking her towards him with a force that made her stumble.

Her cry sliced through the air—sharp, panicked, and more than I could bear.

"Let her go!" I shouted, already moving. My feet weren't thinking. My body wasn't waiting.

A.J. barely looked at me. His grip stayed locked around Emma, his face carved from stone. "Back off," he said, not loud, not angry—just absolute. A voice that didn't entertain the possibility of being ignored.

"Alex," Emma breathed. Her voice was tight, her eyes wide, locked on mine. "Don't."

But I wasn't hearing her. My hand was already in my pocket, already curling around the cold, unforgiving shape of the gun. It felt wrong—like it didn't belong to me—but my fingers tightened anyway. I drew it, heart hammering, the metal shaking in my hands.

"Let. Her. Go. Now."

A.J. turned his head. His eyes found the barrel. No fear, just a flicker of something amused —dark, twisted amusement. "Well, well," he murmured, lips curling. "Look at you, playing the hero."

My hands trembled, but I didn't lower the gun. "Let her go," I said again, firmer, louder. The night held its breath with me.

He raised his free hand slowly, mock surrender in the gesture, while the other loosened just enough to let Emma jerk herself free.

"No need to get dramatic," A.J. said with a smirk, as if this was all theatre and I was the lead in a bad play.

But then Emma's father lunged.

It wasn't rage that fuelled him—it was calculation. A last move. A desperate gamble. He moved with more speed than I'd expected for a man like him, his hands grabbing at my wrist, the gun twisting between us.

The shot went off before I knew I'd pulled the trigger.

A single, deafening roar tore through the air and silenced everything. My ears rang. My breath caught. Time collapsed into a blur of recoil, flash, and silence.

Her father reeled backward, his eyes wide with shock. He clutched at his chest, blood spreading fast beneath his fingers, blooming through his shirt like red ink in water.

Then he dropped.

For a second—just one—the world stood still.

Then came the flood.

Blue and red lights screamed to life, flooding the cracked concrete with colour. Engines revved, tyres screeched, and then the shouts came.

"POLICE! DON'T MOVE!"

Multiple voices, overlapping, harsh and clear and absolute. The sound of boots pounding against gravel. The glint of raised weapons in the flashing light.

"What the—" I began, stunned, but Emma was already beside me, her hand gripping my arm like a claw.

"He called them," she said through clenched teeth. "He set this up. If he couldn't scare us, he was going to get us arrested instead."

A.J. backed away into the shadows he emerged from, hands raised, face blank. A ghost already stepping out of the story.

Emma's father lay bleeding in the dust, his breath a rattling whisper. I stared, numb, the gun still heavy in my hand. My fingerprints. My shot. My moment.

"DROP THE WEAPON!" someone screamed. A rifle pointed squarely at me.

I couldn't move. Could barely breathe.

"Alex!" Emma snapped, stepping in front of me slightly. Her voice was low, tight, and fierce. "Listen to me. Drop it. Now. Let me handle this. Remember to trust me."

More shouting. More movement. Officers surrounding. Every second tighter than the last.

Emma didn't flinch. She stood tall—colder, harder than I'd ever seen her. Like this chaos couldn't touch her.

"Alex," she said again, this time softer, intimate. Just for me. "Drop it."

And I did.

My hand opened slowly, the gun clattering to the ground at my feet.

Then I raised my hands, heart pounding, as the world closed in around us.

Emma

The courtroom was airless—stale, like a hospital waiting room. Except this wasn't a place for healing. It was for judgement. Every movement I made felt amplified. The shift of my skirt. The creak of the chair. The way my fingers trembled just slightly as I rested them on my lap. Measured. Vulnerable. But never weak.

All eyes were on me. Not just watching —scrutinising. The jury leaned forward, expressions tight with expectation, empathy already in their eyes. They didn't want strength from me. They wanted a survivor. Someone broken. Someone believable.

The prosecutor adjusted his glasses, voice calm, coaxing. "Miss Harper, can you describe when Alex's behaviour began to change?"

I looked down, let my lashes fall like a curtain. A moment of stillness. Let them lean in. Then, gently, I spoke.

"At first… he was everything I thought I wanted. The perfect partner. Gentle. Protective. Generous with his time. With his attention. It felt like he saw me, in a way no one else ever had."

A pause.

"But then that attention became… possessive. He'd start turning up places I hadn't told him I'd be. I'd open my door to find him standing there, flowers in one hand, phone in the other, saying he'd just missed me."

A slight catch in my throat. I looked up, gave the jury a glance that said *please understand*. A woman in her forties returned it with a small nod. She understood. Or thought she did.

"At first, I thought it was sweet. That he cared. But eventually… it stopped feeling like affection. It felt like surveillance. Like I was being watched all the time. Smothered."

"And when did that cross the line?" the prosecutor asked, gently.

I nodded slowly. "It was when I had my hours at the coffee shop reduced after Bradley came in and we argued in front of customers, just a silly argument but my manager didn't appreciate it and needed to reduce staffing anyway, so I just gave him a reason to pick me. But Alex said I was encouraging it. Said I was flirting with Bradley, and he was obsessed with me. Told me it was my fault Bradley wouldn't stay away from me, and I needed to be careful."

A sharp inhale from somewhere behind me. I didn't look. Just kept going.

"He promised to make it better, he knew I was struggling for money, so he sent me five thousand pounds out of nowhere, bought me a TV and somehow had my address to have it delivered, then he found me a new job at Westbridge Marketing. Basically my dream job. I thought he was trying to help."

My jaw trembled just enough. "Then I found out he'd forged my reference. Pretended to be my old manager. Lied. Put me in a position where I could've been fired. Where I could've been arrested. But he said it was romantic. He said I needed to trust him."

"And did you?" the prosecutor asked, his tone coaxing.

I looked him in the eye, and then to the jury

again. "Yes. I did. That was my mistake."

I let the silence settle thick and low, heavy with implication. In the front row, a man clenched his jaw. A father, maybe. Someone who'd give anything to protect his daughter from a man like Alex.

"Let's talk more about Bradley," the prosecutor continued.

My heart stilled—but only for effect.

"Bradley was kind. He was the safest thing in my life. A friend. A… quiet place. But Alex… hated him for it. Yes, there was a history between me and Bradley, but I did love him, and he loved me."

"And what did Alex do?"

"He destroyed him." The words came out like smoke—soft but suffocating. "He set him up. Got him in trouble at work so they fired him. And not long after… he was dead. I still remember the last message he sent me. He said, 'We need to talk Emma, it's important.'

Gasps again. I let the tears come, slow and steady. Not hysterical. Not messy. Just enough to sting.

The prosecutor dropped his voice. "Tell us what happened the night your father died."

I lowered my eyes, tilted my face toward the jury so they could see the devastation. "Alex said he wanted to protect me. Said my father was dangerous. Controlling. That we needed to end it once and for all. I thought we were going to confront him. I thought it would be words, not…"

Another pause.

"I didn't know he had a gun."

"And what happened?"

"When my dad arrived, Alex snapped. He screamed. Accused him of things—of controlling me, of ruining my life. I begged him to stop. I grabbed his arm. But he pushed me away and said he'd do whatever it took. That he'd kill for me."

My voice cracked, raw and tight.

"And then he did."

A long silence followed. The kind that makes people look at each other and wonder how it ever got that far. The kind that makes them ask themselves, *how could no one stop this?*

I didn't look at Alex.

I didn't need to.

He was watching me with that same lost expression. Just as I knew he would be.

Let them believe he was obsessed. Let them

believe I was helpless. Let them believe every word I've said is the truth—even if it isn't.

Because in this story, the only thing that mattered was who got to tell it first.

They didn't see the way I'd orchestrated it from the very beginning. How I'd sown the seeds of Alex's obsession, coaxing it to life with every gentle touch and whispered promise until it bloomed into something fierce—something I could use.

They didn't see how I'd baited him, with that message to Bradley telling him to come to the coffee shop, knowing Alex was watching, knowing exactly how it would chip away at his control, how it would ignite a jealousy that I would carefully nurtured.

They didn't see the way I fed his unravelling, drip by drip, pushing him closer to the edge until, at last, he was the one left standing in the ruins with blood on his hands.

No. All they saw was a broken woman.

And that's exactly what I needed them to see.

The courtroom felt like a furnace, every minute stoking the heat, every exchange another turn of the screw. The air was thick with scrutiny—heavy and sharp. Every glance, every whispered note passed between solicitors, every rustle in the gallery landed on me like judgment.

But it didn't shake me.

I knew the narrative I was weaving. I knew what they needed to believe. And I delivered it to them with calculated precision—a picture of quiet devastation, of a woman betrayed, controlled, and clawing her way to survival.

This wasn't about justice. This was theatre. And I was the lead.

~

Alex had taken the stand today, and I'll admit, for the briefest flicker of a moment, something inside me tightened. He was painfully honest, hopelessly devoted. Not like me. He wouldn't twist the truth to survive—he'd cling to it like a cross.

But that was the brilliance of it. His truth would be his undoing.

He sat with his fingers clenched, knuckles pale, his jaw set with that same mixture of weariness and stubborn defiance. The prosecutor approached like a surgeon—calm, clean, and deadly.

"Mr. Turner," he began, voice smooth as glass. "Can you explain why you were at the warehouse that night?"

Alex shifted, spine straightening. "Emma asked me to come," he said, voice firm. "She said her father was threatening her—cutting her out of his will. She was afraid."

"And you believed her?"

"Yes, of course." he answered without pause. "I loved her. I still do."

I bowed my head just slightly, letting my expression crack. The grief had to look real. The ache of betrayal. The pain of lost trust. All part of the show.

"And yet you brought a gun," the prosecutor pressed, voice calm but tightening. "Why?"

Alex faltered. I saw the question land like a blow. "She gave it to me before we got there" he said eventually. "She said I wouldn't need it, and it was in case... in case something happened."

"And when her father arrived?"

Alex's jaw locked. "He was aggressive. He wouldn't listen. He tried to downplay what she was saying. He got too close. He tried to grab the gun."

My solicitor leaned in, playing the part to perfection—concern etched deep on his face.

"And then?" the prosecutor pushed.

Alex's voice thinned. "A.J. stepped in. Grabbed her too. I—" He swallowed. "I didn't have a choice."

"No choice?" The prosecutor's voice sharpened. "You pulled the trigger, didn't you?"

Alex nodded, voice hoarse. "Yes. But I didn't mean to."

There was a stillness in the room then, brittle and tense. The prosecutor held it a moment, then shifted.

"And what about Bradley?"

Alex blinked, thrown. "What?"

"Bradley. Emma's friend. The one who lost his job. The one who died. Did you kill him too, Mr. Turner?"

"No!" The word burst out of him, rough and immediate. "I didn't kill Bradley."

The prosecutor arched an eyebrow. "Then perhaps you can explain why he lost his job after your confrontation."

Alex shook his head. Gripped the wooden edge of the stand like it could keep him upright. "I was angry. But I didn't—"

"You didn't what, Mr. Turner?" the prosecutor pressed. "Didn't threaten him?"

Alex hesitated. The jury shifted. That pause said more than any confession.

"I didn't kill him," he said again, voice frayed.

The prosecutor smiled, almost self-assured that he was going to win this case. He spoke with conviction when he directed the jury to observe the evidence presented on the screen. Up flashed images of bloodied clothing, laid out with evidence markers on them. Stains of blood. Undeniable DNA proof. Alex killed Bradley.

Alex was dumbfounded. He didn't know that the clothes I made him give me, were kept. Stored safely as a security measure. I once again played the threatened, scared girl act again but insisted I hid them because I knew it was the right thing to do. The sympathetic looks from the jury told me they bought it.

"And did you ever feel unsafe?" my solicitor asked me gently.

"Yes," I said instantly. "He had a temper. The

smallest things would set him off. Sometimes it was a tone in my voice, a message on my phone. He'd change. Like a switch had flipped."

"Did he ever threaten you?"

Tears welled. One slipped free, and I didn't wipe it away.

"Yes," I said. "He told me if I ever left him, no one else would ever want me. That he'd make sure of it. He'd mention acid on occasions when he got really angry."

The courtroom sat in complete silence, the gravity of my words echoing through the walls.

And just like that, I had them.

The deliberation felt like it spanned an eternity—each passing second another thread unravelling in a courtroom woven with tension. I sat at the waiting, spine straight, hands knotted tightly in my lap, the picture of poised fragility. My expression was one of quiet dread laced with resilience, the kind that draws sympathy.

Across the room, Alex looked broken. Head bowed, shoulders sagging with the unbearable weight of what he believed had gone wrong. He hadn't even looked at me since the jury was dismissed. Maybe he couldn't. Maybe the penny had finally dropped that this was over, he had lost.

When the jurors finally filed back in, their faces were unreadable, carved from stone. I kept my breath shallow, controlled, every part of me performing a woman on the verge of collapse— but holding on, just barely.

The foreman rose.

"We, the jury, unanimously find the defendant Alexander Turner, Guilty. Of all charges."

A collective exhale rippled through the courtroom, but for me, it was the inhale that mattered. A soft gasp, a trembling hand pressed to my mouth. Tears welled up and spilled over, raw and delicate and utterly convincing.

Alex didn't flinch. He just stared. Not at me. Not at the floor. Somewhere beyond all of it, lost.

The judge called for order, his voice cracking through the stunned silence, but it all felt distant—like I was submerged in something slow and heavy. Beneath the surface, under the sobs and sympathy, was a pulse. Steady. Sure. Triumphant.

I had won.

As the bailiff cuffed Alex and led him from the courtroom, I turned my head just slightly, just enough to catch his eyes. They locked onto mine —pleading, hollow, full of a thousand unspoken things. Searching for something.

Understanding. Mercy. Maybe love.

I gave him nothing.

The room cleared slowly, murmurs trailing behind every closing door. My solicitor leaned in, his voice pitched low for discretion but edged with satisfaction.

"You did well, Emma. Congratulations."

I nodded, offering a fractured, tear-streaked smile. "Thank you," I whispered, just loud enough for him to hear. Just soft enough to make it believable. I rose. Smoothed my dress. Straightened my spine.

And walked out into the sunlight.

Free.

The world saw a survivor. A woman brutalised by love, shattered by loss. They saw pain and courage and a truth so carefully curated they never once thought to question it.

But I knew the truth.

-

Six months had passed since the verdict, and the world had all but wrapped me in its warm, forgiving arms. I was no longer the terrified woman sobbing behind headlines. I had transformed into something else—something sharper. A symbol of strength. A face of survival. The nation's sweetheart with a tragic past and a haunting smile.

Because of who my dad was, the newspapers couldn't get enough. They wrote about my courage in breathless prose, each headline dripping with sympathy and admiration. *'The Girl Who Lost Everything and Fought Back'*. *'From Trauma to Triumph'*. I barely had to lift a finger— just sit still and let them worship the lie I'd built around me.

And now, the story was no longer just something I lived in. It was a brand.

The emails came daily—agents with dollar

signs in their eyes, publishers tripping over themselves to sign me, even producers from LA asking if I'd consider a series instead of a film. They wanted pain they could market. A tragedy they could package with mood lighting, a piano soundtrack and dramatic scenes. I gave them everything they asked for—except the real truth.

Because the truth? The truth was what I said it was.

I sat in my father's study; in the same chair he once lorded over me from. The same desk where he kept his will locked away. Now it was all mine —the oak-panelled walls, the walnut shelves lined with leather-bound volumes nobody had read in decades, the antique decanter I'd filled with wine instead of whisky. His scent still clung to the leather—a trace of dominance that I'd scrubbed away with every glass I drank in this room. Every time I rested my heels on his desk. Every time I breathed, free.

He was gone. And everything he built? I'd inherited it by turning his own sins against him. He never made it to that appointment, as intended.

Perfect.

Bradley had been the first piece of art, even if he never realised it. My father, the second. And

Alex... sweet, loyal, obsessive Alex... he was the masterpiece. The one I'd carved most carefully.

He sat in his prison cell now, somewhere cold and quiet, probably replaying that night in his mind over and over, wondering if there was something he missed. A moment. A sign. He thought he knew me. Loved me. Protected me.

But he never saw the edge of the knife I'd pressed into his hands.

What I miss about Alex isn't the man—no, not really. It's the feeling of owning him. Of watching that haunted devotion in his eyes every time he looked at me, like I was oxygen and he'd forgotten how to breathe without me. There's something godlike about that kind of control.

But gods don't mourn their worshippers. They move on.

And I was already moving.

The public attention was intoxicating. Cameras flashed when I left cafés. Journalists chased me through rain-soaked streets. Fans—actual fans —sent letters to the estate, calling me brave. Beautiful. Tragic. Some days I couldn't decide if they loved me more for surviving... or for suffering.

I gave just enough. A few tearful interviews,

clipped and composed. A delicate balancing act. Cry too hard, and they'd say I was unstable. Smile too much, and the mask might crack.

So, I cried just right. I smiled with restraint. I said things like "one day at a time" and "I'm just grateful to be here." And they lapped it up like obedient dogs.

The book was next. Rachel, my agent, was a predator in heels—sharp-tongued, relentless, and exactly what I needed. She handled the publishers, played them against each other like they were schoolboys fighting over a prom date. The bidding war was obscene. I hadn't even written a word, and already the zeros were stacking up.

The memoir wouldn't be truthful, of course. But it would feel true. That was more important. Truth was subjective. What mattered was the version people needed—wanted—to believe. And I was fluent in that language.

I drifted toward the window, the wine glass swaying gently in my fingers. The gardens below were immaculate, untouched. Tamed. Like everything else in my life now. The hedges were tall enough to keep the world out, the walls high enough to make me feel safe. Not that I needed safety anymore.

But Alex... he was the most beautiful tragedy of

all. Because even now, behind prison walls, he still thought he did it for me. Still thought he was protecting me. He'd built the gallows and stepped onto them with my name on his lips.

I sipped the last of the wine and set the glass down. The sunset soaked the world in gold, warm and soft. Picturesque. Cinematic.

My life looked like a film now. And why not? I'd written every scene.

The book would come. Then the tour. The movie rights. The legacy.

And I would be untouchable. Famous.

Because I'd given them the perfect character— the girl who survived it all. The girl they wanted to believe in.

But I wasn't done. I could feel it, just under the surface—something unfinished. Some new story I hadn't yet written. A hunger that hadn't been fed.

Power wasn't just addictive.

It was insatiable.

And honestly, I was still hungry.

Alex

The first six months inside crawled by like decades. Time didn't move here—it stalled, dragged, twisted into something slow and suffocating. The days bled into each other, indistinguishable from the last, a grey parade of monotony and metal doors slamming like thunder in a sky that never cleared.

But it wasn't the noise that got to me.

It was the silence that came after. That stillness. When the lights dimmed and the voices faded, when the shouting gave way to breathing, to pacing, to sobbing behind walls... that's when she came back.

Emma.

Her name echoed through my mind like a drumbeat, constant and cruel. I saw her every time I closed my eyes—her smile, her scent, the sound of her voice curling around the lie she turned into my reality. She haunted me, not like a ghost but like a fever. Something you survive, but that always leaves you changed.

At first, I waited. I believed. I told myself someone would see through the cracks in her performance, that the truth would rise to the surface like it always does in stories. But this wasn't a story. This was prison.

And in prison, the truth is irrelevant.

Out there, I was the villain. The obsessive. The monster who latched onto an innocent girl, twisted her world, stalked her, threatened her, destroyed everything she loved. The jury hadn't hesitated. The headlines didn't question it. They gave them a simple narrative and a face to blame, and I played the part so well I almost believed it myself.

Almost.

Because beneath the noise, beneath the shame, beneath the slow rot of guilt I wasn't sure I even deserved, there was a kernel of clarity. A memory too sharp to dull.

I had loved her. God help me, I still did.

And she'd destroyed me with the same tenderness she used to seduce me.

That was the part that broke me the most. Not the sentence. Not the cell. But knowing she hadn't just outsmarted me—she'd understood me. She'd seen the obsession behind the affection. The longing behind the loyalty. And she'd used it like a weapon I handed her myself.

Every step, she was ten moves ahead.

Bradley? She baited me. It wasn't a mistake. It was a match lit near gasoline, and I ran straight into the fire.

Her job? She knew about the fake reference. She applied for that job. She let me believe I was saving her, when all along she was threading the noose.

The warehouse? That wasn't chaos. That was choreography. Every word, every glance, every moment now felt scripted. I was just the actor she needed to fall apart on cue.

And her father... the look on her face when the gun went off—God, I see it every night. She didn't flinch. She didn't scream. She watched.

She watched me become a murderer. Again.

Prison strips you. Not just your freedom, but your identity. It peels away your justifications, your excuses, your pride. It leaves you raw and silent and alone with what's left of yourself.

I heard the names. I saw the stares. The officers didn't speak to me unless they had to. The other inmates kept their distance, but their whispers weren't quiet enough. I was the madman who killed for love. A woman-beater. A psychopath. I let the rumours fester. Let them think I was dangerous.

It was safer that way.

But none of their words could match hers.

I replayed her testimony until the words etched themselves into my bones. The tears. The trembling. The carefully broken voice that painted me as the shadow in her life. The storm she couldn't escape.

None of it was real.

But it didn't need to be.

She gave them a story that fit neatly inside a headline, inside a courtroom. And I didn't fight it. Not enough. Not the way I should've.

Because deep down, I still wanted to protect her.

That was the sickest part of it all.

Even now... I miss her.

I hate her. I ache for her. I wake up in the middle of the night with her name on my lips, and I don't know if I want to scream it or whisper it. Some nights, I think I'd still die for her. Other nights, I think I already did.

Twenty-four years. That's what they gave me. A quarter-century locked in a cage, living beneath a lie I helped build. By the time I get out—if I get out—she'll be a survivor.

And me?

I'll still be the villain.

But I know the truth.

She played the victim like a violin. The world sang her song. But behind that face, behind that voice, is something else. Something cold. Something that feeds on power like oxygen.

She won.

But I'll carry the truth with me. Every day. Every breath. Every memory. She gave me the role of the monster.

One day... maybe I'll give her a reminder.

Maybe I'll remind her that monsters don't just disappear.

Some of us bide our time.

Some of us learn how to wait.

And some of us come back.

Emma

I logged into Noted, the usual storm of notifications greeting me before I'd even taken a sip of coffee. Mentions, reposts, follows—a stream of digital noise I'd grown used to. It was like stepping into a party where everyone already knew your name. Familiar, flattering, but rarely exciting.

Until I saw him. Cole.

His profile picture caught my eye like a hook catches skin—subtle, but impossible to ignore. A soft, sunlit candid. He was sitting at a café table, a ceramic mug in his hand, half-smile curling at the corner of his lips, as if someone had just said something that amused him in the most unexpected way. There was no bravado in his expression, no curated cool or try-hard angle. Just ease. Honesty.

He looked kind.

It was that same quiet kind of magnetism I remembered from Alex in the beginning— before everything fractured and curdled. Before obsession. Before consequence.

Cole's hair was a tousled mess, like he hadn't bothered to tame it before stepping out. His hoodie was creased at the collar, and his playlist —God, his playlist—wasn't full of algorithms or trends. It was human. A live recording from some indie band I didn't know, the kind of thing you only found when you really listened.

It had grit. Texture. A song that breathed in the background noise and didn't care about polish.

I clicked the comment box before I even thought it through.

"Great track, love the vibe. You have a good ear for new music! x"

Soft enough to seem harmless. Warm enough to be remembered.

The reply came faster than I expected.

"Thanks, Emma! I'm always looking for recommendations, especially in the indie scene."

There it was again. That feeling. That pulse. Like something dormant flickering back to life.

There was an easiness in the way he wrote—no script, no mask. It was casual in a way that felt genuine. Like he wasn't trying to impress, just trying to connect. It reminded me of when I first spoke to Alex, back when things felt light and open, before they twisted.

I typed back:

"I've got plenty of artists to share if you're up for it. Tell me what you like! xx"

It was beginning. I felt it like an ache beneath my ribs—the slow, delicious burn of possibility. The way words start to thread themselves into something that feels like potential.

I opened his profile again. Studied the way his shoulders curved forward just slightly in the photo, the way his eyes crinkled with sunlight. He looked like someone who didn't know how charming he was. That kind of man was dangerous in a different way. The soft ones, the thinkers, the quietly curious.

Maybe it was nothing. Or maybe it was the start of something new.

That was the addictive part of it—the uncertainty. The not-knowing. Every new connection was a blank canvas. A chance to create, to twist, to rewrite. A new melody to dance through. And Cole? He'd just become the next note in my symphony.

I let my fingers hover above the keyboard, the excitement thrumming under my skin.

Maybe this time would be different.

Or maybe, it would be exactly the same.

Either way, I couldn't wait to find out.

-

Acknowledgements

I would like to thank the small circle of
people that truly supported me, listened
to my ideas and tolerated my silence on
occasion. I can only hope the reviews on this
book will show it was not time wasted.

I would like to thank you for making it far enough
to read this. This is my first self published novel,
and I hope you have enjoyed reading it. I know you
will understand the journey of a writer is to keep
writing and get better, so please stay tuned for more!

On behalf of other independent
authors, we appreciate you.

About the Author

Sam Christopher is a UK-based writer whose work explores the darker sides of love, loss, and human psychology. Drawing on a background in justice work and real-life experiences, he crafts stories that are raw, intense, and unflinching in their look at obsession, grief, and the grey areas of morality.

When not writing, Sam Christopher is often found dabbling in combat sports, cooking and baking and more than anything else, creating music via **@Samtherappermusic** on all major music platforms, or working on change provoking workshops and sessions for the people he works with.

Because of You is his debut novel, with several more projects already underway. Including 'Doing Time' and 'The Good Man Series'

Follow Sam Christopher online:

Instagram- @samchristopherauthor

TikTok- @samchristopherauthor

Email- samchristopherauthor@gmail.com

Thank you for reading! If you enjoyed this book, please consider leaving a review on Amazon. As a independent author, it really does helps more than you know.

Printed in Dunstable, United Kingdom